PRAISE FOR THE *NEW YORK TIMES* BESTSELLING CACKLEBERRY CLUB MYSTERIES

"A merry dose of murder for the holiday season. . . . Frivolity, a frisson of fear, fabulous food, fellowship, and fun. *Eggs on Ice* has all these elements and more."

—Criminal Element

"Tasty and fun." —*Minneapolis Star Tribune*

"Laura Childs once again delivers a delicious platter of thrilling whodunit with a side of friendship and humor, and for dessert—a spectacular collection of recipes sure to quench anyone's hunger for great food!"

—*Las Vegas Review-Journal*

"The scrapbooking mystery series expands with an inviting story that is perfect reading for holiday intrigue."

—Midwest Book Review

"Readers will hit the ground running in this tale."

—Lisa K's Book Reviews

"Twists galore. . . . The entire series is egg-cellent."

—Escape With Dollycas

"Along with toothsome recipes, Childs dishes up plenty of small-town charm." —*Publishers Weekly*

"Childs excels at creating comforting settings in which to put her characters, and the Cackleberry Club is a place you'd like to visit." —*St. Paul Pioneer Press*

Eggs on Ice

BERKLEY PRIME CRIME
New York

BERKLEY PRIME CRIME
Published by Berkley
An imprint of Penguin Random House LLC
penguinrandomhouse.com

ISBN: 9780425281734

Berkley Prime Crime hardcover edition / December 2018
Berkley Prime Crime mass-market edition / October 2019

Printed in the United States of America
1 3 5 7 9 10 8 6 4 2

Cover art by Lee White
Cover design by Sarah Oberrender
Book design by George Towne

Acknowledgments

Major thank-yous are owed to Sam, Tom, Grace, Roxanne, Tara, Jessica, Bob, Jennie, Troy, and all the designers, illustrators, writers, publicists, and sales folk at Berkley. You are all such a wonderful team. Thank you also to all the booksellers, reviewers, librarians, and bloggers. And special thanks to all my readers and Facebook friends, who are so very kind and supportive. I truly love writing for you!

Eggs on Ice

CHAPTER 1

IT was a Dickens of a night. Velvet topcoats worn with silk ascots, fake British accents that echoed through the theater, a key light focused on an antique rolltop desk piled high with black ledgers. Like that.

"It's perfect casting," Suzanne Dietz whispered to her friend Toni as they stood backstage. "Allan Sharp playing Ebenezer Scrooge."

"Our town curmudgeon scored the ultimate role," Toni chuckled. "What's not to like?"

It was Sunday evening, a few weeks before Christmas, and the Kindred Players were holding their first-ever dress rehearsal for *A Christmas Carol*. Suzanne and Toni had ditched their holiday decorating chores at the Cackleberry Club Café in order to help with costumes, sets, and lighting. Now they stood in the darkened wings of the refurbished Oakhurst Theatre, watching their fellow townsfolk do some fairly credible acting.

"Look at Bud Nolden," Toni said. "Who would have thought a big gallumping guy who drives a two-ton snow-plow would make such a believable Bob Cratchit?"

"He's doing great," Suzanne said. "The entire cast is. They've learned their lines and are putting real emotion behind them." Suzanne, who'd never appeared onstage, never even sung in a high school musical, was delighted to remain in the wings. "And take a gander at Mayor Mobley stomping around out there. Even he's giving a hundred and ten percent."

"Which is about what he usually gets after he stuffs the ballot box."

"Still," Suzanne said. "For once Mobley's trying to do his part for the community."

"Which is more than I can say for myself, because I *still* haven't figured out which rope raises the curtain and which pulley lowers the backdrop." Toni let out a long sigh. "And then there are the confounded lights. I don't know a key light from a klieg, which I guess makes me some kind of dim bulb."

"Don't be so hard on yourself," Suzanne said. "We'll get the bugs worked out. That's what rehearsals are all about." For her own part, Suzanne was struggling with the fog machine, trying to figure out how to make it spew just the right amount of moody mist. Too little and everything was out of focus. Too much and the stage looked like a foggy night in the Okefenokee Swamp.

"I gotta get this locked down," Toni said. "Opening night is this coming Saturday and I'm so worried that I bit my press-on nails down to their plastic nubbins." She swiped a hand across her stomach. "And I'm getting a case of the whim-whams to boot."

"Tell you what," Suzanne said. "After everybody leaves

the theater tonight, we'll have our own private stagehand rehearsal. Figure out which pulleys do what. We'll label all the ropes if we have to. Light switches, too. That way there'll be no second-guessing on opening night."

Between Toni and their other partner, Petra, Suzanne was blessed with the cooler head, the more practical approach to everyday life. She was the one who ran interference at the Cackleberry Club, coaxing everyone down from the ledge whenever they dared entertain a harebrained scheme. She also handled the pesky financial and personnel details that made Toni and Petra whimper with fear. In other words, Suzanne was the voice of reason.

Suzanne, who was a few ticks past the age of forty, was also newly engaged to Dr. Sam Hazelet, the town doctor and her own personal hottie. With her shoulder-length silver blond hair and cool blue eyes, Suzanne projected an air of self-confidence that was reflected in her penchant for slim-cut blue jeans and suede jackets, which was the exact combo she was wearing tonight.

Toni, on the other hand, was the Cackleberry Club's self-proclaimed hoochie momma. She favored silver-studded jeans and skintight cowgirl shirts that showed off her cha-chas, and she had never seen a piece of fake Dynel hair that she didn't want to clip into her own mop of reddish-blond hair.

"I didn't realize this show had such a large cast," Toni said. She held her breath as she flipped a switch, dimming the lights right on cue as a half-dozen actors milled about onstage. "Ooh, I did it," she cooed softly. They were coming to the end of the second act and she was still nervous about dropping the curtain. "Eeny, meeny . . ." Toni grasped a thick red rope that led to an overhead tangle of ropes and pulleys. "Is this the right one or should I . . . ?"

Actors streamed past them, coming off the stage and disappearing into the back of the theater: Nolden, Mobley, and six others.

"Don't drop the curtain yet," Suzanne hissed. "You need to dim the lights because the ghost still has to come out . . ."

Toni swatted a switch with the flat of her hand and the entire stage went dark.

"Not that dark," Suzanne said. "The audience has to be able to see *something.*"

Toni's fingers crawled along the entire panel of light switches and settled on one. "Maybe this one?" She flicked the switch and a weird blue light filtered down from above.

"That's the ticket," Suzanne whispered.

"Maybe I am starting to get the hang of things," Toni said. She sounded relieved and a little more confident in her ability as a stagehand.

Suzanne bent down and turned on the fog machine. Instantly, a jet of white fog spewed out and spread across the entire stage.

"Whoa, that might be a bit much," Toni cautioned.

Suzanne dialed her machine back, got it running just right, and then glanced at her script. She was trying to follow along in the dim light. "Okay, so the ghost is supposed to enter stage right . . ."

"Here he comes."

They watched as the ghost floated out right on cue. There was a hush from the other actors, who were all seated in the first few rows of the theater, watching the play, waiting for the next act, when it would be their turn to strut their stuff onstage.

The ghost, dressed in long gray robes and a deep cowl that hid his face in darkness, drifted dramatically about the stage.

"Who is that?" Toni asked as they peered out from the wings.

Suzanne shook her head. "No idea. I wasn't here when Teddy Hardwick had the casting call."

"But the ghost is good. Very believable. Whoever it is."

The ghost postured importantly and lifted his arms as if he were some sort of avenging spirit. "Ooooh." His hollow tones rippled across the stage and filled the near-empty theater.

"Spooky," Suzanne said. "And very realistic." She made a mental note to find out who'd created the ghost costume. With its gray-green color and straggly bits of cheesecloth hanging down, the shroud was very convincing. Like the ghost had actually swept in from the great beyond.

"This is, like, the best part so far," Toni said. She was watching the action with rapt attention.

Suddenly, the ghost darted in close to the Scrooge character and embraced him as he sat at his desk.

"Scrooooge," the ghost lamented. "Scrooooge."

Then Scrooge and the ghost seemed to merge into a single image for a few moments, doing some kind of ethereal dance. The ghost released Scrooge and then floated off into the wings on the opposite side of the stage.

"That's the ticket," Toni said. She grasped the rheostat and slowly dimmed the blue lights to a pale glow that practically pulsed with electrical energy.

"Perfect," Suzanne whispered.

"Suzanne?" came a worried voice from behind her.

Suzanne whirled around to find Bill Probst, one of the owners of the Kindred Bakery, staring at her. His face was scrunched into a nervous expression and he wore a ghost costume made of gray netting.

"I'm sorry," Bill said, "but I completely missed my cue."

"What?" Suzanne blinked rapidly and glanced out at the stage, where Allan Sharp as Scrooge was slowly slumping over his rolltop desk, practically moving in slow motion.

"And now the curtain," Toni said with a triumphant yelp. She had her back to them, hadn't even seen Bill yet, as she released the pulley and a heavy damask curtain came thudding down.

But Suzanne was still staring out at the stage. *Hold everything,* she thought, her mind making a series of nervous blips. *If the ghost is standing right next to me, then who just acted that scene with Allan Sharp?*

"How about an encore?" Toni asked. She raised the curtain halfway up and then glanced toward the stage.

Allan Sharp was still sprawled at his desk as eerie blue light filtered down. His head was bowed low and he looked as if he'd fallen into a trance.

A thin spatter of applause rose from the actors sitting in the first couple of rows. They seemed deeply impressed by such a dramatic climax. But a few moments after their applause died down, Sharp *still* hadn't made a move to get up and take a well-deserved bow.

Is this method acting? Suzanne wondered. *Or is something a lot more sinister going on?*

Just as Suzanne was about to react, Toni jammed an elbow into her ribs and whispered, "Don't you think Sharp is overplaying his role? I mean, he isn't Jeremy Irons and this isn't exactly the Globe Theatre."

Sharp still hadn't moved a muscle, and Suzanne was slowly, almost unwillingly, putting it all together. Connecting the dots between the mysterious ghost, the almost deathlike embrace, and Allan Sharp flopped out there in a heap.

"Holy cats," Suzanne gasped. "I don't think he's acting!"

"What?" Toni cried.

"I think Sharp is . . ."

Without finishing her words, Suzanne rushed out onto the stage. She circled Allan Sharp's crumpled body, reached out a hand to touch the pulse point at his neck, and felt . . . absolutely nothing. There was no sign of breathing, no other vital signs.

Shocked, practically reeling from her grisly discovery, Suzanne spun about and gazed down at a dozen questioning faces in the audience. "Call 911!" she shouted. "Something terrible has happened to Allan Sharp!"

The cast and crew all froze for a long moment, until a few of them had the presence of mind to fumble for their phones. By that time, Suzanne had already turned and sprinted past Toni. Then she dove into the gloom and darkness of the theater's backstage.

Suzanne could hear footsteps—hasty, running footsteps—just ahead of her but could barely see her hand in front of her face. The entire backstage was dark as a tomb except for a single red exit light way at the back. As she dodged past a rack of costumes, in hot pursuit of the mysterious fleeing ghost, she shivered. The dim red light made the Victorian sets look as if they were bathed in blood.

"Stop!" Suzanne shouted. Her voice reverberated back at her as she spun around a row of dressing rooms and spotted the ghost some ten paces ahead of her. "I'm talking to you," she yelled.

The ghost ignored her completely, flinging out a hand to tip over a wooden crate.

Suzanne stumbled, one knee going down to hit the cold cement floor. Then she righted herself and leapt clumsily over the crate. Up ahead, the ghost was moving quickly again, crashing through set decorations, knocking over a Victorian streetlamp, and heading for the back door.

Suzanne pushed herself harder and dodged around a corner, past a dusty grouping of old furniture. Way back here, in the bowels of the old theater, the air was musty and filled with the smell of mildew and rot. Her heart hammered; her temples throbbed with rushing blood. It was like being in a tomb—dark and silent—only she wasn't alone.

She spun around another corner, saw gray cheesecloth fluttering ahead of her, and followed it down a clattering flight of metal stairs.

At the bottom Suzanne hesitated. Was this a good idea? Where was the ghost? Was he lying in wait for her?

Suzanne glanced about for some sort of weapon. In the dim light she saw folding chairs, stacks of old newspapers, and a toolbox. Her hand swept out and grabbed a rusty hammer. She hefted it carefully, feeling the weight, hoping it would be enough of a defense weapon if she needed one.

Sliding ahead, slowly and quietly, Suzanne tried to pick her way through the gloom.

Was the ghost waiting to attack her? He'd already killed one person, so he probably had no qualms about adding another victim to his dance card.

A narrow hallway loomed ahead of her. Her back against the wall, Suzanne eased herself forward.

And there, just ahead of her, heading for the back door of the theater, was the ghost.

"Stop!" Suzanne cried as she scrambled after him.

The ghost slid to a halt and spun around to face her, all dark cowl and quivering cheesecloth. Holding up a mean-looking serrated knife that glistened with a few beads of blood, he jabbed the tip at her.

Suzanne backpedaled mightily, her heart practically beating out of her chest.

Holy crap!

Wide-eyed and practically breathless, Suzanne stood and stared at the ghost. The heavy cowl still obliterated his face; the knife was clutched in his hand. She took one cautious step backward. And then another.

What was I thinking? This is such a bad idea.

The ghost raised his knife and then tilted it in a perpendicular fashion, almost as if he was making some kind of medieval symbol or benediction.

Suzanne's heart fluttered with fear. Had Toni called 911? Had anyone followed her back here? Was she about to become this madman's next victim?

Then, with eerie but coordinated stealth, the ghost whirled about and kicked open the heavy metal stage door. A draft of ice-cold air flowed in as the door banged hollowly against the outside wall, launching a miniature snowstorm of ice rime. Seconds later, the ghost flitted outside, his footsteps crunching hollowly as he disappeared down the back alley into the frozen, dark night.

CHAPTER 2

IT was both a tragedy and a comedy of errors. A tragedy because a man had bled to death onstage, a comedy because Toni was convinced he'd been murdered by an honest-to-goodness ghost.

"The temperature must have dropped thirty degrees when that phantom started whooshing around," Toni said. "And I'm positive I smelled something strange."

"Strange like what?" Suzanne asked.

Toni scrunched her face and made a wringing motion with her hands. "Maybe like . . . brimstone?"

"You're sure it wasn't just cheap drugstore aftershave?" Suzanne asked. Nothing here was particularly funny but she still struggled to keep a straight face.

"No, I think that ghost blew up from the pit of hell."

Sheriff Roy Doogie and Deputy Eddie Driscoll had shown up at the theater almost immediately. They'd rushed down the center aisle in a flurry of khaki, snorkel parkas, and pac boots and checked Allan Sharp's body to make sure he really was dead. Then they listened carefully to Suzanne's eyewitness account of the murder and subsequent chase. Toni's explanation, however, had left them scratching their heads.

"It was a real ghost," Toni insisted.

"If it was a genuine ghost I was chasing, then he was wearing genuine Sorel boots," Suzanne said. "I saw them as he hoofed it out the back door."

"But you didn't see his face?" Sheriff Doogie asked Suzanne.

"Difficult to see a shape-shifter," Toni muttered.

"I never saw the man's face," Suzanne said to the sheriff. "He wore his hooded cowl pulled low the whole time." She turned toward Toni. "We're talking flesh and blood here, Toni, not a ghost."

"You're sure it was a man?" Deputy Driscoll asked. When everybody looked a little sideways at him, he added, "Versus a woman?"

Suzanne gave a brisk nod. "I think so. Even though he wore a costume, he still looked tall and fairly husky. And then when I chased him . . . he turned around and threatened me."

"Threatened you how?" Doogie asked. "Verbally?"

"First he held up a big hunting knife; then he aimed the tip at me like he wanted to kill me."

"I'd classify that as a serious threat," Doogie said. "Did he speak to you? Did you recognize the guy's voice?"

Suzanne shook her head. "Not really. He just kind of grunted, low and gruff, as if he was using a fake voice. You know, the way the actor Nick Nolte always talks?"

"Killer disguised his voice," Driscoll said. He was making notes in a small spiral notebook.

They were all gathered onstage, like some sort of impromptu acting troupe. Suzanne, Toni, Sheriff Roy Doogie, Deputy Driscoll, the play's director, Teddy Hardwick, and the still-very-dead Allan Sharp. Doogie had told the rest of the cast to sit tight in their theater seats.

"I still think it was a genuine ghost," Toni said. "There have been several well-documented cases of hauntings in theaters. There was even a series about haunted theaters on the Travel Channel."

"But this ghost stuck a nasty serrated knife into Allan Sharp's gut and then waved it in my face," Suzanne said.

"Maybe the ghost was running low on ectoplasm," Toni said, reluctant to abandon her theory.

"No, this guy . . . this killer . . . was real. Terrifyingly real," Suzanne said. She'd felt genuine hostility radiating off him.

"What we have here is a straight-ahead homicide," Doogie said. "We don't need an exorcist; we need an investigation." He planted his feet wide apart, grasped his gun belt with both hands, and hitched up his khaki pants. Doogie was a big guy with a shock of gray hair and a meaty face. People thought because he was slow moving that he was slow with his thinking, too. Not so. Doogie was smart and crafty and had the facile mind of a chess player who could see fifteen moves ahead. And just because he was considerate to preachers and little old ladies didn't mean he couldn't be as irritable as a rattlesnake.

"I agree completely," Hardwick said. "We need to solve this murder fast so we can get on with the play. Without any sort of blowback on our actors' reputations." Hardwick was a serious-looking guy in his mid-thirties. Tonight he wore dark slacks and a faded blue sweater and had a long scarf looped around his neck. Artsy-like.

"We need to think logically," Doogie said. "Explore any and all possible motives."

"Maybe the ghost wanted to play the Scrooge role," Toni said.

"It has to be more serious than that," Hardwick said. "There had to be more at stake."

"Who hated Allan Sharp?" Doogie murmured, almost as if he were posing the question to himself.

"Everyone," Suzanne said. "Sharp was a scummy lawyer who dabbled in all sort of things. Politics, shady real estate deals, any kind of kickback he could weasel out of the city or county. And remember, Sharp was booted off the board of directors over at the prison." She was surprised someone hadn't bought him a toaster for his bathtub—he was disliked that much.

Doogie rocked back on the heels of his boots. "Even though Allan Sharp served on the city council, he wasn't what you'd call your upstanding citizen."

Deputy Driscoll made a low sound in the back of his throat. "But we're still sworn to uphold the law. To pursue any and all criminal activity to the best of our ability."

"You don't have to quote law enforcement scripture to me, Edward," Doogie said. "I intend to find Sharp's killer, arrest him, and drag his sorry carcass into court. And if he gets messed up along the way . . . well, those are the breaks."

"Then we'd best get to collecting evidence," Driscoll said.

Doogie nodded. "You grab the crime scene kit from the car."

While Driscoll took pictures and bagged Allan Sharp's hands for possible evidence, Doogie called George Draper, owner of Driesden and Draper Funeral Home.

"You're transporting him to the funeral home?" Suzanne asked.

"No, I only called Draper because he's the one with the meat wagon and the county has a contract with him. I'll have him haul Sharp's body over to the hospital and stash him in their morgue," Doogie said. "You never know; we might end up bringing in an outside forensics expert. Maybe call the state guys up in Saint Paul."

"Then you should check the footprints out back, too."

"Let's go do that."

Suzanne and Doogie wound their way through the back of the theater and down the short flight of steps and pushed their way outside. Snow immediately whipped at their faces, driven by a chill wind. The alley was deserted except for a brown hulking Dumpster, and dark except for a single light from a neighboring building. But the fresh white snow glowed as if touched by a black light.

"Huh," Doogie said. He sniffed the air like a wolf. "He ran out this way, huh?"

"That's right." Suzanne's breath plumed out into the night air and she started to shiver. Not because she wasn't wearing a coat, but because she was thinking how close she'd come to being the second victim. Too close.

Doogie glanced down and pointed at a set of tracks that was mashed into a couple of inches of snow. "Those are his tracks? That's where he ran? You didn't go after him and mess things up?"

"No," Suzanne said. "I was too scared. So those are definitely the killer's tracks."

Doogie pulled out his cell phone, knelt down, and snapped a few pictures. Then he took a pen from his pocket and laid it alongside the tracks for context and snapped a few more shots from different angles.

Suzanne stepped back inside the building and called Sam, wondering just how much she should tell him. Let's see now, a murder, bizarre chase, and a big knife waved in her face. She decided it might be better to wait until she got home; then she could soft-pedal her story.

As soon as Sam answered, Suzanne said, "Apologies, but I'm going to be late tonight. You probably shouldn't wait up for me."

"What's wrong?" Sam asked.

"What makes you think something's wrong?" *Dang, was that a quaver in my voice?*

"The tone of your voice, for one thing. And the fact that my pager just went off with a 187 code."

"Which is . . . ?"

"A homicide."

"Thanks a lot, Doogie," Suzanne muttered.

"Suzanne." Sam's voice was unnaturally sharp and terse. "Wait a minute, you're at the theater? I'm reading this text message. Mmn . . . holy cats, there was a homicide at the theater and you're still *there*?"

"Uh . . . yes."

"Suzanne, are you safe?" Sam demanded.

"I think so."

"What does that . . . ? Never mind, I'm coming right over."

And just like that he was gone.

Putting her phone away, Suzanne walked over to the backstage dressing area. Doogie had come in and stomped the snow off his feet and was poking around with a flashlight. "Find anything?" she asked.

"Kind of a mess back here," Doogie said without looking up.

"We went tearing through here, knocking into things, I guess."

Doogie shone his light on a backdrop that depicted a library scene. The thick paper had been ripped from top to bottom. "Looks like Hardwick's going to have to replace a few pieces of scenery."

"Along with his main actor."

"You know anybody who was vying for that role?" Doogie asked. "The Scrooge role?"

"I don't know anything about it. You'd have to ask Hardwick."

"I will do that." Doogie snapped off his flashlight, leaving them in the dark. "For now I'm going to go out front to interview the other actors."

"I think most of them were seated in the audience when the fake ghost came onstage."

"Somebody must have seen something," Doogie said.

TEN minutes later, George Draper arrived, looking somber in his black three-piece funeral suit and pushing a clanking metal gurney.

Then, a hot minute later, Sam rushed in, right on Draper's heels. Dressed in faded jeans, a gray hoodie, and tennis shoes, he glanced around the theater, a look of panic etched on his handsome face. When he finally spotted Suzanne, sitting in the second row, he raised a hand and called out, "Suzanne!"

Suzanne saw the worry on his face, the tension in his body, and jumped up. She ran to meet him and flung herself into his arms. God, he felt good.

"Are you okay?" Sam asked.

"I am now," Suzanne said.

Sam kissed her on the forehead and then moved down to her lips. But only for a brief moment because now Sheriff Doogie was waving at him and calling his name.

"Lucky me," Sam said in a low voice. "I'm still acting county coroner for another two months."

"And now you've got a murder dropped in your lap," Suzanne said.

"Doc," Doogie called again, more forcefully this time.

"Don't go anywhere," Sam told Suzanne. He vaulted up onto the stage, not bothering with the steps, and walked over to where Doogie and Draper were surveying the body. The three of them put their heads together and muttered in low voices for a few minutes. More photos were snapped. Then they waved at Deputy Driscoll to join them, and together, the four of them rolled Allan Sharp into a black plastic body bag and hoisted him up onto the gurney.

When the body flopped down, a hush fell over the other actors. Somehow the arrival of Dr. Hazelet, the gurney with one squeaky wheel, and the shiny black body bag made Sharp's death feel all too real.

"Wait! Wait!" a strangled voice called out.

Everyone turned as a tall, hawk-nosed man in a long, flapping coat came half running, half stumbling down the aisle.

"Don Shinder," Suzanne said to Toni, who was now seated next to her.

"Allan Sharp's law partner?" Toni asked.

"Sharp Shinder and Young. They've been together almost four years."

"Oh my God!" Shinder shrieked as he drew closer to the stage. He pointed a bony finger at the body bag on the gurney. "Is that Allan? No, it can't be," he said. He stumbled around, looking for a way onto the stage, then finally found the stairs.

Doogie intercepted Shinder before he could reach Sharp's body. He grabbed the man by his shoulders and pulled him to one side. Shinder's narrow face was flushed red and his arms flailed helplessly.

"Allan can't be dead," Shinder cried. "I was just *talking* to him. We just filed a *brief* together, for cripes' sake." He looked forlorn and positively unhinged.

Doogie led Shinder over to a folding chair and Shinder slumped down.

Shinder fought to make his mouth work, then finally croaked out, "What happened?"

Doogie bent down and quietly explained what he understood to be the sequence of events. All the while Shinder kept shaking his head and saying, "No, no, no."

While they talked, Sam helped George Draper lower the gurney off the stage, then walked over to where Suzanne and Toni were waiting.

"There's nothing more we can do here," Sam said.

"You don't have to, like, examine the body?" Toni asked.

"He can wait," Sam said in his quiet, calming doctor's voice. "Come on, let's all go home. Suzanne, Toni? Whose car is here? Who drove over from the Cackleberry Club?"

"Neither of us," Suzanne said. "Junior gave us a ride." Junior was Toni's ne'er-do-well not-quite ex. Four years ago, they'd run off to Las Vegas to get hitched, but before the ink was dry on their marriage license, before the bill for the hotel room came through on her Visa card, Junior was making goo-goo eyes at a waitress at the local VFW. The one with the cheap mohair sweater and hot pink extensions in her hair.

They drove over to Toni's apartment, Sam's BMW cranking out heat as tiny pellets of snow ticked hard against the windshield.

"Take care," Suzanne said as Toni hopped out.

"I will," Toni said.

"Lock your doors," Sam cautioned.

And then they were alone, snuggled together in the warmth of the car. They drove down Main Street through the center of Kindred, past Founder's Park, past hundred-year-old redbrick buildings that still housed small businesses like Kuyper's Hardware and Rudd's Drugstore. At one street corner a city worker was up on a cherry picker, putting up strings of brightly colored lights and green garlands. Christmas decorations.

Neither Suzanne nor Sam spoke a word until they were a few blocks from home. Then Suzanne, sensing there might be something left unsaid between them, asked, "Is something wrong?"

Sam didn't mince words. "I don't want you to get involved."

"I'm already involved. I saw Allan Sharp get stabbed."

"You know what I mean."

"Not really," Suzanne said, even though she knew exactly what Sam was driving at.

"Doogie told me you chased after that guy," Sam said. "And that he turned and pulled a knife on you. Almost killed you."

Thanks a lot, Doogie.

"Doogie might have exaggerated that part a bit."

"No, I think you're the one who's probably underplaying the truth. And I think I know why."

"Excuse me, but what are we really talking about?" Suzanne asked.

"I'm asking you not to stick your neck out," Sam said.

"I can handle myself, you know."

"Like Allan Sharp did?"

He had her there.

Sam was silent as he turned into their driveway. The

headlights swept the frozen pavement, which still held a thin skim of snow. "Suzanne, I'm the coroner. I don't know what I'd do if I had to . . ."

"Nothing's going to happen to me," Suzanne said.

"Just, please, I'm asking you to be careful."

"Come on, Sam, you *know* me." Suzanne tried her best to sound calm and even a little lighthearted.

"Indeed I do, my dear. Which is why I'm begging you to take care."

CHAPTER 3

"I already heard about the murder," were Petra's first words as Suzanne and Toni tumbled through the kitchen door of the Cackleberry Club Monday morning, ushering in a whoosh of frigid air. "I've been listening to WLGN since the sun came up, and Allan Sharp's murder has been positively splashed across the news. They even had it on before the farm report. First a nasty murder and then hog prices." Petra gazed at Suzanne and Toni with a mixture of shock and awe. "And to think you guys were there." She shoved both hands deep into the pockets of her checkered apron and shook her head. "Must have been awful."

"It was spooky," Toni said, eyes sparkling as she shrugged out of her coat.

"No, Petra's right," Suzanne said. "It was awful."

"And there isn't a single suspect?" Petra asked. She was a big-boned Norwegian lady with a kind face, no-nonsense short silver hair, and warm, expressive hazel eyes. Now in her early fifties, Petra was confident and satisfied and wore her age like a badge of honor.

"Could have been a ghost," Toni said.

"Could have been someone who had a major beef with Allan Sharp," Suzanne said.

"Now, there's a major shocker," Petra said. "Half of Kindred had a beef with that dingbat Allan Sharp. If Sheriff Doogie tries to narrow down a list of people who *didn't* like Sharp, he's going to be interviewing people until the spring thaw."

"Doogie's going to have to figure something out," Suzanne said. "People are really shaken up by this."

"Will the Christmas play still go on?" Petra asked.

Suzanne shrugged. "I have no idea."

"The show must go on," Toni said. "Isn't that the tried-and-true saying?"

"But maybe not when the principal actor has been murdered in cold blood," Suzanne said.

Petra picked up her spatula, bent over a frying pan, and started shoving hash browns around. "Mmn, don't like that word, 'murder.' Let's just keep all that investigative nonsense out of my kitchen. It not only puts me in a downer mood; it's bad karma to boot."

"Toni," Suzanne said, "why don't you unlock the front door and make sure the tables are all set for breakfast? I'll print out our specials on the chalkboard." She gave Petra a sideways look. "I'm assuming we have a few specials?"

"Killer specials," Petra said. Then she put a hand up to her mouth and said, "Well, you know what I mean." She dug in her apron pocket and handed Suzanne a three-by-five-inch recipe card with writing on it. "Here you go, Suzy-Q."

Suzanne glanced at the list of specials. "Elvis French toast?"

"What the heck is that?" Toni asked.

"It's French toast stuffed with peanut butter and bananas," Petra said.

Toni perked up. "Sounds pretty good."

SUZANNE and Toni pushed through the swinging door and got busy in the café. They snapped on lights, jacked up the thermostat a few degrees, and glanced around. The tables were covered in cheery yellow and white tablecloths and had salt and pepper shakers and sugar bowls ready to go. But they needed to be set with napkins, silverware, pitchers of cream, and ceramic coffee mugs. When the morning rush started—and it would probably begin in the next ten minutes—they had to be ready. Hungry truckers and farmers would be bulldozing their way in, anxious to order their hearty and delicious breakfasts.

While Toni worked on the tables, Suzanne put on two pots of coffee, French roast and a Kona blend. She also got hot water ready for tea and pulled out a pretty Coalport teapot in the Ming Rose pattern, as well as a Chinese blue and white teapot. More and more she'd weaned her customers away from tea bags and had them enjoying fresh-brewed tea leaves, especially in the afternoons, when she offered cream teas and special event teas.

"Got sticky buns fresh from the oven," Petra called out.

Suzanne leaned forward and saw that Petra had pushed two trays of glazed cinnamon and pecan rolls through the pass-through. Good. She stacked the rolls carefully in the glass pie server that sat atop her old-fashioned ceramic counter, the counter that came as a sort of bonus gift when she'd scrounged the old-fashioned soda fountain backdrop from a long-defunct drugstore.

The rest of the Cackleberry Club was equally charming. Funky metal signs and colorful painted plates adorned the walls, along with a few of Petra's hand-stitched wall hangings. There was an oak cabinet that held candles, vases, linens, and glassware, and wooden shelving that ran all around the room and served as a perch for Suzanne's vast collection of ceramic chickens. She had everything from salt-and-pepper-shaker chicks to enormous red and green roosters.

Across the café were the Book Nook and the Knitting Nest. When Suzanne had acquired and renovated the building, what had been an old Spur station, those two extra rooms had been a kind of lucky-strike extra. Now one was filled to capacity with bestsellers, the other jammed full of quilting fabrics and colorful skeins of yarn, a nod to Petra, who also gave knitting and quilting lessons a couple of times a week.

"The chalkboard," Toni called out. "You gotta put up the specials."

"I'm on it," Suzanne called back, realizing she'd kind of spaced out for a few minutes. Thinking about Allan Sharp . . . and the mysterious ghost.

So . . . rosemary scones and sticky rolls. Elvis French toast. Hash browns and turkey bacon. Breakfast burritos. Peach cobbler pancakes. Scrambled eggs and veggie omelets. Everything farm-to-table fresh, but hearty enough to keep a person fueled for the cold.

When she'd finished, Suzanne walked to the front window, pushed back the café curtains, and stared out at the blanket of snow. It made everything—the driveway, trees, small buildings across the way—look pristine and softly mounded. Then she remembered the drops of bright crimson blood dripping from the ghost's knife last night and felt a sudden tickle of apprehension. Was she safe? Was any-body in Kindred really safe with a killer on the prowl?

THREE minutes later, their first customers began to arrive and Suzanne was caught up in the morning rush. She greeted people, seated them at tables, poured coffee, and listened to gossip about last night's murder as it swirled around her like an ill wind. She took orders, delivered them to Petra, then ran back out into the café and took more orders.

"Are you picking up snippets of the conversation du jour?" Toni asked when she and Suzanne met behind the counter. "Everyone seems to be gossiping about Allan Sharp's murder."

"Because everyone knows about it by now," Suzanne said.

"Small-town folk," Toni said. "Our underground network has better communication ops than the US military."

"And everyone's got a theory on whodunit."

"Guy at table eight suspects al-Qaeda," Toni said. She tapped a finger against her head. "Ca-rack-pot."

Suzanne grabbed three breakfast orders that were up, delivered them to her customers, and then glanced out the window again. Then, seeing a familiar face bobbing across the parking lot, she hurried to the front door with a big smile on her face.

"Reverend Yoder," Suzanne said as she held the door open. "We haven't seen you in a while." Reverend Yoder was the heart and soul of the Journey's End Church, which was just across the parking lot from the Cackleberry Club. He was tall and thin and had a strict Calvinistic aura about him. Once you got to know him, however, he turned out to be one of the gentlest, most kindhearted people in Kindred.

Reverend Yoder bustled in, shivering and smiling as he clapped his gloved hands against the sleeves of his thin coat. "I finally got to the point where I couldn't resist the temptation of all the delicious aromas emanating from your fine kitchen."

"You see," Suzanne said, "there *is* such a thing as good temptation."

"I'd like you to meet a colleague of mine," Reverend Yoder said. "This is Ethan Jakes."

"Wonderful to meet you," Suzanne said, shaking hands with the young man who'd accompanied Reverend Yoder. She noted that Ethan Jakes seemed to be a stark contrast to Yoder. Jakes had a pinched face and a furrowed brow and wore what looked to be a permanent scowl.

"Reverend Jakes is newly ordained and going to be our new assistant pastor," Yoder said.

"Wait . . . don't tell me you're leaving us," Suzanne said, surprise and dismay evident in her voice.

"Not for a while, anyway," Reverend Yoder said. "But it never hurts to be prepared."

Suzanne led the two men to a table, got them settled, and then poured each of them a cup of coffee. "You heard about our trouble last night?" she asked. "At the theater?"

"Such a terrible tragedy." Reverend Yoder shook his head. "Poor Mr. Sharp."

That seemed to be a cue for young Ethan Jakes to come alive with a fiery Bible verse. "For he is God's servant for your good," he suddenly sang out. "But if you do wrong, be afraid, for he does not bear the sword in vain. For he is the servant of God, an avenger who carries out God's wrath on the wrongdoer."

"You think Allan Sharp was a wrongdoer?" Suzanne asked. She was taken aback by the man's intensity.

"He most certainly was," Jakes said. "One of my first missions when I arrived in Kindred was to approach Allan Sharp. I wanted him to be my champion at the city council and help sponsor a day of prayer. Instead, Sharp scoffed at me." Jakes's lip curled in disdain and he shook his head. "With the evil pull of technology, pornography, and drugs in our society, a day of prayer is practically a requirement!"

"Well, I'll settle for Sheriff Doogie sorting out the wrongdoers here in town," Suzanne said. "Along with administering just punishments." She smiled at Reverend Yoder. "I'm guessing you're here for one of Petra's omelets?"

"With vegetables and cheese," Yoder said. "And a cup of tea. Something with a little body."

"I'm just brewing a pot of Assam."

"Perfect," Yoder said.

"And you?" Suzanne asked Jakes.

He stared at her with dark-rimmed eyes. "Just a simple poached egg on dry toast."

AT eleven o'clock, Sheriff Doogie came drifting in. Most of the breakfast crowd had departed and it was too early for the luncheon crowd, so he glanced around, seemingly pleased that he wouldn't be bothered, and stomped over to the counter. Slouching down on his favorite stool, he swiped off his Smokey Bear hat and set it on the stool next to him. It was a clear warning that no one should infringe on his personal space.

Suzanne poured Doogie a cup of black coffee, then placed two sticky buns on a plate and set it in front of him.

The sheriff was like a trained bear; he responded positively to sugar.

"How late were you at the theater last night?" Suzanne asked.

Doogie blew on his coffee, then took a quick sip. "Don't ask."

"It was that bad, huh?"

"Ah, it is what it is. Problems and vexation come hand in hand with the gold star."

"How did your interviews with the other cast members go?" Suzanne asked.

"They weren't terribly productive. Can I get some butter, please?"

"Does that mean you didn't come up with any decent leads?" Suzanne gave him four pats of butter.

"Can't say that I did," Doogie said. He slathered butter on his sticky roll, took a bite, and chewed thoughtfully. "I was hoping that maybe you remembered something else. You know, in the cold, clear light of morning." He shifted on his stool. "Since you've had some time to ruminate, is there anything else you can tell me? Anything your mind might have dredged up overnight?"

"All I saw was the ghost," Suzanne said. "Only it was a fake ghost."

Doogie glanced around, then leaned forward on his stool and gave Suzanne a conspiratorial look. "But that's what makes this case so weird . . . some crazy jackhole had that costume all ready to go." He enunciated his words carefully. "Which means Allan Sharp's murder was *planned*."

"Premeditated," Suzanne said. She shivered at the connotation the word carried. She hadn't thought about the costume aspect last night, but now it seemed obvious.

"Planned and carried out by someone who was reckless

and brazen enough to murder Allan Sharp in front of a dozen people," Doogie said.

"Maybe the killer is just plain crazy," Suzanne said. "A dangerous psychopath."

"There's always that theory," Doogie agreed. "But most times . . ." He hesitated, looking thoughtful now. "When a man commits murder, there's a reason that drives him to it."

"A motivating factor," Suzanne said.

Doogie bobbed his head. "Anger, resentment, jealousy, political ideology, that sort of thing."

"You asked the all-important question last night," Suzanne said. "Who hated Allan Sharp?"

"I asked and then answered my own question. Pretty much everybody in town."

"That makes for a pile of suspects."

"And the pile keeps getting bigger with every person I talk to," Doogie said. "Seems nearly everyone had some kind of gripe with Sharp. Hell, even I had words with the guy on more than one occasion. He was a real jackass."

"So, what now?" Suzanne asked.

Doogie looked troubled. "I'll keep asking around. Dig into Sharp's finances and different business interests. See if that leads anywhere." He took a slurp of coffee. "People are really freaked-out about this. I'm catching a lot of heat. Mayor Mobley convened a special meeting with the city council."

"It's only natural for people to be scared."

"I understand that," Doogie said. "But it doesn't make my investigation any easier. Hell, the guy who killed Sharp could have been here for breakfast this morning, stuffing his face with flapjacks, chuckling to himself because nobody was the wiser."

"Now you're trying to scare me."

"Didn't mean to. It's just that this feels like a very strange case. And between kids racing their cars on a half-frozen lake and a couple of home invasions to investigate, I've got a lot on my plate."

"Well, let's put some bacon and eggs on your plate right now. Give you some protein to speed you through the day." Suzanne turned to the pass-through and called in an order to Petra. And thought about what Doogie had just said. That the killer could have come here for breakfast or could be on his way in for lunch. And there wasn't a thing she could do about it.

Or was there?

CHAPTER 4

"DIDN'T you just do that?" Toni asked.

Suzanne turned toward her, a piece of yellow chalk clutched in her hand. "Do what?"

Toni gestured at the chalkboard, where brightly colored puffy letters danced across the black surface and starbursts highlighted some of the specials. "Print the menu."

"You see how time flies when you're having fun?" Suzanne said. "This is the luncheon menu I'm putting up."

Toni's eyes goggled and she hastily looked at her watch. "Holy smokes, is it that late?" She tapped a finger against the crystal. "Dang thing stopped on me again."

"Is that the watch Junior gave you for your birthday?"

"Yeah. Although I think he got it from one of those claw machines at the county fair. Fished it out of a pile of junky cigarette lighters, Kewpie dolls, and tin belt buckles."

"Maybe he got it at the pawnshop."

"Junior does love his pawnshops," Toni agreed. "If he's

not buying something he can't afford, he's trying to hock something. Tools, tires, fishing gear, an outboard motor." She took a step back and squinted at the board. "What's that say? Parrot soup?"

"Carrot soup," Suzanne said. "Along with chicken meatballs, a black and blue burger, and a grilled ham and cheese sandwich. Oh, and a winter salad plate."

"Guys don't generally dig salads."

"This one is fairly hearty. It's got apple bits, walnuts, feta cheese, dried cranberries, and a balsamic vinegar dressing. Besides, if guys don't like it, they can just order something else. Here." Suzanne handed Toni her piece of chalk. "Why don't you finish up while I run into the Book Nook and unpack all those boxes that UPS unceremoniously dumped on our doorstep this morning?"

Once she was in the Book Nook, Suzanne grabbed a knife and busied herself with slitting open all the cartons. Then she set about shelving the new arrivals. There was something very satisfying about the shiny, colorful book jackets and the way the shelves came newly alive with gardening, mystery, romance, and history books. She was also glad to see that copies of *Kiss the King* by Carmen Copeland, a local romance writer, had arrived. In fact, the publisher had shipped an entire case of Carmen's books.

Suzanne decided she'd have to schedule a book signing for Carmen, though sometimes those events could turn slightly unpleasant. Carmen, who lived in a sprawling Victorian mansion in the nearby town of Jessup, was a wealthy, somewhat snobby one percenter who never let the other 99 percent forget it.

With all the new volumes shelved, Suzanne grabbed a few children's books so she could make a Christmas display. The Book Nook had limited space, but she'd managed to cram in a couple of rump-sprung easy chairs along with a battered wooden table. That table now held a small, twinkling Christmas tree along with some cotton batting that was meant to represent drifting snow.

As Suzanne hummed along, adding a couple of fuzzy reindeer to the display, as well as a few kids' picture books that were all about reindeer, her thoughts circled back to last night's catastrophe. She'd *tried* to dredge her memory for some sort of clue that would help Doogie; she really had. But nothing had surfaced yet. Maybe if she put what had been a harrowing experience on her brain's back burner, something would eventually pop. Hopefully it would, because Doogie seemed to be counting on her.

"Suzanne?" Toni leaned in the doorway of the Book Nook. "A little help, please?"

Suzanne looked up. "Pardon?"

"The café is filling up and I've already taken a dozen orders."

"Right. Okay," Suzanne said as Toni disappeared. "I'm on it."

At the exact moment Suzanne hustled back into the café, Mayor Mobley walked through the front door.

Mobley cocked a mournful eye at her and said, "Suzanne," in a voice that sounded as if he was about to make a major proclamation.

"Mayor Mobley," Suzanne said. "How was your emergency meeting this morning?"

Mobley's florid face pulled into a frown. "How'd you know about that?"

"In case you hadn't noticed, this is a café," Suzanne said. "Everybody talks. They gobble donuts and sticky buns, choke down enough coffee to kill a horse, get their sugar buzz going, and gossip to their hearts' content. It's like a relentless twenty-four-hour cycle of fake TV news."

"I don't like to hear that," Mayor Mobley said. He was overweight and sneaky as a weasel and had a pugnacious nature that was reflected on his pudgy face. This was Mobley's third term as mayor and probably the third time he'd stuffed the ballot box. The citizenry not only didn't like Mobley; they didn't particularly trust him. Then again, that's what happened when you had a reputation for sticking your fat fingers into all sorts of shady deals. Mayor Mobley and Allan Sharp were the deal brokers in town. Now, with Sharp dead and gone, it would be up to Mobley to carry on their nefarious tradition.

Suzanne seated Mobley at a small table by the window. Mobley, who was perpetually cranky and a genuine snake in the grass, got right down to business.

"If you know about our meeting, then I guess you've heard about Allan Sharp."

"Are you kidding?" Suzanne said. "I was *there* last night, working in the wings. I watched all of you guys come trooping offstage; then I saw Sharp get stabbed!" What was wrong with Mobley? Had he left his brains in his sock drawer this morning?

"Oh yeah, I guess I did see you there," Mobley muttered. He wasn't one bit flustered by his mistake. Then again, he never was. He seemed to perpetually exist in his own self-important world. He'd also managed to cobble together a web of informants who kept him apprised of everything.

"Allan was a good man," Mobley said in carefully measured tones.

"Yet you didn't ask him to run your last campaign,"

Suzanne said. Mobley and Sharp had always been thick as thieves. But not lately. Something major had happened in the last couple of months. Some sort of disagreement had driven a huge wedge between them.

"No, I hired someone else." Mobley's eyes were a pair of hard gray marbles as he stared at Suzanne. "Pretty much had to. Allan went out and got himself elected to the city council. I had to cut him loose because I didn't want anybody screaming foul play or accusing us of having an old boys' network."

Even though you really are an old boy with a network, Suzanne thought. Then she decided to have a little fun. It wasn't often that she got a chance to needle Mobley and maybe do some investigating at the same time.

"But right after the election you *did* have a major falling-out with Allan Sharp, isn't that right?"

"Not really," Mobley said. "We both had what you'd call . . . um, other interests." Then Mobley's face creased in a knowing crocodile smile. "But getting back to the murder, I guess you don't know everything, Suzanne."

"What don't I know?"

"That Sheriff Doogie already has a prime suspect."

Suzanne was shocked. Was this really true? Was Doogie hot on the trail of someone but had purposely played it cool with her? Or had this suspect just popped up in the last thirty minutes?

"Who is it?" Suzanne asked.

Mobley lifted a pudgy hand and made a childish zipping motion across his mouth. "You'll have to wait and see, Suzanne, just like every other law-abiding citizen in Kindred. Much as you have a reputation for meddling, you're not gonna get involved in this investigation." Mobley favored her with a knowing, smarmy smile. He was doing his level best to be intimidating, but Suzanne wasn't buying what he was selling.

Suzanne whipped out her order pad. "What can I get for you, Mayor?" She wasn't about to play Mobley's silly games. She'd worm the suspect's name out of Doogie later. The sheriff might talk tough but he was terrible at keeping secrets.

Mobley squinted at the chalkboard. "I'll have your ham and cheese sandwich with extra cheddar."

"On whole wheat toast?"

"Sourdough. And have Petra grill it in butter."

"Any sides?"

"Large order of French fries. Make sure they're nice and hot."

Suzanne decided that much grease would definitely make him a cardiac patient–in–waiting. One EKG special coming right up.

"Was that fat tub of lard giving you a hard time?" Toni asked. She was standing behind the counter, packing up a to-go order. Wrapping the pickles in plastic so the juice wouldn't leak everywhere, snapping lids on small containers that held potato salad.

"Mobley's just being Mobley," Suzanne said. "Nothing I can't handle."

"Are you sure? Because I'd be happy to mosey over there and spill something on him. I just brewed a fresh pot of Sumatran blend that's hotter'n blue blazes. I could dribble some down the front of Mobley's shirt or I could even try for a crotch shot."

"You're a good friend, Toni, but he's not worth the effort."

Suzanne and Toni went back to work, taking orders and serving luncheon entrees, doing a choreographed dance that was worthy of Martha Graham. Petra kept things churning in the kitchen, sending out orders and beaming whenever one of their customers ordered a nice slice of her fresh-baked pecan pie for dessert.

At two o'clock, Petra pulled a pan of scones from the oven and turned her attention to making dainty tea sandwiches. By two-thirty a few customers had wandered in for afternoon tea.

When the Cackleberry Club first opened, customers had come in looking for mid-afternoon pie and coffee. But with a little coaxing and a lot of charm, Suzanne had turned those confirmed pie and coffee lovers into fans of afternoon tea. Of course, Petra's chocolate chip scones, chicken and chutney tea sandwiches, and pink and yellow macarons had helped turn the tide as well.

As Toni poured steaming cups of Darjeeling into their treasured Shelley Primrose Chintz teacups, a young woman in a navy blue puffer coat stepped through the front door. But instead of sitting down at one of the empty tables, she stood there, looking nervous and a little timid.

Toni hurried over to the young woman. "Help you, honey?" she said. "We just started serving our afternoon three-course tea if you're interested."

"I . . . I'm looking for Suzanne Dietz," the young woman said. "Is she here?"

"She's working in the Book Nook," Toni said, gesturing across the café. "You head in there and when you encounter a fine-looking blond lady who looks like she could serve high tea while whipping an ornery bronc into shape . . . you'll have found our boss lady. That'll be Suzanne."

SUZANNE was sitting behind the front counter, writing up book orders and sipping a cup of tea, when the young woman approached her.

"May I help you?" Suzanne asked without looking up. She was just tallying her order amount. And it came to . . . a lot.

"I hope so."

Now Suzanne glanced up with a friendly smile. "We just received the new Lee Child thriller, and Carmen Copeland's newest romance is . . ." She stopped mid-sentence, a little startled because she was pretty sure she recognized this young woman. "Wait. I know you."

The woman touched a hand to her chest. "Amber. Amber Payson." She was in her late twenties, very pretty, even though she wore a somber expression. A cherubic flow of auburn hair enhanced her lovely peaches-and-cream complexion. She looked, Suzanne thought, as if her portrait should be done in stained glass in some medieval cathedral.

"You used to work at the Westvale Clinic with Sam," Suzanne said. "At the front desk. You sat right behind Esther." She noted that Amber, though dressed in a navy blue puffer coat, still managed to look fashionable and just this side of sexy.

"I wish I still worked there," Amber said.

"It's nice to see you again," Suzanne said. "And I didn't mean to push our new bestsellers at you."

"That's okay." Amber shifted from one foot to the other. She seemed to be working up to something.

"If you're not in the market for a book, maybe I could interest you in a pot of Darjeeling or Assam tea?" Suzanne said. "Or Japanese green tea if you're in the mood to stretch your taste buds."

Amber shook her head. "Thank you, but I . . . I don't want any tea." She leaned forward, placed her hands on the counter, and dropped her voice. "I came here hoping you could help me."

"Help you?" Suzanne cocked her head to one side. "I'm not quite sure I understand what you're getting at."

"You and I have a mutual friend."

"Okay." Suzanne waited patiently for Amber to make her point.

"Missy Langston."

"Yes, Missy is a dear friend. But what does that . . . I mean, how may I help *you*?"

"There's a rather difficult situation that's come up," Amber stammered. "And Missy told me that you were really, really smart and . . . that, um, maybe you could give me some assistance."

"If you're asking for advice, perhaps you'd better tell me what this situation is all about," Suzanne said. She was starting to get a weird, jangling vibe from this girl.

"The thing is . . . I just came from the Law Enforcement Center," Amber said. "Where they asked me all sorts of questions about Allan Sharp."

"You mean Sheriff Doogie asked you questions?" Suzanne said. "Or one of his deputies did?"

"It was the sheriff."

"You must be one of the actors from last night," Suzanne said, though she didn't remember seeing Amber at the theater.

Amber shook her head. "No."

"Then why on earth would they ask you questions about Sharp?"

Amber drew a deep breath and said, "Because they think I killed him."

CHAPTER 5

"MAYBE you should start from the very beginning," Suzanne said. "Tell me the whole story." She'd immediately hustled Amber into her small office adjacent to the Book Nook. Now she sat in her leather swivel chair while Amber faced her across a desk cluttered with invoices, orders, vendor product sheets, and recipes. "You're an honest-to-goodness suspect in Allan Sharp's murder?"

Amber gave a sorrowful nod. "According to Sheriff Doogie I am."

Suzanne shook her head. "I find that hard to believe since you weren't even at the theater."

"No, I wasn't. I didn't even know about the play until this morning."

"Then why is Doogie questioning you? What's the connection?"

"After I left the clinic I went to work for Mr. Sharp at his law firm."

"Oh," Suzanne said. "You mean at Sharp Shinder and Young."

"I thought it was going to be my dream job. I'd have lots more responsibility, practically be on par with a paralegal. It was going to be a fabulous opportunity for me to learn about the law." Amber drew a quick, shaky breath. "Unfortunately, things didn't turn out the way I hoped, so I resigned."

"How long ago was that?"

Amber thought for a few moments. "It's been two months. And my departure didn't exactly happen on friendly terms."

"In other words you quit," Suzanne said. "Why?" She knew there was more to this story. That the other shoe was about to drop with a loud clunk.

Amber could barely meet Suzanne's eyes. "I quit because of Mr. Sharp."

"Did Allan force you out because the two of you didn't get along? Did he overburden you with extra work so you'd have to quit?"

"No, the workload was nothing I couldn't handle. In fact, I enjoyed the legal aspect and I'm a pretty hard worker. It was . . . all the other stuff."

Suzanne's blood ran a little cold. "The other stuff," she said. "Go on."

Amber looked pained. "I'd been there maybe a month before Mr. Sharp began to harass me unmercifully. He was constantly making comments about how I looked, how pretty I was, and how I dressed. Then he started finding excuses to brush up against me or whisper in my ear. He even drove by my house a couple of times—a duplex over on Mason Street."

Right about then, Suzanne started thinking that Sharp's

death might not have been such a bad thing after all. "What else?" she asked.

Amber couldn't meet Suzanne's eyes. "He asked me out to lunch as well as on a couple of dates. When I continued to say, 'No, thank you,' he started bringing me cornball gifts. Teddy bears, candy, funny trinkets for my desk. Then one day . . . he brought me a present of black frilly lingerie."

Suzanne grimaced. There were no words. She'd always known Sharp was a sleazeball; she just hadn't realized the full extent of his sleaziness.

"I always tried my best to keep our relationship strictly professional," Amber said. "That's what I was taught to do at business school." She glanced sideways at Suzanne. "I don't know, maybe things have changed?"

"No," Suzanne said in a firm voice. "Nothing's changed. If anything, women are standing up to this kind of crappy, rude behavior. They're fighting back."

Amber nodded. "That's what I figured. But it's difficult to stand up for yourself when your boss refuses to take no for an answer. When you're terrified that he'll badmouth you all over town."

"Did Sharp do that? Try to damage your reputation?"

"Some."

"Oh Lord." Suzanne leaned back in her chair and steepled her fingers. "You don't need me, honey, you need an attorney."

Amber curled a lip. "You mean like Allan Sharp's partner?"

"No. Definitely not him. Someone who specializes in workplace harassment. Wait, don't tell me you had a problem with Don Shinder, too?"

"No, I never did."

"Did Don Shinder know that Sharp was sexually harassing you?"

"I don't think so," Amber said. "Mr. Shinder was out of the office an awful lot and I didn't feel it was my place to bring it up to him. For one thing, I didn't know if I could trust him."

Suzanne sat there thinking.

"Was Missy right?" Amber asked. "Can you help me?"

"Maybe I could talk to Sheriff Doogie," Suzanne said slowly. "He's a good friend and might listen to me." She tapped a finger against her desk. "Did you tell Sheriff Doogie about Sharp harassing you?"

Amber hung her head. "No, because it's too embarrassing."

Suzanne thought some more. "But somebody out there put a bug in Doogie's ear that you were angry at Allan Sharp."

"I have no idea who that would be," Amber said.

"*Someone* said something to Doogie. And it carried enough weight for him to bring you in for questioning. Unfortunately, it looks as if you have an enemy, someone who wants to bring serious trouble down upon your head."

"It's terrifying to think someone would hate me that much."

"Is there anyone else who's been causing problems for you? Old employer, old boyfriend, jealous girlfriend, roommate?"

"I'm not employed right now and I don't have a roommate."

"Boyfriend, then?" Suzanne asked.

"Even if it was an old boyfriend, I don't think Curt would be that nasty."

"You never know," Suzanne said. "Did you ever tell this guy, Curt, about Sharp's bad behavior?"

"Some."

"Hmm."

Amber sat bolt upright in her chair and turned mournful eyes on Suzanne. "So, was Missy right? Can you help me?"

"Amber, I'm going to try. Believe me, nobody wants to figure this out as much as I do."

AN hour and a half later, Suzanne, Toni, and Petra were gathered in the deserted Cackleberry Club for what Toni liked to call an executive board meeting. Which meant Petra had brought her knitting and Toni was fussing with a new set of purple press-on nails.

"What are you working on?" Toni asked Petra.

"Just something I want to show my knitting class," Petra said. "It's a sweater made with a blend of arctic fox yarn."

"Are you serious?" Toni asked.

"Well, it's thirty percent arctic fox and seventy percent merino wool," Petra said.

"You mean this wool was once alive?" Toni asked.

Petra chuckled. "Most types of wool were. Or are."

Suzanne sat down at the table with Toni and Petra. "Are you ready?" she asked. She'd tossed around the idea of telling them about Amber's problem but had decided to hold off until she talked the whole thing over with Sam. So, instead, Suzanne just told Toni and Petra that she wanted to go over their plans for the coming week.

"We're gonna be super busy," Toni said immediately. "Day after tomorrow is our Christmas Tea, which is sold out, by the way. And then we kick off our toy drive on Friday."

"Is Junior still planning to bring us a few boxes or bins for collecting toys?" Suzanne asked.

"He promised he would," Toni said.

"And we're probably going to need posters," Suzanne said.

Petra waved a hand. "I'm already on it. But we need more marketing juice than just that. We gotta let people *know* that we're collecting toys."

"I've got that covered," Suzanne said. "Laura Benchley at the *Bugle* is going to do a write-up in the newspaper and I'm already booked on Paula Patterson's *Friends and Neighbors* radio show. Paula promised me a two-minute segment."

"That's perfect," Petra said. "So what else is hot?" She looked around the café. "Oh. Holiday decorating."

"Consider it done," Toni said. "I'm the garland and tinsel queen." She made a grand gesture and one of her nails popped off. "Oops." She grabbed it and stuck it back on.

"Then you'd better get your tinsel in gear," Suzanne said. "Because we need to be gussied up in time for our Christmas Tea." She glanced at Petra. "You're all ready for that? Ingredients have been ordered?"

"Orders are in, menus are planned," Petra said. "Now I'm working on Saturday afternoon's wine and cheese fund-raiser for my church."

"And Saturday is opening night for our play," Suzanne said.

"The play," Toni said, sticking on another purple nail. "We got so busy, I kind of forgot about that." She drummed her fingers against the table, testing the stick-on power of her new nails. "Is dress rehearsal still on for tonight?"

"No," Petra said. "It's been cancelled." She made a face. "I forgot to tell you guys. Teddy Hardwick called during lunch and said rehearsals are off for tonight, but they'll start up again tomorrow night."

"Must be out of respect for Allan Sharp," Toni said. "Why else would there be a delay?"

"I think," Petra said, "they're hoping to find someone to step in and play Scrooge."

"Another victim," Toni said.

Suzanne sighed. "Let's just hope there isn't a Christmas jinx."

ON her way home from work, Suzanne decided to stop at Alchemy Boutique and talk to Missy. Missy was, after all, Amber's close friend. Maybe she'd be able to shed a little more light on why Amber had come begging for help this afternoon.

Alchemy Boutique was a contemporary upscale clothing shop that shouldn't have been particularly well received in the small midwestern town of Kindred but had proved to be a rip-roaring success. Alchemy carried the latest trend-driven fashions—7 for All Mankind jeans, cold-shoulder sweaters, shredded hoodies, suede booties, and designer looks by Rag & Bone, Vince, and C&C T-shirts.

Suzanne let herself in the door and instantly felt her spirits lift. Candles flickered; Adele's "Set Fire to the Rain" oozed over the sound system; beautiful clothing beckoned from tasty little please-touch-me displays. Olive drab jackets, camo jeans, and suede boots were gathered in one section; another table was stacked with orange-, red-, and plum-colored sweaters. An old-fashioned cabinet held a wealth of bags and dreamy wool scarves. For a few seconds, Suzanne had an image of herself dressed in caramel-colored leather slacks and a matching sweater. The slacks would be soft as butter, the sweater embellished with bits of suede fringe and exotic feathers. A camel's-hair coat would be draped carelessly over her shoulders as she posed next to a silver Mercedes-Benz. Then she shook her head and the Suzanne-as-runway-model dream burst like a soap bubble.

At the same moment a loud, excited shriek erupted from the back of the shop. "Suzanne! I haven't seen you in *forever.*"

Missy Langston bustled toward her, all long blond hair, fair skin, and boundless enthusiasm. Up until a year ago, Missy had been endowed with a lush, positively ripe figure. Now she'd dieted down to a teeny-tiny size, the better to squeeze into the extra small fashions that the store carried. Suzanne wondered whether the weight loss had been Missy's idea, or if she'd been coerced by Carmen Copeland, the snooty romance writer who also owned the store.

Suzanne and Missy exchanged de rigueur air kisses and friendly hi-how-are-yous. Then Suzanne got right down to business.

"One of your friends stopped by to see me today," she said.

Missy gave a knowing nod. "Amber. I told her that you could probably help her."

"The influence I have over Sheriff Doogie is basically zero to none," Suzanne said. "What Amber really needs is a good attorney."

"Couldn't you do for her what you did for me?" Missy gave a little shudder. "I'll never forget how you pulled my fat out of the fryer when Doogie accused me of murdering Lester Drummond."

"Yes, but I *knew* you so I could vouch for you wholeheartedly. I don't know a thing about Amber, other than the fact that she worked at Sam's clinic for a few months."

"Well, can't you talk to Sam? Or ask somebody at the clinic?"

"Sam doesn't want me to get involved in the Allan Sharp case. In fact, he was quite adamant about it."

Missy smiled. "When have you ever done what someone told you to do, Suzanne? Long as I've known you, you always follow your head and your heart and do the *right* thing."

Yes, but is this the right thing? Suzanne wondered.

Missy reached out and grabbed Suzanne's hand. "Listen, Suzanne, I swear on my mother's grave that Amber is good people. And right now she's being falsely accused of a crime she didn't commit."

"It makes me nervous that somebody went out of their way to accuse Amber," Suzanne said. "That she's made an enemy somewhere."

"Doesn't matter who started the lie," Missy said. "Amber's in trouble and she needs help."

"Like I said, she needs a lawyer."

"She needs a friend."

Suzanne raised an eyebrow. "And I'm supposed to be that friend?"

"Isn't there some kind of saying about how your enemy is my enemy?" Missy asked.

"I think that's only in B movies that involve swords, armor, and fur capes."

"But it could work the other way, too, couldn't it?" Missy pleaded. "My friend is your friend?"

"I suppose so."

Missy continued with her impassioned plea for Amber, begging Suzanne to step in and help. Suzanne listened carefully but still wasn't convinced.

Finally, Missy said, "Look, I'll make a deal with you. You do what you can for Amber—running whatever interference you can with Sheriff Doogie—and I'll help you out.

I could . . ." She glanced around the boutique. "I could stage a mini fashion show for you."

"What are you talking about?" Suzanne asked.

"Well, I know you're having your big Christmas Tea this Wednesday. What if I brought a few girls and some fun clothes over to the Cackleberry Club and we staged a mini fashion show for you?"

"A fashion show," Suzanne said, liking the idea.

"It would be an impromptu surprise. Kind of like a Christmas gift for all your guests. What do you say, Suzanne?"

"I think it's a great idea. But you don't have to bribe me. I'll talk to Doogie and try to run interference . . ."

"You'll really help Amber?" Missy cried.

"Yes, I will," Suzanne said. She'd take a giant step in and use whatever influence she could muster. "For you, Missy, I'll try to help Amber. I really will."

BY the time Suzanne arrived home, it was well after six o'clock. She kicked off her boots, stowed her coat in the front hall closet, and wondered where her dogs were. There was usually the telltale click of toenails on floorboards and then two warm muzzles snuffled her hand, a lovely doggy greeting. But when Suzanne walked into the kitchen and found Sam feeding jerky treats to Baxter and Scruff, she knew her work here was done.

"Hey," Sam said, a grin splitting his face. "You're home."

"*You're* home," Suzanne said. Sam was generally the one who was the late arrival. Also, though this was slightly picky, it technically wasn't Sam's home yet. They were, as Suzanne liked to say, living in sin. But since they'd be getting married in a few short months, it made no earthly sense for Sam to keep his apartment. After all, Suzanne had plenty of room upstairs in her king-sized bed.

"Are you actually cooking something or just puttering around, trying to look busy?" Suzanne asked as Baxter and Scruff finally came over and stretched their noses up, hoping for a pet. Or another treat.

Sam fixed Suzanne with a dazzling smile and her heart leapt at the idea that this man, this slightly *younger* man, not only loved her, but had asked her to marry him.

"What I'm doing couldn't exactly be classified as cooking," Sam said. "It's more like prowling through the refrigerator and pulling out a few choice ingredients that will hopefully inspire you." He took two quick steps in her direction, wrapped his arms around her, and pulled her close. Delivered a kiss that was long and sweet. Then his lips moved down to impart tiny butterfly kisses on her neck. "You're the one who's the gourmet chef, after all," he murmured.

"Mmn," Suzanne said, her appreciation apparent as she snuggled even closer to him. *Never mind the gourmet chef part. Just please don't stop those kisses. In fact, let's just save the calories and chuck the whole idea of dinner so we can go upstairs and . . .*

"What about lamb chops?" Sam asked. Regrettably, he'd come up for air and the kisses had stopped.

"I take it you're hungry?" she asked.

"Famished. After a day of appendectomies, broken wrists, and a possible E. coli outbreak, who wouldn't be?"

Me, Suzanne thought. *I'd never eat a speck of food again if I had to deal with that stuff.* Now that Sam's mind had methodically switched over to food, she knew the kissing and hugging portion of the evening was over.

"How about I do a quick grill on some lamb chops and serve them with American fries and broccolini?"

Sam grinned. "I'd go out and commit highway robbery just for your delicious taters."

Suzanne got busy then. The nightly routine of cooking a complete meal appealed to her. It felt somehow comforting and brought a sense of closure to her day. Afterward, she and Sam would hunker down for the night, enjoying their almost-family. No more simply eating a sandwich alone in front of the TV.

Sitting at the dining room table in a warm spill of candlelight, Suzanne waited until they were halfway through their dinner and the better part of a bottle of Montrachet before she told Sam that Amber Payson had stopped by to see her.

"Amber?" Sam said, his brow puckering. "You mean our Amber from the clinic?" Baxter and Scruff perked their ears forward when he spoke. Sam was more liberal than Suzanne about feeding dogs at the table, so there was always the chance of a choice tidbit.

"Well, she hasn't been your Amber for a good six months," Suzanne said. "In fact, she's been working for Allan Sharp."

That grabbed Sam's immediate attention. "You're not serious."

"Not only that; Amber seems to be in a bit of trouble." Suzanne went on to explain about Amber showing up at the Cackleberry Club, the accusations from Doogie, and Amber's subsequent plea for help.

Sam was dumbfounded. "Now Amber's a suspect in Allan Sharp's murder? I can't believe it."

"She was terribly upset about being questioned by Doogie, so I know she didn't just make it up."

"And Amber wants you to step in and help her? Use whatever influence you have with Doogie?"

"That was the basic gist of her request, yes."

As always, Sam's practicality came to the forefront. "Amber doesn't need you; she needs an attorney."

Suzanne aimed her fork at him. "Thank you very much. That's exactly what I told her."

"And it was excellent advice. It means you won't get dragged into some weird investigation."

"But I didn't say I *wouldn't* help her," Suzanne said, her eyes focused on Sam.

"Advising her to hire an attorney was all the help she needs," Sam said. He popped a bite of lamb chop into his mouth, chewed appreciatively, and said, "This is really delicious, you know? And your glaze—I don't know how you do it—is to die for." Baxter stood up and his ears pricked forward.

Suzanne continued to look at Sam until, eventually, his chewing slowed. Then he swallowed hard. "No," he said. "Oh no." Baxter lay back down.

"I'm not going to get *involved* involved," Suzanne said. "I'm just going to ask Doogie a few simple questions. Probe around, try to find out who Amber's accuser was."

Sam set down his fork. "Allan Sharp was *murdered*, Suzanne. His killer *threatened* you. Do you not get that? On top of that, we don't *know* Amber very well. She could be under the influence of drugs. Or . . ." He searched for the right word. "Delusional."

"She wasn't delusional when she worked for you a few months ago. Besides, Missy Langston says Amber is to be trusted. They're apparently very good friends and Missy firmly believes that Amber is levelheaded. And you know I'll be careful." Suzanne stood up, grabbed her plate, and then reached over to clear Sam's plate. Smiled sweetly as she did so.

"No, you'll take chances," Sam said. "You always do."

"Mmn, how can I convince you otherwise? Perhaps with a slice of peach pie for dessert?"

Sam frowned. "You're trying to change the subject."

Suzanne set the dishes back down, stepped around the table, and kissed him. Her lips were gentle at first; then she gradually increased the intensity. "No," she whispered, "*this* is changing the subject."

Sam pulled back from her a quarter inch. "You're not playing fair. You won't get away with this."

But in the end, she did. Because Suzanne could be quite convincing when she wanted to be.

CHAPTER 6

FRYING pans sizzled, eggs bobbed in bubbling water, and copper pots clunked as Suzanne, Toni, and Petra prepped for the coming day.

"Eggs on a cloud this morning," Petra boomed out. It was one of her favorite breakfasts, a poached egg perched on a flaky buttermilk biscuit. "Plus pumpkin breakfast casserole and blueberry flapjacks."

"What's the difference between pancakes and flapjacks?" Toni asked. She was slicing oranges for fresh orange juice but having trouble because of her press-on nails.

"Flapjacks are more hearty and country-style," Petra said. "And, Toni, if one of our customers finds a sliver of purple plastic floating in their orange juice, I'm going to rip every one of those stupid things off your fingers."

"Yeah, yeah," Toni said. She sliced a couple more oranges and then glanced at Suzanne, who was arranging a stack of plates. "You're awfully quiet this morning."

"Oh, I've been noodling something around," Suzanne said.

"A good something or a bad something?" Toni asked.

"More like a questionable something," Suzanne said.

Petra looked up from her griddle. "Uh-oh. Does this have to do with Allan Sharp?"

"Yes, it does," Suzanne said. "Now . . . promise me you ladies won't breathe a word?"

"Spit it out," Toni said. "You've really got me dancing on tenterhooks."

"Here's the thing," Suzanne said. "Amber Payson dropped by to see me yesterday."

"The girl who used to work at Westvale Clinic," Petra said.

"That's right," Suzanne said. "Only it turns out Amber's most recent job was working as a paralegal for Allan Sharp."

Petra paused, a large wooden spoon in her hand.

"And Amber's been accused by someone . . . I don't know who exactly . . . of murdering Allan Sharp," Suzanne said.

"Holy butterballs!" Toni cried. "That girl who stopped in yesterday is a genuine suspect?"

"Apparently Doogie questioned Amber at some length," Suzanne said.

"Wait a minute," Petra said. "Even if someone's spreading false rumors, why would they be about Amber? I mean, why would they think *she* had a bone to pick with Sharp?"

"Probably because she quit working for Sharp right after he started harassing her," Suzanne said. There. She'd spoken the dreaded words out loud and felt somewhat relieved. At least she wasn't carrying around that deep, dark secret anymore.

Toni's eyes went wide as saucers. "You mean he was, like, *sexually* harassing her?"

"Sharp tried to canoodle with Amber on numerous occasions," Suzanne said. "The final straw came when he started buying her gifts."

"What kind of gifts?" Toni asked.

Suzanne took a deep breath. "Lingerie."

"That freak," Petra spat out. She slammed a lid down on top of her soup pot and stared at them. "That stupid, arrogant pig. Maybe Allan Sharp deserved to get knifed after all."

"Maybe he did," Suzanne said. "But I don't think it was by Amber's hand."

"That ghost looked big to me," Toni said. "That girl Amber looked kind of thin and wispy."

"On the other hand, the ghost was wearing a costume," Petra said. "So it could have been, you know, built up to make the ghost appear larger."

Suzanne thought about the navy blue puffer jacket she'd seen Amber wearing. That coat, under a costume . . . ?

"Jeez Louise," Toni sputtered at Petra. "You think Amber did it?"

Petra shook her head. "That's not what I said."

"Amber denies anything and everything," Suzanne said. "Swears she hasn't seen Sharp in several weeks."

"Do you believe her?" Petra asked.

"I don't know," Suzanne said. "I think so. I'd really prefer to give Amber the benefit of the doubt."

Petra pulled a pan of biscuits from the oven and set it on the butcher-block table next to Suzanne. "I need to tell you something. A few weeks ago, I heard a rumor about Amber."

Suzanne was taken aback. "What did you hear?"

"That she and Allan were going steady," Petra said. "That they were officially an item."

"Where did you hear this?" Suzanne asked.

"At church," Petra said. "After bingo."

Toni shook an index finger at her. "That's not a very churchy thing to spread around."

Petra gazed at her. "Which is why I never said anything about it, why I never repeated what was probably a stupid, empty rumor."

Suzanne considered Petra's words. Could Amber have lied to her? Was there a bigger story here than she'd been led to believe? And if so, what exactly was going on? Because stabbing someone for payback seemed way over the top. What someone in law enforcement would term "overkill."

"You know," Suzanne said, "Missy Langston was the one who sent Amber to me for help. Missy essentially vouched for her."

"Missy *is* a sweetheart," Petra said. "And trustworthy, too."

"Yes, she is," Suzanne said. "She even offered to do a fashion show at our Christmas Tea."

"Just like that?" Toni asked.

"She meant it as a trade-off," Suzanne said. "If I'd try to get Doogie off Amber's back, then she'd help us with the fashion show."

"Are you sure that's a fair quid pro quo?" Petra asked. "You'd be sticking your neck out . . ."

"I already made up my mind to help Amber," Suzanne said. "Even before Missy offered to do a fashion show."

"So both things are a done deal," Petra said.

"I like the idea of a fashion show," Toni said. "It'll add extra panache to our Christmas Tea."

"I'm just worried about Suzanne," Petra said. "Getting dragged into the Allan Sharp case."

Toni favored Suzanne with a sly look. "Maybe she wants to get dragged in?"

Suzanne didn't say a word. She was too busy thinking. Wondering who was trying to heap blame on Amber's head. And what exactly was their reason for doing so? The easy answer, of course, was that it was Sharp's killer at work. That he'd tried to throw up a smoke screen. But that still begged the question—who was the killer?

As customers began to arrive, Suzanne, Toni, and Petra got to work. Petra cranked up activity in the kitchen while Suzanne and Toni ran orders out to their customers. They remained organized in their tasks, like SEAL Team Six dropping out of a black helicopter to take out the bad guys. Only in this case, the bad guy was whoever had murdered Allan Sharp.

Just as Suzanne delivered two orders of cheese omelets to table six, Toni waved to her.

"What?" Suzanne mimed.

Toni held up the telephone and waggled it back and forth. "Call for you." She dropped her voice. "It's some guy. Not Sam."

Suzanne came around the counter and grabbed the phone. "This is Suzanne."

"Suzanne?" came a deep male voice.

"Yes," she said. She couldn't quite place the voice. A mystery caller?

"It's Don Shinder."

Holy cats, it's Allan Sharp's partner!

"Mr. Shinder," Suzanne said, recovering her composure. "You have my deepest sympathies. I am . . . well, all of us at the Cackleberry Club are so very sorry about your partner."

They really weren't all that sorry, but Suzanne knew condolences were a common courtesy.

"That's very kind of you," Shinder said. "But I'm actually calling for another reason. There's going to be a visitation for Allan tomorrow night at Driesden and Draper Funeral Home and I was wondering if your restaurant could cater the event."

"The event?" Suzanne said. "Tomorrow night?"

"If this is too short notice . . . I suppose I could call someone else."

There isn't anyone else, Suzanne thought. Unless he went to the Save Mart and bought chips and onion dip.

"I'm sorry, I'm . . ." Shinder coughed nervously into the phone. "This is difficult for me. I've never had to organize anything like this before."

Neither have we, but there's always a first.

"I'm sorry, Mr. Shinder," Suzanne said. "I didn't mean to give you the impression that we weren't interested. Of course we're happy to help in any way we can."

"Thank you." He sounded genuinely relieved.

"Did you have something special in mind? Desserts or . . . ?"

"No . . . not really . . ." Shinder's voice trailed off.

"You obviously have a lot going on right now," Suzanne said. "And I'm afraid I'm just making things more difficult by asking questions. Why don't I put together a quick proposal and drop by your office later today?" It had just occurred to Suzanne that stopping by Shinder's law firm presented her with a dandy opportunity to ask questions and kick off her own investigation.

"You're very kind," Shinder said.

"It's the least I can do," Suzanne said. "I'll see you after lunch."

* * *

"MAKE way, make way." The front door bumped open and a huge cardboard barrel appeared in the doorway. It started to push its way through, got hung up, then finally squeezed in. Junior Garrett, Toni's soon-to-be ex, followed in the barrel's wake.

"Junior," Suzanne said. She was setting up the tables for lunch, keeping an eye on two customers who were just finishing a late breakfast.

"Got your barrels for you," Junior said, patting the large cardboard receptacle. "Plus there's two more out in my truck."

"For our toy drive," Suzanne said, looking pleased. "They look great. Where did you get them?"

"Bundy Brothers' Meatpacking."

Suzanne made a face. "These came from the meatpacking plant?"

Junior held up a hand to calm her. "Before you go all off-the-wall bonkers on me, Suzanne, I can assure you these bins are nice and pristine. No hog snouts or chicken guts were ever packed inside them. They're clean as a whistle, never been used."

"You're sure of that?"

Junior half closed one eye and gazed at Suzanne. "Would I lie to you?"

"Yes," Toni said. She'd come from the kitchen and was holding a tray of just-washed cups and saucers. "You lie to me all the time."

"That's 'cause we're married," Junior said. "That's what married people do. Make excuses and tell tall tales. But I'd never lie to Suzanne, no, sir."

"Right," Suzanne said. She knew that Junior was basically

an overage juvenile delinquent who wasn't particularly trustworthy. Today he was dressed in his trademark saggy jeans and studded motorcycle boots and had pulled on a ratty plaid jacket. A hank of dark hair dangled over his forehead, a tribute to James Dean, Elvis, and all the bad boys who had come before him.

"Now that you're here, I suppose you expect us to provide breakfast," Toni said.

"I wouldn't say no, seeing as how much hard work I done already," Junior said.

"Right," Toni said. "Seeing as how you're basically unemployed and probably stole those barrels from the warehouse."

"Cover them over with fancy Christmas wrap and nobody'll be the wiser," Junior said.

Suzanne decided it was time to step in. "Why don't you sit at the counter, Junior, and I'll have Petra fix you a plate of scrambled eggs."

Junior almost broke his leg getting to the counter. "With cinnamon toast?"

"Sure," Suzanne said. She figured it was the least she could do. The barrels really were perfect. Now they just had to fill them with toy donations.

Suzanne called in Junior's order to Petra and poured herself a cup of coffee. She held it up. "You want coffee, too?" she asked him.

"Naw, just a Coke." Junior drank something like a dozen cans of Coke every day. No wonder he was as jittery as a chipmunk on crack.

Junior spun around on his stool, doing a slow three-sixty. "This is real nice sitting here at the counter. I can see why folks like to come here and enjoy a friendly, educated conversation."

"With your tenth-grade education, what would you converse about?" Toni asked. "The works of Aristotle?"

Junior waved a finger at her. "Don't go knockin' that guy. He married Jackie O, didn't he?"

Toni just shook her head and retreated to the kitchen.

When Suzanne set Junior's eggs and toast in front of him, she said, just to be friendly, "How's your car wash coming along, Junior?" She knew Junior had been negotiating like crazy to buy the defunct Typhoon Car Wash out on the south edge of town.

Junior ducked his head, looking dismayed at her question. "Sadly, I had to abandon that dream, what with the cold weather and all."

"You know, Junior, most people think it's important to keep their cars clean in winter, too. All that salt and road gunk is tough on a car's finish and undercarriage."

"Yeah, but I couldn't find any girls who'd work in wet T-shirts during the winter."

"Ah." Suzanne had somehow forgotten that Junior's dream had been to open either a topless or wet T-shirt car wash. "I see where that might be a problem. For the girls anyway."

Junior gave a solemn nod as he tucked into his eggs. "Occupational hazard."

"I guess it wasn't in the cards," Suzanne said. *Thank goodness.*

"That's the least of my worries right now."

"Excuse me?" Suzanne said.

"I had to up and move my trailer."

"You're not parked out by the town dump anymore?" Junior had been living in a ratty house trailer that had been parked illegally near the dump.

"Not since this past Saturday. That jerk Allan Sharp evicted me. Claimed he owned the land."

"What did you say?" Suzanne demanded. Had she heard Junior correctly? Allan Sharp had evicted him?

"Yeah, that jerk Sharp got something called an injunction," Junior babbled on. "I cussed him up and down, but, in the end, Deputy Robertson served me with legal papers and told me I had twenty-four hours to relocate my trailer." Junior scrunched up his face. "Can you imagine that? I had to borrow Buddy Breggeman's tow truck and haul my trailer over to my new spot near the old gravel pit. Then I had to jack up the trailer, put it on cement blocks, and hitch up the water line and electrical. Been workin' on that non-stop for the last three days."

Suzanne stared at Junior. "Then you haven't heard?"

Junior stuck a finger in one ear and rotated it hard. "Heard what?"

"Allan Sharp was murdered Sunday night."

Junior reacted as if somebody had touched a red-hot wire to his spine. "Say what!"

"Somebody murdered Allan Sharp," Suzanne repeated. "Stabbed him with a knife."

"I'll be jim-jammed!" Junior cried, slapping a hand against his chest. "Who'd go and do a thing like that?"

"A ghost," Toni said. She'd been listening in on their conversation and had crept back out into the café.

Junior's eyes popped open wide as he did an almost cartoon double take. "You mean like a spooky-haunt?"

"No," Suzanne said. "Like a person dressed up in a ghost costume."

"So you say," Toni muttered.

"It happened during dress rehearsal at the Oakhurst Theatre," Suzanne told Junior.

"Where?"

"Right at the end of act two."

"I mean where was he stabbed on his person?"

"Oh," Suzanne said. "I guess in his stomach. All I know is that major organs were involved." She grimaced. Were they ever.

"Jeez," Junior said. "Are there any suspects?"

"Probably you," Toni said, poking at him with an index finger. "I overheard your remark about how you cussed out Allan Sharp because he made you move your trailer. I hope you didn't go spouting off about that in public."

Junior looked sheepish. "Ah jeez . . . I may have let fly a few choice words when I was in Schmitt's Bar Saturday night. Of course, that's 'cause I was in a relaxed state after downing a couple of crapple bombs."

"You didn't just fall out of the stupid tree," Toni said. "You were dragged through dumb-ass forest."

Junior hung his head. "It was only a few drinks."

"You were off on a toot," Toni said. "Jeez, Junior, the last thing we need is a murder suspect in the family."

Junior peered at Toni. "How can you call us a family when we don't even live together?"

"Don't get technical," Toni said. "And you know darned well why we don't live together. Because we're getting a D-I-V-O-R-C-E."

"Ah, you've been threatening that for three years and it ain't happened yet." Junior gave her a cockeyed grin and stuck his tongue out the side of his mouth. "I think you're still sweet on me."

Toni shook a fist at Junior. "One of these days, buster. Just wait and see."

Junior focused on Suzanne. "I can't believe somebody went and killed old Allan Sharp."

"Believe it," Suzanne said.

"So there must be a big manhunt under way," Junior said. "Wow. That's just crazy."

"Better keep your head down," Toni said.

"Hey, sweet cheeks, you'll change your tune soon enough when I'm walking around all flush with a pocket full of cash like Daddy Warbucks," Junior said.

"What are you talking about?" Suzanne asked. With Junior it was like channel surfing with the sound turned down. You never knew what you were going to get. Could be a documentary on dung beetles, could be a Lifetime movie.

"I'm going to the Shooting Star Casino tonight—just wait until I win the Mega Millions!" Junior cried.

"That's the lottery, dingdong, not the casino," Toni said.

"Doesn't matter," Junior said. "I can feel it in my bones. Something big is going to happen tonight."

"Yeah," Toni said. "You're probably going to get arrested."

CHAPTER 7

BREAKFAST morphed into lunchtime. Toni buzzed back and forth from the kitchen to the café like a demented hummingbird, all the while grumbling about Junior.

"That boy's brain is set on a totally different frequency," she told Suzanne as they were standing at the pass-through window. "One that none of us can pick up."

"Junior doesn't mean any harm," Suzanne said. "He's basically an overgrown kid."

"Who sticks his foot in his mouth and gets in trouble as regular as clockwork. Jeez, Suzanne, what if Sheriff Doogie gets wind that Junior was badmouthing Allan Sharp?"

"Then Junior is probably in deep doo-doo." But Suzanne wasn't so much worried about Junior blipping up on Doogie's radar as Amber already being there. That was clearly a problem.

Lunchtime rolled around and Petra did the Cackleberry Club proud with her lunch offerings. Crab cakes, slow-cooker sweet-and-sour pork, egg drop soup, and small sausage pizzas topped with a fried egg.

Suzanne was just taking an order for two of the pizzas when Sheriff Doogie came stomping in. He hastily covered the distance from the front door to the counter and heaved himself onto a stool. Suzanne quickly shoved her order through the pass-through and turned to face Doogie.

"Anything?" Suzanne asked as she poured him a cup of coffee. It was hot and strong, just the way Doogie liked it.

Doogie hunched up his shoulders. "I got one suspect, yeah, but I'm sitting on the fence about it."

"Amber Payson," Suzanne said.

Doogie's coffee cup was almost to his mouth, but at hearing Suzanne's words he jerked it away fast, slopping coffee down the front of his khaki shirt.

"Doggone it, Suzanne!" he exploded. "Look what you made me do. And this shirt was fresh from the laundry. With extra starch."

"Amber Payson," Suzanne said again. Clearly she was on the right track if just the mention of Amber's name caused Doogie to jump like that.

"How did you find out about her?" Doogie asked. He was gruff, just this side of angry, as he grabbed a bunch of paper napkins, wadded them up, and sopped at his shirt.

"I keep my eyes and ears open," Suzanne said. "But what I really want to know is, how did *you* find out about her? Who was the jerk who pointed a finger at Amber?"

"That's classified information," Doogie said.

Suzanne stared at him. "Let me make a wild guess. You received a tip. An anonymous tip."

Doogie glowered at her, the skin crinkling at the corners of his eyes. "For your information it *was* a tip."

"And you happily bought into it?"

"That's how law enforcement agencies operate, Suzanne. We get tips that turn into actionable information."

"Mixed in with a lot of false accusations," Suzanne said.

"Not always."

"Amber didn't murder Allan Sharp. If you waste valuable time questioning her, trying to background her every move for the last month, you'll let the real killer slip right through your fingers."

"Why are you such a cheerleader for Amber Payson?" Doogie asked.

"I'm not."

"You sure seem to be pleading her case."

"I'm funny that way," Suzanne said. "I have a soft side for underdogs and people who are wrongfully accused." She knew that if she argued any more, Doogie would dig in his heels and get obstinate. So she said instead, "You must have other suspects."

Doogie leaned forward across the counter. "Don't breathe a word of this to Toni, but Junior was heard making disparaging remarks about Allan Sharp the other night at Schmitt's Bar."

"Toni already knows about that. And for your information, that's just Junior shooting off his fool mouth. He might cuss and talk tough, but he wouldn't hurt a fly."

"Those are the kinds of guys sitting on death row, Suzanne. Those are the ones who profile as serial killers, sweet to their hound dogs and old grannies but hostile to the civilized world."

"Not Junior."

Doogie took a sip of coffee. "Still, that boy does seem to be a few bricks short of a full load."

Suzanne flipped open her order pad. "What's it going to be today, Sheriff? The crab cakes or the egg drop soup?"

Doogie waved one of his big paws. "Aw, can you have Petra grill me a burger?"

"It's not on the menu, but I suppose we can manage." Doogie never ordered off the chalkboard like a regular customer. Instead, he acted like he was some big-shot Hollywood producer who'd swaggered into Spago or the Ivy, where the chefs were falling all over themselves, happy to cater to his every whim.

"And have Petra throw a slice of Muenster cheese on my burger, too. And some fried onions. While she's at it, she may as well add an order of home fries on the side."

"Very heart-healthy," Suzanne said.

Doogie wasn't amused. "Yeah, yeah."

Toni sidled up to them on her way to the kitchen. "You're kind of a light eater, Sheriff."

Doogie turned, looking slightly pleased. "You think?"

"As soon as it gets light you start eating," Toni cackled.

"Gosh darn it, Toni, I don't have to take crap from you," Doogie snorted.

"Hey, did I tell you about my new exercise routine?" Toni asked. She leaned forward and grinned. "Every day I do diddly-squat."

ONCE the lunchtime crowd began to dwindle, Suzanne ducked out and drove over to Don Shinder's law firm. The offices of Sharp Shinder and Young were located in downtown Kindred, in one of the rehabbed brick buildings that lined Main Street.

She entered the lobby, checked the register, and walked up a flight of polished wooden stairs. At the top of the stairs were a pair of smoked glass doors that were inscribed Sharp Shinder and Young.

A young woman looked up from behind a wooden counter. "Help you?" she asked.

"I'm here to see Don Shinder. Suzanne Dietz."

"Of course. He's expecting you," the girl said. "Hang on a sec while I buzz him."

Two seconds later, Shinder was front and center. He greeted Suzanne, then led her through a doorway and down a wood-paneled hallway into his office. Tall windows let in scads of daylight, which played against a lovely buff-colored brick wall. There were two old-fashioned barrister bookcases that held papers and books, as well as two brown leather chairs that faced Shinder's desk. Suzanne sat down in one of the chairs and faced him.

"This is a lovely old building," Suzanne said. "How long have you been here?"

"We signed a lease, let's see, two years ago," Shinder said. "Got three more years to go."

"So you're planning to keep this office space? Even though Allan . . ." Suzanne's words trailed off when she saw Shinder's downcast look. He really was taking his partner's death hard.

"Look at this," Shinder said. He jumped up and tapped a framed photo that hung on the wall. "It's when Allan and I went fishing for marlin down in Cabo San Lucas."

Suzanne stood up and studied the photo; then she moved on to a second one. This photo showed the two of them, tan and happy-looking, hoisting bottles of Cerveza beer on an outdoor patio, the Pacific Ocean sparkling in the background. There was another photo of the two of them posing in front of a slot machine along with two bored-looking showgirls in glitzy gold costumes and plumed headdresses.

"That was taken when Allan and I attended the Midwest Law Conference in Las Vegas," Shinder said. He shook his head and tears sparkled in his eyes. "I'm really gonna miss that guy."

Shinder beckoned for Suzanne to sit back down. He sat down heavily and rested his elbows on his desk, pushing aside large stacks of paperwork that threatened to tip over.

"I'm curious," Suzanne said. "About a former employee of yours. Amber Payson."

"I know she's a suspect," Shinder said right away.

"So Sheriff Doogie informed me," Suzanne said. "But I'd like to know what you think."

Shinder put his chin in his hand and leaned sideways in his chair, as if considering Suzanne's request. "I never got to know Amber very well," he said. "Allan hired her . . . what?" He scratched his chin. "I guess six or seven months ago, but she only ended up staying something like three months." He shrugged. "What can you do when these . . . what's the term for them? Millennials? They job hop constantly." He shook his head. "I find it strange but they're very big on job hopping."

"I understand Amber resigned."

"Is that so?"

"Excuse me, but I thought you worked with her." Suzanne was confused. It was a four-person office and one of the partners didn't know Amber had resigned?

"Not at all," Shinder said. "Amber worked for Allan. Her desk was right outside his office. As you can see, I'm on the far side. Our semiretired partner's office is in the middle."

"That would be Pete Young? Where is he now?"

"Down in Islamorada, Florida. Probably catching bonefish even as we speak."

"Whatever the office arrangement was, I can't believe Amber would have such hard feelings for Sharp that she'd actually plot to kill him," Suzanne said.

"That's the crazy thing," Shinder said. "I get clients in here every day who swear on a stack of Bibles that they're innocent, that they have no idea who could have killed their wife or embezzled the company finances. And you want to believe them . . . *I* want to believe them. And then the evidence begins to mount against them and you think, 'Jeez, this case isn't a slam dunk after all. If we're lucky it's going to be a plea bargain.'" He paused, looking a little disheartened. "It's a darn shame."

"Actually, it sounds soul crushing," Suzanne said.

"It can be."

Suzanne got down to the real business at hand, which was showing Shinder the menu she'd drawn up for Allan Sharp's visitation. It was fairly straight ahead, three varieties of tea sandwiches—chicken salad, ham salad, and cucumber and cream cheese—along with brownie bites and coffee.

"Are you going to have those church basement funeral bars?" Shinder asked.

Suzanne frowned. "What do you mean?"

"You know. Those graham cracker bars with nuts they always serve in church basements after a funeral."

"Okay, we can definitely include something like that."

Suzanne went on to explain that everything would be easy to transport from the Cackleberry Club's kitchen to what would probably be a hastily set-up folding table at the back of the funeral parlor.

"Good, very good," Shinder said as Suzanne continued talking. But in the long run he wasn't much interested in hearing any details. His responses were merely polite and pro forma.

Suzanne decided that Don Shinder must be very sad indeed over losing his partner.

CHAPTER 8

BY the time Suzanne got back to the Cackleberry Club, afternoon tea was almost finished. A half-dozen tables were occupied and Toni had set out the good Coalport china and was using the fancy Chinese blue and white teapots. Suzanne was just about to put on an apron and help Toni when the phone rang.

It was Amber. And of course she wanted to know if Suzanne had made any progress.

"Not really," Suzanne told her, a blip of worry making her heart contract. "I talked to Sheriff Doogie over lunch and he said you were a suspect by dint of someone phoning in a tip."

"A tip about me?" Amber sounded startled. "Who would do that?"

"I have no idea. Doogie said it was an anonymous tip."

"Then it's no tip at all," Amber said, bristling. "It's somebody being horribly mean . . . some crackpot playing a joke."

"And a pretty bad joke at that. Unfortunately, Doogie seems to be taking the tip seriously." Suzanne paused. "Amber, when you spoke with Sheriff Doogie, you should have *told* him about the unwanted advances from Allan Sharp."

"I just couldn't. It's too embarrassing." She paused. "Did you tell him?"

"No, but I think it's time that *you* made it perfectly clear to Sheriff Doogie that you left the law firm under duress. And that even though you might have felt *unhappy* about Allan Sharp's actions, there's no way you would ever be angry or impulsive enough to consider any form of retaliation."

"You want me to call Doogie up and say all that?" Amber asked.

"No, I want your attorney to handle it. Couched in careful legalese that will hopefully extricate you from what could turn into a very bad situation."

"I thought you were going to help me."

"I just don't think I'm the one you want on your side," Suzanne said.

"I really have to call an attorney?" Amber asked in a small voice.

"And you can always talk to me, too," Suzanne hastened to say. "But purely for moral support."

"I suppose that's fair advice," Amber said in a tone that sounded completely dispirited, as if she knew Suzanne was trying to bail on her.

"You know what?" Suzanne said. "Why don't you come to our Christmas Tea tomorrow? We can talk some more afterward, see what we can figure out." Amber sounded so disheartened that Suzanne knew she had to do something to help boost the girl's spirits.

"Really?"

"Absolutely. Come as my special guest. Gratis. I promise

the tea will be lots of fun. Missy has even promised to stage a surprise fashion show."

"Thank you, Suzanne. That's very kind of you. I look forward to it."

JUST as Suzanne was standing behind the counter, sorting through tins of Assam and oolong tea, Teddy Hardwick, the director of *A Christmas Carol*, came bustling in. He wore a navy pea coat with a beige cashmere scarf draped artfully around his neck and carried a large shopping bag. His expression was intense and he looked discombobulated.

"Teddy," Suzanne said. "Can I offer you a nice cup of tea to warm you up and help you relax? And I think . . . I'd have to check with Petra on this . . . but we might be able to scrounge up a raspberry scone."

Teddy shook his head. "No time, Suzanne. I'm out canvassing the town, trying to hustle up interest for a replacement Scrooge. I already asked Sheriff Doogie if he'd step in, but he claims he's way too busy, what with investigating Allan Sharp's murder."

"Actually, it sounds more like a conflict of interest," Suzanne said.

Teddy waved a hand as if to dismiss that thought. "What I'm wondering now is, do you think Sam would be willing to take over the part?"

"I guess you'd have to ask Sam," Suzanne said.

"But you'd put in a good word for me? You'd kind of encourage him?"

"You want me to twist his arm?"

Hardwick smiled, lots of teeth but very little warmth. "That'd be wonderful if you could do that, Suzanne."

Wonderful for you, not so good for Sam.

"I'll pitch him on the idea," Suzanne said. "But I can't promise anything." She doubted that Sam would want to play the part of Scrooge. Learn all those lines in just a matter of days? And then there was the precedent of the recently murdered Scrooge to consider.

"Is Petra around?" Hardwick asked.

"We pretty much keep her locked in the kitchen."

Hardwick looked antsy as he bounced on the balls of his feet. "Could you tell her that I'm here? It's pretty important." He held up the bag. "I need to talk to her about a costume change for the play."

Suzanne leaned forward and called through the passthrough. "Petra. Teddy Hardwick needs to talk to you. He says it's important."

Petra's voice floated back to them. "I'll be right there."

WHILE Petra took Hardwick into the Knitting Nest for a discussion about costumes, Suzanne served coffee and a scone to a trucker who had pulled in for coffee and cake but was thoroughly won over by Toni's description of their chocolate chip scones. Or it could have been Toni's low-cut green silk blouse with the yellow embroidered roses that sealed the deal.

Then the front door swung open to reveal a familiar figure.

"Dale," Suzanne said. It was Dale Huffington, who worked as a guard at the nearby Jasper Creek Prison. He was a big guy, pleasant-natured, with a friendly, open-looking face.

"Am I too late?" he asked.

Suzanne waved Dale over to the counter. "You're late, but I'm sure we can scrounge something up for you." She called to Toni, who was bustling around in the kitchen now. "Are there any scones left?"

"No," Toni said. "Sorry."

Dale plopped down on the middle stool and put his elbows on the counter. "Coffee and a cookie is good," he said.

"Did you just get off work?" Suzanne asked. She poured the last of the coffee into a large ceramic mug and plated a sugar cookie for Dale.

"Yep, they're changing schedules again. You never know when you're supposed to be on duty. Could be daytime, could be midnight."

"Must make things difficult for you," Suzanne said. She put the coffee and cookie in front of him.

"It surely does. Especially since I got that part in the play," Dale said. "I've already missed three rehearsals. Now with the Allan Sharp thing . . . well, you were there that night. You saw what a mess it was, everybody running around in a blind panic. Who knows what's going to happen now?" He took a bite of cookie. "If you ask me, the play might even get cancelled."

"I don't think so," Suzanne said. "Teddy Hardwick is meeting with Petra in the Knitting Nest right now. Something about a costume change, I guess."

Dale looked encouraged. "So the play is still set to go on?"

"Apparently. Though Teddy Hardwick still hasn't recast the Scrooge role." Suzanne gave a rueful chuckle. "He was lobbying me to try and talk Sam into being our new Scrooge."

"Aw, Sam's not near enough cranky to play that role."

"What with Sam's schedule, I don't think he'd even consider it," Suzanne said. "But I feel bad for Hardwick. I mean, he's down to the final hours. Plus, he pretty much saw everything unravel. It must have been awful to watch the star of your play murdered before your very eyes."

"Well, he didn't exactly see it," Dale said. He took a slurp of coffee and another bite of cookie.

"What do you mean?" Suzanne asked. "Sure he did."

Dale waved his cookie in front of him. "No, no. I don't think Hardwick was sitting out front when that ghost attacked Allan Sharp." Golden crumbs tumbled down the front of his shirt.

"Sure he was," Suzanne said. "He said he was. At least I think he did."

But Dale was sticking to his story. "No, ma'am. I was in the audience with the rest of the cast members. Didn't see hide nor hair of Hardwick until afterward."

"Then where the heck was he?"

"Backstage with you, I guess." Dale chewed the last bite of cookie. "Do you have any more of these, Suzanne?"

"That was the last one," Suzanne said in an absent tone. Dale's words had thrown her for a loop. Because Hardwick definitely hadn't been backstage with her. At least she didn't recall seeing him. So where had Hardwick been? She didn't like the crazy direction her suspicious mind wanted to go. But . . . could there have been a problem, an issue, between Hardwick and Allan Sharp? Was that possible?

"Suzanne?" Dale said. "Seems like you kind of drifted away for a minute."

"Sorry, Dale. How about I get you a brownie instead? On the house."

"Sure. That'd be great."

As Suzanne grabbed a brownie for Dale, she continued to wonder about Teddy Hardwick. And worried about the funny vibe that was rattling through her brain, conjuring up strange ideas.

"I was just thinking," Dale said, snatching up his

brownie, "that Hardwick's got a lot going on right now, poor guy."

"You mean with directing the play? Recasting Scrooge?"

"That's not even half of it. He's having major problems with the developer who built his town house."

"What do you mean?" Suzanne said.

"Yeah, Hardwick's only lived in his new place for, like, seven months and the foundation's already cracked in two spots," Dale said. "You know how that happy crap goes. If it doesn't get fixed pronto, it'll turn into a real mess. Groundwater seeps in and then it's only a matter of time before the whole dang house collapses."

"Do you have any idea who the developer is?"

Dale shook his head. "No idea. But whoever built those places, they're in for a boatload of trouble." He chewed some more. "And lawsuits up the wazoo."

"Toni," Suzanne said, once Dale had left. "I think I need your help."

"Yeah?" Toni said. She was sitting at one of the tables in the café, refilling the sugar bowls.

There were still two people lingering over tea, so Suzanne just said, "I'll talk to you later."

"About what?" Toni asked.

"Investigating."

CHAPTER 9

WITH narrowed, suspicious eyes, Suzanne watched Petra walk Teddy Hardwick to the door and bid him good-bye.

"Everything okay?" Suzanne asked, once he had gone.

"Fine," Petra said, giving an abstract smile. "Just last-minute costume stuff to deal with."

"You've got a knitting class tonight?"

Petra nodded. "My Woolly Mammoth class."

Suzanne practically laughed out loud. "What on earth is that?"

Petra crooked a finger and led Suzanne into the Knitting Nest. She picked up a skein of soft, fluffy yarn. "You see this? It's spun from reindeer fur." She picked up another skein. "And this one's a hundred percent llama from Peru. Now, this yarn"—Petra grabbed a squared-off skein of cream-colored fiber—"is fifty percent yak fiber from Central Asia blended with fifty percent virgin wool."

"Where did you get all this stuff?"

"I imported it. You should know: you get the bills. I also have a knitter friend up in Alaska. They play with crazy yarns all the time, even spin fibers from the fur of sled dogs."

"That's amazing," Suzanne said. "Actually, you're amazing."

Petra blushed. "I wish you wouldn't say things like that. Makes me feel very uncomfortable."

"No need to feel that way; you're a true fiber artist."

"I'm just a lady who knits."

"And quilts."

"Well . . . yes," Petra said. "I do love quilting, too."

Suzanne looked around at the floor-to-ceiling shelves filled with yarn, and the bundles of fabric that were stacked everywhere. Tall wicker baskets were stuffed with yarns by Berroco, Appalachian Baby, Sirdar, Malabrigo, and lots more in all sorts of colors. There were bright colors and sun-washed, almost Santa Fe–looking colors, as well as heavenly cream, alabaster, and stone colors.

"I hadn't realized our inventory was so jam-packed for the holidays," Suzanne said, looking at Petra's display of quilting fabric. She reached out and touched a piece of fabric that was soft and silky. She could just imagine it being stitched into a cozy quilt.

"Those are our new quilt squares," Petra said. "You can see that I've got them bundled according to color and motif." She smiled. "You see those squares that are all ivory and cream-colored?"

"Uh-huh."

"I call that group Cream and Sugar." Petra's hand moved to indicate another bundle. "And these indigo and Persian blue squares are my Dark Dreams bundle."

"I bet we'll sell a ton of them," Suzanne said, pleased.

"I hope so," Petra said.

Toni poked her head into the Knitting Nest. "Are you guys heading out?" she asked. Toni had wound a long pink and yellow scarf around her neck and shoulders and now looked like a human burrito.

"I am," Suzanne said. "And I need to talk to you."

"And I've got a class tonight," Petra said. She started bustling around the Knitting Nest, grabbing a basket of knitting, arranging chairs in a semicircle. "So I'll see you ladies tomorrow."

"Night-night," Toni called out.

Suzanne and Toni pulled on their coats and walked outside. A thin sliver of silver moon hung tilted in a purple-blue sky.

Toni looked at Suzanne. "Okay, we're alone. What exactly do you have up your sleeve? Earlier you said you wanted to do a little investigating?"

"More like checking on something to satisfy my curiosity."

"Yeah, right. Tell me, does this have anything to do with . . ." Toni pulled her mouth into a crooked line and made a slashing gesture across her throat.

"I'm afraid it does."

"Uh-oh, better lead on, then, Sherlock."

IT was full-on dark now as they drove through Kindred. The wind had come up, whipping bare trees into a frenzy and blowing twisted wisps of snow across the road in front of Suzanne's headlights. Even though they were still in the middle of town, the atmosphere felt foreboding.

Toni, meanwhile, had turned on the radio, listening to the five-o'clock drive-time news. She'd also slipped out of her boots and put her stocking feet on the dashboard, right next to the heat vent.

"You don't mind my stinky feet, do you?"

"Not unless you do," Suzanne said.

"Just walking across our parking lot made my toes feel like Mrs. Paul's frozen fish sticks." Toni shivered as she snuggled lower in her seat. "So tell me where we're headed again. Oh wait, you said you wanted to stop at a local watering hole first and pick up a couple of hot dudes."

"You wish. No, we're going to take a cruise out to that new town house development. Whitetail Woods, I think it's called."

Suzanne made a turn on Lindahl Avenue and cruised past a car dealership, Rush Street Pizza, and Kerkow's Garden Center, which was closed for the season except for a small Christmas tree lot that was strung with colored lights. Now they'd left the more residential part of Kindred behind and were headed into suburban territory.

"What's clicking in that supercomputer brain of yours?" Toni asked. "You going to sell your big house and buy a townhome? Move to the burbs?" She scraped a bit of ice off the passenger side window and peered out. "What there are of them."

"I've got a funny idea rattling around inside my head and I need to check something out. See if my suspicions are legit."

"Then afterward do you want to stop at Schmitt's Bar and have a couple of bumps? I think they got two-for-one Passion Puckers tonight."

"I don't even know what those are."

"They're cocktails made with apple schnapps, cranberry juice, pineapple juice, and a couple more tutti-frutti juices. Kinda tastes like cough syrup."

"Sounds challenging," Suzanne said. "On the other hand, maybe a couple of drinks will help make tonight's rehearsal run a lot smoother."

"I just hope Teddy Hardwick's found a new Scrooge," Toni said.

"And I hope it's not going to be Sam."

They drove out to Whitetail Lane and then turned into a new residential development that had stone pillars on either side of the road and a large sign that said Whitetail Woods. They bumped over frozen ground past one row of townhomes and into an area where cinder blocks, pipes, and pallets of construction materials were scattered about.

"I thought this development was completely finished and move-in ready," Toni said. "But it looks like they've had some major problems. Like they need to redo the siding or the sewer system or something."

"Or something," Suzanne said. Her eyes focused on a row of townhomes that were completely dark. Obviously, no one had moved in yet, though they looked completed. Across the road, however, was a row of six townhomes where lights burned brightly. Some lights shone out of first-floor windows and a few porch lights twinkled, making the townhomes look lived-in and cheery.

"So why are we really here?" Toni asked. She turned off the radio, dropped her feet down, and pulled on a pair of brown suede boots that were beaded and fringed like moccasins.

"Because this is where Teddy Hardwick lives and I heard a rumor that he was in a huge fight with his developer."

"Uh-huh. And who's the lucky developer?"

"That's what we're here to find out."

"Something tells me you've got a sneaking suspicion," Toni said.

"Maybe I do."

Toni turned in her seat. "If I'm gonna be part of this stealth operation, you'll have to do better than that, girlfriend. You have to level with me."

Suzanne tapped her gloved fingers against the steering wheel. "Okay, here's the deal. I think Allan Sharp was the developer."

Toni stared at her openmouthed. "You mean deader-than-a-doornail Allan Sharp?"

"Remember, the operative words are 'I *think* he was the developer.'"

"So we're here to confirm that? Okeydoke." Toni put her hand on the door, ready to jump out.

"Wait a minute. That's a lot easier said than done," Suzanne said. "We're gonna need a good story to back us up. We can't randomly go knocking on doors."

Toni grinned. "Oh yeah? Watch me."

TONI was as good as her word. She strolled up to the town house on the end, hit the doorbell, and then banged on the screen door. When a woman in gray wool slacks and a blue and white Norwegian ski sweater opened the door a couple of inches, Toni said, "Hiya. I'm looking for the sales office. Can you point me in the right direction?"

The woman peered out at them, her body language betraying a hint of nervousness. Then when she saw Suzanne also standing on her porch, looking friendly and relatively nonthreatening, she said, "There was a sales office, but they closed it last month."

"Aw, rats," Toni went on, "I'm in the middle of a divorce

and I'm looking to buy a property. My friend here has been urging me to buy a house, but since there's just little old me now, these town houses look like they might be perfect." She paused. "If there's no sales office anymore, maybe I should go directly to the developer."

The woman made a downcast face. "That's going to be a problem," she said.

"All the units are sold?" Toni asked.

"No, I'm pretty sure there are units still available. The thing is . . . the developer is dead."

Toni clapped a hand over her mouth and reeled backward. "What?" She spun about. "Suzanne, did you hear that?"

"Yes, I did," Suzanne said, wishing Toni wasn't being quite so theatrical. Then again, with acting skills like that, maybe *Toni* should be the new Scrooge.

"His name was Allan Sharp," the woman said. "And he was murdered just two nights ago." Her eyes darted back and forth, as if Sharp's killer might be lurking nearby, ready to pounce on them at any moment.

"How awful," Toni said.

"I think it had something to do with a play he was in," the woman said.

Suzanne could barely contain her excitement. If Teddy Hardwick was unhappy with his town house construction, and he was angry with Allan Sharp but wasn't getting any results, then maybe Hardwick had taken matters into his own hands?

"Well, that changes everything," Toni said. "Guess I'll have to call a Realtor and see if they can help."

"Or the First Heartland Bank," the woman said. "I think they provided some of the financing."

"Thank you," Toni said. "You've been more than helpful."

* * *

BACK in Suzanne's car, Toni was crowing about her performance. "Did we figure this out or what?"

"*You* put on a great performance," Suzanne said. "Very convincing."

"The only sticking point," Toni said, "is that Hardwick was going up against Allan Sharp. Being a scummy lawyer, couldn't Sharp have just done some legal mumbo jumbo to make Hardwick go away?"

"If Hardwick killed him, maybe that's the reason right there," Suzanne said. She backed her car up, made a K-turn, and headed back toward town. "Because Sharp was stonewalling him."

"So what now?" Toni asked. "I've got bumps and chills that we uncovered a possible suspect. Now the question is—what do we do about it?"

Suzanne thought for a moment. "I think we should stop by the Law Enforcement Center and lay this squarely in Sheriff Doogie's lap." *Nice and neat, just like when Baxter brings me a dead squirrel in tribute and drops it on my back porch.*

"This new information does cast a pretty bad light on Hardwick," Toni said.

"And it might take some pressure off Amber."

But when they went looking for Doogie at the Law Enforcement Center, he was nowhere to be found. The place, which was normally bustling with activity, was relatively quiet. End of day, end of watch. Only two deputies were on duty and Suzanne didn't know either one of them particularly well. She was afraid if she spilled her recent findings to them, they'd write her off as the nosy, kooky neighbor lady. Or, worse yet, a Miss Marple type.

"Maybe Doogie skedaddled on home," Toni said. "It is almost five o'clock."

They walked back down the long corridor, where fluorescent lights buzzed overhead and posters warned about drunk driving and fire safety.

"What about . . . ?" Suzanne stopped and put her hand on the door that was marked Dispatch.

"Good idea," Toni said. "We'll ask Marilyn."

But when they asked Marilyn Grabowski, the official dispatcher, purveyor of home-baked cookies, and den mother to the sheriff's department, she informed them that Doogie was out on a call. "And he told me he wouldn't be coming back," Marilyn said.

They walked outside and climbed into Suzanne's car.

"You think he went home?" Toni asked, pulling the seat-belt strap across.

"Let's take a cruise through downtown," Suzanne said. "See what we can see."

"And then for sure hit Schmitt's Bar."

Main Street twinkled like a fairyland. City workers had finally finished putting up all the Christmas decorations. Now green garland and colored lights were wound around lampposts and stretched across all the downtown streets. Many of the small businesses located in the historic brick buildings had also strung up colored lights and hung holiday wreaths.

"There's Doogie's cruiser!" Toni cried suddenly.

"Where?" Suzanne said. "Oh, never mind, I see it."

His maroon and tan cruiser with the whip antenna was parked right outside the Kindred Bakery.

"And there's Doogie himself," Suzanne said. He was just coming out of the bakery, khaki parka zipped up tight over his bulging belly, clutching a white bag in his hand. "It looks as if he just bought himself a sack of donuts. Talk about a tried-and-true cliché."

"Doogie eats so much junk food he oughta change his middle initials to KFC," Toni snickered.

Just as Doogie was about to climb into his car, Suzanne pulled up next to him and tooted her horn. Doogie tossed his bakery bag onto the front seat and turned toward them, a quizzical look on his face.

Suzanne buzzed the passenger side window down and called across Toni, "Hey, Doogie, got a minute?"

Doogie's shoulders slumped as he held up two padded fingers of a gloved hand. "I was this close to a clean getaway."

"We got some red-hot information for you," Toni said. "Really good stuff."

Doogie leaned against their car, his breath pluming out in the bitter cold. "You ladies stirring up more trouble?"

"We're trying to *save* you some time and energy," Suzanne said.

When Doogie cocked his head in a what's-up? gesture, Suzanne hastily told him about the rumor she'd heard concerning Teddy Hardwick's foundation. Then she explained how they'd driven out to Whitetail Woods and learned that Allan Sharp had been the property's developer. She wrapped up by postulating that Hardwick might have been so incensed, so clouded by worry over his foundation woes, that he took matters into his own hands.

All through the telling of her story, Doogie's face remained impassive. When Suzanne had finally finished, Doogie tipped his hat back and said, "I knew Sharp had a couple of real estate developments cooking, but I didn't know Hardwick bought a house in one of them. That's . . . interesting."

"More than that, it changes things a bit, don't you think?" Suzanne asked.

Doogie was slow to agree. "Maybe." Then, "You're sure Teddy Hardwick owns one of those town houses? And that the foundation's kaput?"

"Pretty sure," Suzanne said. "That's what Dale Huffington told me, anyway."

"Need to check deeds and property tax records," Doogie said. "Get some confirmation."

"You don't believe us?" Toni asked. "After our careful and profound analytical analysis?"

Doogie cocked an eye at her. "Wouldn't that be a redundancy?"

"So what if it is?"

"Hardwick, huh?" Doogie was mumbling to himself now. His lips moving, his head tipping from side to side, trying to see if the pieces might fit. "And Dale says he didn't see Hardwick when Sharp got stabbed?"

"That's right," Suzanne said. "So it could have been Hardwick who killed Sharp. He'd know about the ghost costume—he could have easily made a second one himself. Then he ran out the back door, went around to the front, and slipped back inside the theater. The place was in an uproar, so Hardwick could have easily snuck in."

"Stashed his costume, too," Toni said.

"Maybe," Doogie said.

"As far as the real estate angle, it would be interesting to know what other real estate deals Allan Sharp was involved in," Suzanne said. "There could be others—buyers or tenants—who had a bone to pick with Sharp."

"It's possible," Doogie said. He hadn't discounted Suzanne's story, but he hadn't completely bought into it, either.

"If I were the suspicious sort, I'd keep a keen eye on

Mayor Mobley, too," Suzanne said. She had no idea where that idea had originated from; it just flew out of her mouth like a bad, hacking cough you didn't realize was coming and couldn't hold back.

Doogie flinched but didn't say a single word, just pressed his lips together tightly.

"What?" Suzanne asked.

"I didn't say anything," Doogie said.

"You didn't have to," Suzanne said. "You made a weird face. Like you poured too much sriracha sauce on your scrambled eggs. Is something going on with Mayor Mobley? Wait." She peered at him. "Is he a suspect, too?"

Almost reluctantly, Doogie said, "Ah, Mobley and Allan Sharp were partners in an apartment complex a while back. I don't know all the details, but the deal went sour and they ended up at loggerheads."

"There you go!" Toni cried.

As if to punctuate Toni's sentence, the radio in Sheriff Doogie's car suddenly crackled to life. Doogie reached in, grabbed the mic, and said, "Ten-four, Doogie here, go ahead."

Marilyn's voice came across the radio, carrying lots of static and a hint of panic. "Ten-fifty-F in progress."

"Holy cripes!" Doogie yelped. He jumped into his car and pulled the door closed. He had an animated forty-five-second conversation with his trusty dispatcher, then rolled the window partway down and gazed at Suzanne and Toni.

"What's the problem?" Toni asked. "You look like somebody just snapped your suspenders in a random act of kindness."

Doogie stared at her. "Junior's trailer? It's caught on fire. The guy who called it in said it's burning like there's no tomorrow!"

CHAPTER 10

A zombie apocalypse couldn't have kept them away from the fire. Suzanne stomped down hard on her accelerator in an effort to keep pace with Sheriff Doogie's car as he sped away from the curb. But with his bigger, souped-up cruiser, he was way ahead of her in a matter of minutes, his lights blazing and siren wailing as he fishtailed through the snow.

Toni scrunched down in the passenger seat of Suzanne's car and jammed a fist against her mouth. Over and over she kept muttering, "Oh no, oh no. Faster, Suzanne, faster. Please drive faster."

Suzanne spun around a corner, skidded sideways, and almost clipped a white Jeep that was parked on the side of the road. She fought hard to regain control, then finally got her Taurus straightened out again. "I'm sure it's just a grease fire," she said, though she knew it wasn't. "It'll probably be out by the time we get there."

Toni put her hands over her eyes.

Suzanne punched on her brights and rested one hand on the horn in case she had to blare out a warning to anyone in her way. She was hitting speeds of forty, fifty, and now sixty miles an hour—and she still hadn't caught up to Doogie. With his powerful V-8 engine, he'd pretty much left her in the proverbial dust. Or, in this case, dirty churned-up snow.

"That knucklehead," Toni said through gritted teeth. "If he used a blowtorch to grill hot dogs again, I'm gonna beat him like a cheap carpet. Then I'm gonna have him committed to a state mental hospital."

"Everything's okay," Suzanne said. "I can feel it in my bones."

But tonight Suzanne's bones were dead wrong. Because when they finally came out on Silver Creek Road, roaring past Ed's EZ Storage and Seifert's Grain Mill, they could see the fire burning up ahead. Red, yellow, and blue flames swirled and twirled thirty feet into the air like some kind of hellish tornado. Junior's squat little trailer was completely engulfed in fire, with flames crawling up the sides like scrabbling bugs.

"Dear Lord," Toni moaned. "What if Junior's inside? What if he's being cooked and crackled like a Christmas goose?"

"Hang on," Suzanne said. She swerved off the highway, heading for a bright red fire truck, then skidded into a shallow ditch and felt her car bottom out. Pumping her brakes hard, Suzanne slewed her way through a good eight inches of snow. She was hoping to end up right behind the fire truck, but Toni threw open the door and jumped out of the car before she managed a complete stop. When Suzanne popped out, too, pulling on a knit cap, she saw more than a dozen firemen working the scene. Wearing helmets and heavy dark slickers that were already coated with a thin skim of ice, they were manning the hoses, aiming two powerful jets of water at Junior's burning trailer.

Toni screamed out Junior's name as she fought to break through their line. Luckily, one firefighter grabbed her around the waist and hauled her back, away from the danger.

"Let me go!" Toni screamed as she kicked her feet, ready to attempt a return run. "Junior's in there!"

Suzanne caught up with Toni and wrapped her arms around her tightly. "You can't go in there, honey. It's like a microwave gone berserk. Just stay put and let the firemen do their job."

The firemen were coordinating their efforts, doing a masterful job. They continued to shoot great gluts of water at Junior's trailer, moving in as close as they dared. One of them pulled on breathing apparatus and dashed up to a window. With one quick punch of his ax he shattered the glass.

"Do you see him?" Toni called out. "Is Junior in there?" But there was too much noise and chaos for her voice to be heard.

"Shush, take it easy," Suzanne said. Her hands felt clammy inside her gloves despite the bitter cold. Because . . . what if Junior really was inside? What if he was curled up on the floor, passed out from smoke inhalation, flames licking at his hair and clothes?

Suzanne and Toni clutched each other, praying, freezing their buns off, watching the fire dance and sizzle. After a few minutes, Suzanne realized that Doogie was standing right next to them.

"He's not in there," Doogie said.

Worry and anguish were etched into Toni's face. "But what if . . ." she started to say.

In that split second there was a huge explosion. The noise sounded like two locomotives meeting in a head-on crash. Then a bolt of blue flame shot skyward.

"Gas tank," Doogie said, almost matter-of-factly.

They all watched in awe as the little trailer swelled up like a pan of Jiffy Pop and then twisted apart at the corner seams. Seconds later, blackened debris shot up into the air.

"Get back, everybody back," a fireman shouted.

They all moved back as debris rained down around them, almost in slow motion, settling in the snow with soft *plips* and *plops*. Cups and plates, tools, a flaming blanket, a tire, a radio, charred bits of God knows what.

"Oh no," Toni moaned.

But the firemen moved in closer now, steadily knocking down the flames, finally getting the whole mess under control. Five minutes later, it was all over except for the acrid stink.

Fire Chief Mulford Finley used a long metal tool with a hook to pop open the trailer's door and then peered inside. "Nobody home," he said, sounding vastly relieved.

Toni collapsed into Suzanne's arms.

Then Chief Finley stomped over to confer with Sheriff Doogie.

"Looks like it might have been arson," Finley said. "It caught fast and burned hot, which is often a dead giveaway for an accelerant. But we'll still have to run some tests."

Suzanne and Toni overheard Finley and turned toward the two men.

"Who would deliberately set a fire?" Toni demanded.

Doogie was the one who answered her. "Could have been anybody. Just some bum cruising through who thought the trailer was vacant and needed a place to crash. Maybe he lit a fire to stay warm. Or it was kids up to no good. Maybe they didn't figure anyone was living there. Just saw a shabby, rickety trailer and thought it was a junker."

"Kids, especially, will do that," Finley explained. He was short, squat, and in his mid-fifties, with a scrub of yellow-white hair. "Remember all those Dumpster fires last summer?"

Doogie nodded. "Just dumb kids."

Toni, who was watching the firemen stow their gear while chewing the end of her glove, was the first one to hear Junior's car. The knocking cylinders and screeching brakes gave it away.

"Junior!" she cried, waving her arms at him.

Junior careened to a stop next to the fire engine and jumped from his shuddering car. "Holy crap!" came his high-pitched squeal. He started hopping up and down, flapping his arms like a flightless bird that desperately wanted to go airborne. "What happened to my trailer?" He stared at the smoldering ruins as if he couldn't quite believe it. "Did somebody torch it?" Then, without waiting for an answer, he sprinted for the blackened door, which dangled by a single hinge. "I gotta get in there and save my stuff!"

"Junior, no!" Suzanne shouted. She made a grab for him, but Junior was too fast for her. Her fingers skittered off the back of his cracked leather motorcycle jacket.

Fortunately, two firemen were able to grapple with Junior and pull him back to safety.

Doogie dropped a kindly hand on Junior's shoulder. "You can't go in there, buddy. It's completely trashed. Besides, it's a crime scene now."

"Crime scene?" Junior dropped his head. "I can't believe this. Who'd set all my stuff on fire?"

"That's what we have to figure out," Doogie said. "Chief Finley needs to investigate."

"You're saying I can't go in there at all?"

"Not a good idea," Doogie said.

Junior looked around at what remained of his possessions. "What about all the stuff that blew out of there?" he asked. "That's all over the ground? Can I at least salvage *some* of that?"

Now Toni spoke up. "You gotta let him, Sheriff. It's all he's got left."

"Aw," Doogie said. "I guess it's cooked down enough. Go ahead."

A devastated Junior started poking around in the snow, picking up what he could and piling it into the trunk and backseat of his old junker. Once Toni joined in the recovery, Suzanne decided she'd better pitch in as well. Show a little solidarity for Toni and some compassion for Junior.

Amazingly, they were able to salvage quite a few of Junior's belongings. Yes, his Captain and Tennille tapes were singed beyond belief, but his tools seemed to have come through the fire and subsequent explosion just fine. Tempered by fire, Suzanne told herself, so probably still usable.

"I'm running out of room," Junior said, as he wedged a still-smoldering tire into the backseat of his '98 Chevy Corsica. He threw Suzanne a pleading look. "Do you think I could stash my toolbox in the backseat of your car? I can't jam much more into Blue Beater." Junior named all his vehicles. The dilapidated junker he drove tonight had been christened Blue Beater. He called another car Old Yeller and his pickup truck Old Faithful.

"Go ahead and stick 'em in there," Suzanne said. It was hard to say no to Junior in light of his tragic loss. Not that he'd lost anything of particular value.

"Thank you," Toni whispered to Suzanne.

But there was still one more hurdle to be crossed.

"Where am I going to sleep?" Junior moaned. "I can't camp out in this weather. I'll freeze my wazoo."

Suzanne pretended not to hear him. Sam would kill her if she dragged Junior home with her, like a dejected stray dog. Besides, there'd be the eventual issue of how to get rid of him.

Finally, Toni took pity on Junior and told him he could bunk with her for a while.

Junior perked up instantly. "Hey, babe, that'd be swell. I figured you'd come through for me."

"I said bunk at my apartment, Junior, not sleep together," Toni said. "As in *you're* the one sacking out on the lumpy sofa."

"Aw, babe."

WHEN Suzanne finally got home, her clothes still smelling faintly of smoke, Sam was stretched out on the sofa in the living room, perusing medical journals.

He smiled at her as he took off his reading glasses. "How was rehearsal?" he asked.

Suzanne collapsed into the chair across from him. "A funny thing happened on the way to the rehearsal. We never made it."

Baxter and Scruff got up from where they'd been sleeping, padded over to Suzanne, and sniffed her clothing from head to toe. From the sour looks on their doggy faces, they weren't one bit pleased.

"What happened?" Sam's feet hit the floor as he sat up. "Did you quit the play? That doesn't sound like you."

"Let's just say there were extenuating circumstances."

Now Sam's brows pulled together and a hint of alarm crossed his face. "Something happened?"

Suzanne drew a deep breath, then proceeded to tell him all about the fire at Junior's trailer. When she finished with her tale of woe, she said, "So you see, yet another cause for concern."

Sam continued to stare at her. "This is very weird. Every time you come home, something horrible has happened. You're like the angel of death, the harbinger of bad news."

"That's me," Suzanne said. "I'm the town jinx."

Sam cleared his stack of magazines away. "Come sit with me." He patted a sofa cushion.

Suzanne was delighted to sit next to him and have his arms around her. After her crazy night she finally felt cozy and safe.

Sam planted multiple kisses on her lips and cheeks and said, "So . . . was it awful?"

"Terrible. Toni was going berserk, and when Junior showed up he completely freaked out. I actually felt sorry for him."

"Of course you did. Because you're a sweet and caring person."

"Oh, maybe," Suzanne said to herself. Then, louder, "Did you eat?"

"Peanut butter and jelly on a toasted English muffin, so I'm fine. But what about you?"

"Starving. I'm going to fix a little something."

"In that case I'd be happy to keep you company. Food-wise, I mean."

Suzanne futzed around in the kitchen, fixing them a simple supper of leftover chicken-and-rice soup and slices of grilled focaccia. As she filled in a few more bits of information about the fire, Baxter and Scruff remained underfoot. Suzanne gave them each a jerky treat and sent them on their way. Temporarily, of course, because she knew they'd be back.

When the food was ready, Suzanne and Sam ate at the kitchen counter, sitting on stools, their knees and shoulders touching. Staying connected.

"I find this all very strange," Sam said as he spooned up his soup. "First a murder, then a fire. Wait, was it arson?"

"Fire Chief Finley wasn't sure. He said he has to run a few tests."

"Mmn . . . Do you think Allan Sharp's murder and Junior's fire are somehow connected?"

"No idea," Suzanne said.

"Lots of strange things going on," Sam mused. "What's next on the docket? Locusts and frogs?"

"Or flies and boils?"

Sam shuddered. "Please, no boils. Reminds me too much of when I was in med school."

"To change the subject, did Teddy Hardwick ever get hold of you? About taking over the Scrooge role?"

"Yes, he did," Sam said.

"And?"

"I told Hardwick I'd do it. Starting tomorrow night."

"Why on earth would you agree to take on that role?" Suzanne asked. "That gives you, like, two days to memorize all the lines and get up to speed. And right now you're especially busy at the clinic and . . . um . . ."

"I'm busy with you," Sam said.

"Well, yes."

Sam eased an arm around her and pulled her close. "I figure that if I'm in the play, I can keep a careful watch on you."

"You're sweet," Suzanne said, giving Sam a kiss. She wondered if she should tell him about Teddy Hardwick's bad foundation and Hardwick being furious with Allan Sharp. But, no, better to hold off. There was only so much bad news you could spring on your fiancé in a single night.

CHAPTER 11

CURIOSITY may have killed the cat, but a determined Suzanne was fearless. Which was why this Wednesday morning she was slogging a path on an unshoveled sidewalk to the front door of the county courthouse.

Last night, Doogie had mentioned something about checking on deeds and property tax records, which Suzanne thought was a spectacularly clever idea. So here she was, stomping snow off her boots in the entryway, then walking down a cavernous corridor to the door where pebbled glass was etched with the words County Records.

Luckily, the crabby lady who sometimes clerked in the records department was nowhere in sight today and Bonnie Saefer was working behind the wide wooden counter. Bonnie was a sometime Cackleberry Club customer, so Suzanne figured Bonnie would gladly do some digging for her.

She figured right. Bonnie was a former secondary

school teacher just like Suzanne was—a sweet-natured woman who favored twinsets and still wore her blond hair in a modified pageboy. Only on her it managed to look cute.

"Suzanne," Bonnie said, sounding genuinely happy. "How are you?"

"Never better," Suzanne said.

"How are Toni and Petra?"

"Working hard as always. Getting ready for Christmas."

Bonnie lowered her voice. "I heard about the fire last night. At Junior's trailer? Where's that poor boy going to live now?"

"Toni took him in temporarily."

"Mmn." Bonnie pursed her lips. She knew it wasn't a good idea.

Then, after a three-minute discussion on the merits of sweet scones versus savory scones, Bonnie nodded agreeably to Suzanne's request. She put on a pair of purple half-glasses and proceeded to pore through a thick brown binder. "Yup," she said finally. "Teddy Hardwick does indeed reside at 316 Whitetail Lane."

"And the property taxes?" Suzanne asked.

"Fourteen hundred annually," Bonnie said. "Of course, that'd be on top of your mortgage and your monthly HOA."

"Any liens or foreclosures against the development in general?"

"None that I can see." Bonnie closed the book. "Are you thinking of picking up stakes and moving? Buying Teddy's place if it goes up for sale?"

"Maybe," Suzanne hedged. "I heard him talking about his town house and I started to get curious. Although I understand there are still a couple of brand-new units for sale."

"That could be tricky," Bonnie said. "In light of . . ."

"I know. Allan Sharp being the developer. But I figured that since the bank probably handled financing, I could talk to them."

Bonnie nodded. "That's exactly right. That's where I'd start, too."

Heavy footfalls sounded in the hallway outside the office; then voices boomed loudly. The noise level continued to increase until it exploded into a very heated argument.

Bonnie rolled her eyes.

"What?" Suzanne whispered.

"Mayor Mobley's yelling his fool head off again," Bonnie said in a low voice. "That man is always upset about something."

"I suppose you get quite an earful working here."

"Do I ever. Before . . . well, when Allan Sharp sat on the city council, he and the mayor used to go at it tooth and nail. Their arguments pretty near blew the roof off this place. I think they even threw a few punches once."

"The two men really hated each other?" Suzanne asked.

"'Loathed' is the word that comes to mind. I don't know what happened between them; they used to be birds of a feather when it came to cooking up dirty little schemes and bilking the poor taxpayers. But then . . . wham. Suddenly it was World War III and Sharp was constantly haranguing Mobley about financial impropriety."

"You think there was funny business going on here?"

"I know there was. Is."

Suzanne rapped her knuckles against the counter. "Thanks for your help, Bonnie."

"Don't mention it. You take care now. Say hi to Toni and Petra for me."

Suzanne walked out into the hallway, where Mayor Mobley was still screaming. His victim was a young man in an oversized suit jacket and wire-rimmed glasses. Mobley was red-faced and gesturing like mad, really ripping him a new one, lost in a bombastic rant. He glanced at Suzanne as she went by him, but nothing seemed to register. He never faltered in his scathing tirade.

Yup, Suzanne thought to herself, *that pompous blowhard is definitely a suspect. His anger level is about 7.6 on the Richter scale and his blood pressure has to be off the charts. Which probably puts him in the crazed-killer category.*

SUZANNE pulled off one glove and dialed her phone from the car. When Toni answered she said, "Hey, it's me."

"Who's me?" Toni asked.

"Very funny," Suzanne said. "I just wanted to let you know I'm on my way in. I just have one more stop to make."

"Alrighty, cupcake," Toni said. "But sooner is better than later. Don't forget we've got our Christmas Tea this afternoon and then we're catering Allan Sharp's visitation tonight."

"On my way." Suzanne paused. "How did you fare with Junior last night?"

"I can't even," Toni said.

"Sorry I asked."

As Suzanne navigated the slippery streets, a fine snow began to fall, probably due to another chinook that dipped down out of Canada. *If this was only early December, what was it going to be like in February?* she wondered. Probably ten-foot-high snowdrifts.

Suzanne drove down Arcade Street and eased to the curb in front of Fabrique, Kindred's one and only fabric store. Not a lot of women sewed their own clothing or draperies these days, yet Fabrique managed to somehow stay in business. In fact, the gold lettering on their front window advertised Fabrics, Draperies, Upholstery Materials, Classes.

Upholstering, Suzanne thought. That'd be the day. She'd watched a demo once, a lady upholstering a wing chair. Punching through heavy fabric with a circular needle, she'd taken teeny-tiny little stitches. Talk about dedication.

When Suzanne walked into Fabrique, the shop was empty of customers but packed to the rafters with bolts of fabric. Colorful felts, corduroys, and wools caught her eye. As well as tartans, checks, calicos, quilted fabrics, flannels, and fleece.

Andrina Chamberlain, the shop's owner, emerged from the back and hurried to greet Suzanne. She was tall and dark-haired and always had a tape measure slung around her neck and a narrow pair of reading glasses slipping down her nose.

"Suzanne, how are you?" Andrina asked. "What can I help you with? We're running a terrific special on our quilted fabrics. They're normally seven ninety-nine a yard, but for the holidays we've marked them down to four ninety-nine a yard."

"I'll be sure to tell Petra," Suzanne said. "You know how much she loves to quilt."

"Don't I know it," Andrina said. "She's one of the movers and shakers behind our annual Quilt Trail."

"What I'm shopping for today is a little information," Suzanne said.

"Concerning our classes?" Andrina pushed up her glasses.

"Noooo. I was wondering if anyone, specifically someone of the male persuasion, purchased a few yards of cheesecloth or muslin lately."

"Funny you should ask. We did have a man in here about a week ago. I remember it quite distinctly because this shop doesn't generally attract many men."

"And you remember what this guy bought?"

"Oh yes. It was practically a full bolt of cheesecloth."

A satisfying ping registered inside Suzanne's brain. "Was the cheesecloth dark green?" She wondered if someone might have created a ghost costume. An alternate ghost costume.

"Not green," Andrina said slowly. "Because we only carry it in a natural cream color. But he did ask me about dyeing it. You know, what type of dye to use, do you soak the fabric in a large vat or what?"

Suzanne knew she had to ask. How could she not? "Who was it, do you remember?"

"It was that young man who's come here to help Reverend Yoder. You know, at the church right across the parking lot from your café."

"Ethan Jakes," Suzanne said.

"I believe that's his name, yes."

"Did he say what he wanted the cheesecloth for?"

Andrina shook her head. "I just assumed it had something to do with Christmas. Maybe some sort of swag or backdrop for a church pageant? Why, is there a problem?"

"None at all," Suzanne said. "I'm sorry I bothered you."

ALL the way back to the Cackleberry Club, Suzanne's mind was running in overdrive. Reverend Ethan Jakes had bought almost a full bolt of cheesecloth. But why? What would he use it for? Yes, she knew Jakes had had a nasty tiff with Allan Sharp, but would a man of the cloth (an ironic term in this case) actually commit murder?

Better to find out what the cheesecloth was used for. So she could cross him off her list.

"Hey there," Petra said when Suzanne walked in the back door. "Look who finally turned up."

"Apologies," Suzanne said as she traded her winter coat for a black French waiter's apron. "Have we been terribly busy?" The kitchen smelled of bacon, warm cinnamon, and melted cheese. In other words, heavenly.

Toni came through the swinging door at that exact moment. "Naw," she said. "We didn't do very many covers this morning. Probably because of all the snow. It's keeping a lot of folks at home."

"I'm worried about people not showing up for our Christmas Tea this afternoon," Petra said.

"Don't be. We're completely sold out," Suzanne said.

"Yeah, but that doesn't mean they'll all show up," Petra said. She turned back to her frying pan, where red peppers sizzled alongside rings of sweet Vidalia onion. Garnish for her chicken and wild rice sausages.

Toni, meanwhile, was still jacked up about the big fire last night.

"You should have seen it," she said to Petra. "Flames shooting almost fifty feet in the air!"

"So you told me," Petra replied. "About five times already."

"It was like the fiery tornado in the Bible where it says, 'I have come to cast fire upon the earth,'" Toni said.

"Luke 12:49," Petra responded. "But tell me, if Junior's trailer was completely destroyed, that pretty much leaves him homeless, right?"

Toni nodded. "That's the awful part of it."

"So where's Junior going to live? Can he even afford a room at Motel 6?"

Toni shrugged. "Dunno. Maybe that one room behind the Dumpster that nobody ever wants. Or he might have to rough it and sleep in one of his cars." Junior had his small collection of junker cars parked behind Matson's Body Shop.

"Junior's cars never run properly," Petra said. "That fool boy will end up carbon monoxiding himself to death."

"You better tell her," Suzanne said to Toni.

"Tell me what?" Petra said. A certain *tone* had crept into her voice.

"I told Junior he could stay with me for a while," Toni whispered.

"Oh, girlfriend, no." Petra turned and put a hand on her hip. "You took him in like a stray cat? Say it ain't so."

"Just temporarily, until Junior finds himself another trailer."

"Dear Lord," Petra said. "That could be decades."

THEY were right on the cusp between breakfast and lunch, so Suzanne busied herself getting ready for their Christmas Tea. Toni (bless her heart) had managed to come in early to string lights and garland around the windows and on the shelves. Now the only thing left to do was put up the Christmas stockings Petra had knitted and hang two dozen or so white cardboard snowflakes from the ceiling. Just as she was dreading dragging out the ladder, Junior came swaggering in.

"Junior," Suzanne said, pulling out the box of decorations. "How are you doing?"

"Not too bad," Junior said. "I managed to get a good night's rest, so I feel halfway recovered from last night."

"That's good to hear. I'm very sorry about the fire. Losing your trailer and all your . . . um, stuff."

"I went out to look at it first thing this morning." Junior shook his head. "Just ashes and embers, that's all that's left. Like you'd see after a weenie roast. Except, of course, the axles are still sitting there."

"So what are you going to do now?"

"I dunno. Hang out at Toni's place, I guess."

Junior looked like he was at odds and ends. And why wouldn't he be? No job, no place to call home, no insurance . . .

"Junior, could you . . . would you . . . grab the stepladder and help me hang these snowflakes?" Suzanne asked.

"Sure thing," Junior said. Then his face took on a cagey expression. "But maybe I could have some breakfast first?"

"Not a problem," Suzanne said, relieved that he was willing to pitch in and help. "You go sit at the counter over there and yell out to Petra what you want. Hey, are you really feeling okay?"

"I guess," Junior said. As he wandered over to the counter, he seemed to have a wad of something stuck in his cheek. Chewing tobacco?

Petra leaned through the pass-through and gazed at Junior. "What's wrong with your teeth?"

"What? Nothing." Junior snapped his teeth together a couple of times to demonstrate. "See? My choppers are all present and accounted for. Well, I did lose one of my incisors in a motorcycle crash last summer."

"Are you sure? Because it looks like *all* your front teeth got knocked out."

"Naw, I've just been eating black licorice." Junior dug in his jacket pocket and pulled out a sticky glob. "Want some?"

"No, thanks," Petra said. "So, whadya want to eat?"

"Sausage and eggs?"

"Coming right up."

* * *

STRANGELY, Junior was as good as his word. As soon as he finished his breakfast, he helped Suzanne wrap Christmas paper around the toy bins and then set up the ladder and began hanging snowflakes from the ceiling. He'd decorated half of the ceiling when Toni came out and said, "You're doing it all wrong. You've got to hang the snowflakes at different lengths. Some should dangle six inches down, some ten inches down."

Junior eyed his handiwork. "I think they look better when they're all even."

"No, they don't."

"You don't have to be so bossy, Toni. I can make a few adjustments."

But ten minutes later Toni still wasn't happy.

"Now some of them are *too* long. People are going to get bashed in the head," Toni said.

Junior gave her a dismissive look. "Only if they're going to be walking around the café on stilts. Like some kind of stupid circus act."

"If at first you don't succeed, try doing it the way I told you," Toni said, a trifle harshly.

"Why are you always nagging me?" Junior asked. "Just because you woke up on the wrong side of the bed this morning, you've gotta yammer at me about how to do my job? It's a bummer. Why can't we work together in peace? Let all the workers have an equal say?"

"Who do you think you are? Leon Trotsky spouting the *Communist Manifesto*?" Toni shouted. "If you can't do the job right, then get out!"

Junior scrabbled down the ladder, grabbed his jacket, and strode defiantly out of the Cackleberry Club. As the door slammed shut behind him he was mumbling to himself that it was time to watch *The Price Is Right* anyway.

"You don't think you were a little hard on him?" Suzanne asked. She'd watched their squabble from the doorway of the Book Nook.

"You're probably right," Toni sighed. "But, holy cow, Junior sure does bring it on himself. This morning, before I even opened my peepers, he managed to knock over a plant stand, mess up the carpet, and break my favorite coffee mug. And then he had the gall to turn around and ask if I'd buy him an Xbox. Just like that. Said he was bored hanging around my place. Already! I was so furious I wanted to rip out his gizzard and fry it up in a pan." Toni scrubbed at her hair with both hands. "Look at me. Junior's been under my roof for less than twelve hours and he's already turned me into a raving shrew."

Suzanne put an arm around Toni. "Yes, but you're *our* little raving shrew."

CHAPTER 12

"LUNCH is super abbreviated today, right, Petra?" Suzanne asked. Now she was the one peering through the pass-through.

"Just three entrees," Petra said. "Denver omelets, chicken and waffles, and three-bean chili. Of course we've still got our usual complement of sticky buns, scones, and muffins. But I'd feel a lot better if you guys could kind of hurry our lunch guests along."

"I'll have Toni wait on them. With the mood she's in, she'll have them fleeing like rats from a sinking ship."

"If it means anything to you," Toni called out, "I'm over my crabby mood now. I feel a lot more composed."

Suzanne smiled. "I'm glad Junior didn't get the best of you."

"Only my best years," Toni grumped.

Clearly she wasn't over it.

Suzanne printed their abbreviated luncheon menu on the

blackboard while Toni finished hanging the snowflakes. Then Petra came out to eyeball the café's décor.

"Everything looks great," Petra said. "Very festive. Oh, and, Suzanne, you put up my Christmas stockings." She smiled at the red stockings that were hung on the walls.

"Of course I did," Suzanne said. "I know that the money from every sale goes right into your church coffer."

"Don't you just adore the yarn I used? It's beaded mohair from Artyarns," Petra said.

"And what's with the little knit teddy bears?" Suzanne asked. "I saw you had a couple sitting by the cash register."

"Those are part of Operation Cuddle Bear. My knitting group has been making little bears that we give out to the sheriff's department, fire department, highway patrol, and the EMTs."

"Um . . . why?" Suzanne asked.

Petra saw the confused look on Suzanne's face and laughed. "Oh no, the bears aren't for them. Well, not directly anyway. They're to be handed out to kids in crisis situations. You know, if there's been a car accident or fire . . . it helps soften the impact of a disaster."

"That's a fabulous idea," Suzanne said.

Toni had crept up behind them. "You see how the snowflakes are hung at different lengths?" she asked Petra.

"I hadn't really noticed," Petra said. She was suddenly shifting from one green Croc to the other, twisting a dish towel between her hands.

"What's wrong, Petra?" Toni asked. "You look like you're as nervous as a ceiling fan salesman with a bad comb-over."

"I think I might be coming down with a case of the collywobbles," Petra said.

"Is it catching?" Toni asked.

"No, I'm just nervous about serving lunch, then fixing all the tea sandwiches and baking scones for our party," Petra said. "And then I've got to turn around and do it all over again because we've got that catering job for Allan Sharp's visitation tonight."

"We'll all pitch in and help," Suzanne assured her. "We'll get everything done in no time flat."

"No time," Petra said. "That's the problem."

Suzanne followed an anxious Petra into the kitchen. "Petra, how well do you know Reverend Ethan Jakes?"

"I really don't know him at all," Petra said. "Because I don't attend his church. You know very well that I'm a confirmed Methodist." Petra grabbed a spoon and stirred her pot of chili. "Why are you asking?"

"No reason."

She sprinkled in a helping of cayenne pepper. "Suzanne, you always have a reason."

"Okay. I happen to know that Reverend Jakes had a serious dustup with Allan Sharp . . ."

Petra turned toward her, mouth gaping, eyes suddenly gone wide. "And . . . don't tell me, you think the reverend might possibly have killed Sharp? That Jakes was the one who wore a fake ghost costume and stabbed him onstage?"

"The thought had flitted briefly through my mind."

"Well, get rid of it," Petra said, sounding more than a little irritated. "Don't even go there."

"Okay, I won't." *Or maybe I will.*

"Honestly," Petra huffed. "To suspect a man of the cloth."

Cheesecloth, Suzanne thought. She knew she couldn't march over to the Journey's End Church and start firing questions at Reverend Jakes. That wouldn't work. But she did need to find out about the cheesecloth he'd purchased.

In other words, Suzanne needed a plan. Or, at the very least, a darned good story.

LUNCH flew by amazingly fast. Suzanne and Toni took orders, smiled prettily, did their jobs to perfection, and didn't linger with any extra conversation. So, wonder of wonders, the café cleared out by one-fifteen, just as Joey, their teenage busboy, arrived.

"What up, Mrs. D?" Joey asked as he bounded through the door. He was sixteen, dressed like a rapper in baggy pants and an oversized denim jacket, and sporting a neck full of cheap gold chains.

"You're right on time," Suzanne said, pleased. "I was worried about all this snow." She winked at him. "Makes it tough to skateboard, huh?" Joey was a skateboard fanatic.

Joey shook his head. "Rode my bike today."

Toni walked into the café and said, "No, you didn't."

Joey gestured out the window. "I sure did. My dad changed out my regular tires for studded tires. Now I can go anywhere I want, even on ice."

"Well, don't go breaking your leg," Suzanne said.

"That's not going to happen to me," Joey said. "I'm immortal."

"Petra's waiting for you in the kitchen," Toni told him. "This Christmas Tea is gonna make for a super busy day."

"A tea party, huh?" Joey said. "I can handle it."

Suzanne smiled at him. She was always tickled by Joey's crazy, upbeat attitude. "I believe you can."

TWENTY minutes later, Missy Langston showed up. She had three giggling, long-limbed models in tow along with two rolling racks stuffed with clothes. It looked as if Kim Kardashian was about to have an over-the-top session with her fashion stylist.

"Seriously, Missy?" Suzanne said. "What kind of production do you have planned for us?"

"One filled with holiday fabulosity," Missy said. She grabbed Suzanne by the arm and pulled her aside. "Have you told anyone about the fashion show?"

"Only Toni and Petra. So your show's going to come as a huge surprise to our guests."

"Wonderful, that's exactly what I was hoping for. Now . . . where do you want us to hang out until the big reveal?"

"Probably in the Book Nook," Suzanne said. "There's plenty of room and a mirror in my office so you can . . . Well, you'll figure it out."

Missy drew even closer to Suzanne. "Have you talked to Amber recently?" she asked in a low voice.

"Yesterday. In fact, I invited her to the Christmas Tea."

Missy looked surprised. "And she's coming?"

"She said she would."

"Wonderful!" Missy winked at Suzanne as she slipped away with her models and racks of clothes.

Suzanne and Toni had already put on bright red sweaters to complement their white blouses and black slacks. Now they were doing a last-minute perusal of the café, making sure everything was in full holiday mode.

In other words, white linen tablecloths, red napkins, bouquets of red roses and greenery adorning each table. And for the pièce de résistance, they were using creamy white china with silver rims as well as silver candleholders with white tapers.

"If we dim the overhead lights a little, I think the

colored lights and flickering candles will look even more perfect," Toni said.

"Then let's do it," Suzanne agreed.

"Mmn, really nice," Toni said, once she'd hit the dimmer switch. And the décor did look great, with twinkling Christmas bulbs shimmering and reflecting off the crystal goblets and silverware in a million points of light.

They did one final check in the kitchen, where Petra, much to everyone's surprise, seemed to have everything under control. Unlike a three-course tea, where every course was served separately, they were doing a one-shot deal today, using their large three-tiered tea trays. That way, an abundance of scones, tea sandwiches, and desserts piled on each tray would not only look spectacular; it would make serving a whole lot easier.

"Okay," Petra said, flapping a tea towel at them. "You've seen where I am. Now, out, out, out. You two are starting to make me nervous all over again."

"That was precisely our intention," Toni said.

Petra flapped her towel again. "Oh, you."

Back out in the café, Suzanne gave everything a final glance. "It looks positively magical. I think we're all set."

"Music," Toni said. "We need to put on some Christmas music."

Suzanne knelt down, rummaged through her CD collection, and popped one into her CD player. Immediately, the strains of "White Christmas" echoed throughout the café.

"What about when Missy's fashion show starts?" Toni asked. "What kind of music should we play?"

"Missy already gave me a CD," Suzanne said. "*Evolve* by Imagine Dragons. She said the music's got lots of sharp edges so the models can really strut their stuff."

They stood together, admiring the gleaming tables and

the lovely décor and enjoying the peace and quiet. Then Toni said, "What if nobody shows up because of all this snow?"

"Then we'll be stuck with a ton of food."

"Maybe we could open a pop-up tea shop on the side of the road. Until the food starts to freeze, that is."

But in the end their worries were unfounded, because not two minutes later the first SUV bumped its way into their parking lot and four guests spilled out. Another ten minutes later and the parking lot was practically full, with three dozen guests tumbling through their front door.

Suzanne greeted everyone, shaking hands and hanging up coats on the temporary coatrack they'd stuck by the door. Toni checked off each guest's name and led them to their assigned tables.

The door flew open again and Laura Benchley, the editor of the *Bugle*, rushed in.

"Suzanne," Laura cried, throwing her arms around Suzanne's neck. She was a dark-haired woman, even skinnier than Toni, bubbling over with energy and enthusiasm.

"Delighted you could make it," Suzanne said.

"You know I never miss one of your Christmas Teas," Laura said. "Never miss one of your Valentine or Easter Teas, either."

"And I thank you wholeheartedly for all the publicity you've graciously given us."

Laura leaned in close. "It seems you in particular have scored a little extra ink this week."

"What are you talking about?" Suzanne asked.

"Gene Gandle, our intrepid reporter, mentioned your name prominently in the article he wrote about Allan Sharp's murder. Well, you can read it for yourself when the paper comes out tomorrow."

Suzanne winced. She really didn't relish *that* kind of

publicity. "I was just in the wrong place at the wrong time," she said. Then, glancing around the café, she saw that Toni was already making the rounds, pouring tea. Thank goodness.

"Too bad this community play turned into a total washout," Laura said.

"What do you mean?" Suzanne asked. "Wait a minute, do you know something I don't?"

Laura stared at her, practically bug-eyed. "Suzanne, you mean you haven't heard? The play's been cancelled!"

"What?" Suzanne could hardly believe it. "No, I hadn't heard that at all. In fact, I'm downright shocked." The Cackleberry Club was usually ground zero for any faint rumblings or whiffs of hometown gossip. But today they seemed to be the last ones to know. Suzanne wondered if Sam had been informed that the play was cancelled, or if he'd started memorizing his lines, unaware. Then she decided that, between dispensing antibiotics, making rounds at the hospital, and suturing the occasional cut, he probably hadn't had time to glance at his script.

"I hope you're not too disappointed," Laura said, peering at Suzanne.

"About the play? No, I suppose I'm not," Suzanne said. "What does disappoint me is that Sheriff Doogie hasn't made an arrest yet."

"But he will, I'm positive of it."

Suzanne peered at Laura. "Do you know something else that I don't?"

Laura smiled sweetly. "I think I've probably said too much already."

JUST as Suzanne was about to get the event started, Amber Payson came flying through the door. She looked very cute in her red coat and cream-colored mittens and scarf and immediately began thanking Suzanne for the invitation.

"My pleasure," Suzanne said, eyeing the tables crammed full of guests. There were only two seats left. One for Amber and one for someone who probably wasn't going to show.

"I've never been to a fancy tea before," Amber said. "This is a first for me."

"I hope you enjoy it," Suzanne said as she gently guided Amber to one of the empty seats.

"Is Missy here already?" Amber asked.

Suzanne put a finger to her lips. "Shhh. That's a secret for later."

Finally, with "Joy to the World" playing over the stereo system, Suzanne stepped to the front of the room. Toni rang a tiny tinkling bell and the conversation and excited chatter immediately dropped to a low buzz.

"I'd like to welcome everyone to our Christmas Tea," Suzanne began. "We're thrilled to have you as guests of the Cackleberry Club, and I'm delighted to tell you about the lovely three-course tea that Petra, Toni, and I have prepared for you. On the top tier of our serving trays today you're going to find Petra's special cranberry and walnut scones. To complement those scones, we'll be serving a Chinese black tea infused with orange and rose petals. Your next course will consist of three different tea sandwiches. A ham, pineapple, and cucumber sandwich. A chicken salad sandwich with chutney. And an egg salad sandwich with tarragon. We created an in-house blend of jasmine and pouchong tea to accompany those particular sandwiches. For dessert you'll find butterscotch and pecan shortbread as well as hummingbird cupcakes on your tea tray. And we'll be pouring a delicious peach-apricot tea."

There was a round of applause and then Suzanne held up a finger.

"As a very special treat, Missy Langston and her Alchemy gang will also be presenting a holiday fashion show . . ."

Now everyone beamed and the applause ratcheted up a hundred percent.

". . . with some absolutely spectacular clothing from Alchemy Boutique. And trust me, ladies, I took a sneak peek at the clothes and they are to die for." Suzanne took a single step in the direction of the kitchen and spread her arms wide. "And now . . ."

Toni and Petra emerged, perfectly on cue, each carrying an enormous silver three-tiered tea tray laden with goodies. They placed their trays in the center of the nearest tables and dashed back for more. This time, Suzanne was right on their heels. Seconds later, the three of them appeared with more tea trays, and their Christmas Tea was off and running.

It was, Suzanne decided some thirty minutes later, one of the best events they'd ever had at the Cackleberry Club. Jenny Probst from the Kindred Bakery had shown up, as had good friends Lolly Herron, Pat Shepley, and Bea Strait. The kinship and camaraderie in the room were off the charts. And when one of her guests raised a hand in the air and yelled, "Women power," everyone chimed in with good-natured hoots and applause.

Grabbing a pot of black tea, Suzanne made the rounds, filling teacups, chatting with her guests, and saying hello to old friends she hadn't seen in months.

"Suzanne." Tiny Agnes Bennet, the organist at Petra's

church, put a gnarled hand on Suzanne's arm. "How is Toni holding up? I heard her husband's trailer caught fire."

"Toni's doing okay," Suzanne said. "Probably better than Junior."

"That boy does seem to be a trial," Agnes said. "I remember one time when he ran short on spark plugs and used a live bullet instead. As soon as his engine heated up, the bullet exploded and shot right up through the windshield. Good thing he's not a particularly tall man."

"Good thing Toni keeps him on a short leash," Suzanne said. She moved to another table and refilled teacups for Anna Bartlett and Faith Jorgenson.

"How's your son, Noah, doing?" Suzanne asked Faith.

Faith beamed. "Wonderfully well at his new school. Thank you for asking."

Then Toni was at her elbow.

"Missy wants to know when she should start the show," Toni asked.

"Our guests are just finishing their tea sandwiches, so I'm guessing in about five or six minutes," Suzanne said. "The fashion show will be the perfect accompaniment with their desserts."

"Along with peach-apricot tea."

Suzanne poured the last of her tea and said to Helen Winder, "I know you've got a sweet tooth, so wait until you taste—"

Wham! Bam! Whap!

The front door whooshed open, bringing in a gush of frigid air, followed by an angry-looking Sheriff Doogie. He stood there, eyes blazing, head and shoulders dusted with snow, breathing hard, looking like a reincarnation of the Abominable Snowman.

Heads turned, chairs creaked, and one woman let loose

a little scream in the back of her throat. A buzz of questions suddenly rose, building to a steady, confused hum.

Suzanne, poised with teapot in hand, was thoroughly taken aback. She gaped at Doogie, ready to demand answers. Why would he burst in like this? What was this rude, unwelcome interruption all about?

But before she could open her mouth, Doogie gazed across the crowd, steely gray eyes ignoring bewildered glances.

Then Doogie shouted, "Where's Amber Payson!"

CHAPTER 13

This is so not happening! was Suzanne's first thought. *Not in the middle of my Christmas Tea!*

Like an avenging angel, Suzanne rushed to intercept Doogie. She was beyond angry and outraged at his boorish intrusion.

"What do you think you're *doing*?" she hissed.

Doogie scrupulously ignored her. His eyes continued to scan the crowd until he finally located Amber. He pointed a pudgy hand at the trembling girl and said, "You need to come with me, young lady."

"Are you *arresting* her?" Suzanne asked.

"Taking her in for questioning," Doogie said.

"I need to know why," Suzanne said. She glanced back over her shoulder and realized that absolutely everyone in the room was staring at them, absorbing every word that was being exchanged. "Excuse me." Suzanne gripped

Doogie's arm and pulled him through the swinging door into the kitchen.

"Who's making that awful noise?" Petra demanded.

"It's the cops!" Joey cried.

Petra straightened up from her cutting board, took note of Doogie's angry face and Suzanne's smoldering look, and said, "*Now* what's wrong?"

"Doogie came here for Amber," Suzanne said.

Petra didn't utter a word, just stared at both of them as if they were two ornery bulls, pawing and stomping, getting ready to lock horns. Joey stood in the background, all ears and big eyes.

"Now, tell me exactly *why* you had to bust in here and disrupt my Christmas Tea?" Suzanne said to Doogie.

Doogie folded his arms across his chest in a protective gesture. "I already told you. I need to talk to Amber."

"You need to talk to her or you're going to take her in for questioning?"

"Both."

"Why? Please tell me what's going on," Suzanne said.

"I don't have to explain myself to you," Doogie said.

"You're on my premises so, yes, I think you do," Suzanne said.

Doogie wrinkled his nose, rolled his eyes, and looked in Petra's direction, hoping for an ally.

Petra just shrugged, interested to see who was going to come out on top.

Suzanne tapped a toe. "I'm waiting."

"Ah . . ." Doogie was supremely unhappy now, his face flushed red, his jowls sloshing in protest. "I sent Deputy Driscoll over to Amber's house to ask her a couple of follow-up questions, routine questions . . ."

The kitchen door creaked open and Amber crept in. She

stood right behind Doogie, quiet as a mouse, but with every nerve quivering.

Suzanne made a rolling motion with her hand. "And . . . ? Come on, what's the rest of the story?"

"Driscoll found a can of gasoline sitting on Amber's front porch."

"Gasoline," Suzanne said. She was struggling to make any sort of connection. Then her eyes widened and she said, "Surely you're not trying to pin the fire at Junior's trailer on Amber? Wait . . . are you?"

"The gasoline may be circumstantial, but it bears looking into," Doogie said.

"It's not mine," Amber shouted, causing Doogie to jump in surprise. He hadn't realized she was lurking behind him. "Someone must have put it there!"

Doogie spun around to peer at her. "I'll be the judge of that, young lady. In the meantime, we need to collect fingerprints. So it's in your best interest to come along with me to the Law Enforcement Center."

"This isn't right," Suzanne said. "You come in here and humiliate this poor girl in front of everyone. Intimidate her . . ."

Doogie managed an offhand toss of his head. "I'm only doing my job."

"No, you're not," Suzanne said. "You're trying to make impossible connections. Tell me, what reason would Amber have to burn down Junior's trailer?" Doogie started to open his mouth, but Suzanne steamrolled right over him. "I'll tell you what. She had no reason. None at all!"

"Yet Chief Findley found evidence of arson," Doogie hurled back at her. "Somebody doused Junior's trailer with gasoline."

"That could have been anyone. Like you said the other

night, kids or someone who passed by and decided to get his jollies."

"And then we have the fact that somebody gutted Allan Sharp with a hunting knife!" Doogie cried.

"But it wasn't Amber."

Still, Doogie stood his ground. "I don't know what's behind either case. Or if they're even related. But I swear to God I'm going to find out. I'll get to the bottom of this if it kills me."

In the end, Amber went willingly with Doogie. Suzanne had put up a good argument, but there wasn't much else she could do.

BACK out in the café, Suzanne started to offer a halting explanation to her guests. But Toni, knowing what really mattered, quickly popped Missy's fashion show music into the CD player. Two seconds later, the music of Imagine Dragons throbbed throughout the Cackleberry Club. Then the models came strutting out and the guests started smiling and clapping.

So much for an apology, Suzanne decided. Sometimes it really was better to keep calm and carry on.

"Holy bejeebers," Petra called to her through the pass-through. "That had to register a good ten points on the weirdness scale." Suzanne was standing behind the counter, brewing two more pots of tea, so she leaned down and looked in at Petra. "Do you think Doogie was right to take Amber in?"

"I didn't at first, but now that I mull it over, I'm not so sure."

"Why would Amber want to murder Allan Sharp and then set Junior's trailer on fire?"

"Maybe she didn't mean to set it on fire," Petra said. "Maybe she was trying to kill him, too."

"Petra!" Suzanne watched a swirl of purple and peach mohair go by on one of the models, but she wasn't so caught up in the fashion show that she couldn't be outraged.

"I don't know what to think," Petra went on. "Because it's all so awful. The murder . . . the fire . . . it all seems crazy to me."

"Because it is crazy," Suzanne muttered. "It's kapow-crazy."

At the end of the day, when Suzanne counted up their sizable receipts, she was pleased with the Christmas Tea, but still upset by Doogie's little storm-trooper routine. In fact, his bursting in to accost Amber had made her want to double down on her investigation. Now she resolved to dig deeper into why Allan Sharp had been murdered and why Junior's trailer had been set on fire.

Toni poked her head into Suzanne's office and said, "How'd we make out?"

"With the tickets we sold for the tea and all the knitted Christmas stockings that sold, it comes to well over nine hundred dollars."

"But some of that money goes to Petra's church."

"Um, a hundred and twenty dollars does. As well as fifty dollars to Joey."

"Still, we did really good."

"Yes, we did," Suzanne said. They were heading into the final days of a rather profitable fiscal year. There'd be Christmas bonuses for everyone.

"And now we have to get ready for Allan Sharp's visitation tonight." Toni shuddered. "Ugh, I hate going to funeral homes and looking at dead bodies."

"Then don't look at him," Suzanne said.

"Easier said than done. You know what? Junior told me that a person's fingernails and hair keep growing even after they're dead."

"Gross."

"Yeah, but do you think that's really true? Could you ask Sam about it?"

"I don't think so," Suzanne said. "Why don't we drop the subject and check in with Petra. See what she wants us to do."

Amazingly, Petra had lulled herself into a state of almost tranquility.

"I told myself to stop worrying," Petra said. "I've already got the dough for the scones sitting in the cooler and the tea sandwiches won't take more than a half hour to whip together."

"What time does the dead-body preview start?" Toni asked.

"It's a *vis-i-ta-tion*," Petra enunciated.

"Seven o'clock," Suzanne said.

"Wait a minute," Petra said. "Won't you two be missing rehearsal?"

"I guess you haven't heard," Suzanne said. "The play's been cancelled."

"What?" Petra said. "Seriously? It's been called off? Was this Sheriff Doogie's idea?"

"I don't know," Suzanne said. "Maybe. I'm going to call Sam and let him know about this before he starts memorizing lines. He's not just a type A; he's a type A squared."

She went out into the café, dialed the clinic, and asked to be put through to Sam. When he finally came on the line she said, "Have you heard?"

"Heard what?" Sam asked. There was another voice in the background and then Sam said, "No, it should be amoxicillin, not ampicillin. Amoxi has better efficacy in treating middle ear infections." He muttered something else and then was back on the line. "I'm sorry, Suzanne, what were you saying?"

"Have you heard that the play's been cancelled?"

"You mean rehearsal's cancelled? For tonight?"

"No, forever. The whole play has been called off."

"Seriously?" Sam said. "Well . . . humbug to that."

"Come on, you didn't really want to play Scrooge."

"Sure I did. I was looking forward to it."

"Liar."

Sam's throaty laugh filled Suzanne's ear.

"Something else happened, too," Suzanne said. "Something I need to tell you about."

"Please don't tell me extraterrestrials crash-landed. And that you're about to run off with one that's cuter and even more charming than I am."

"One of Doogie's deputies found a can of gasoline sitting on Amber Payson's front porch."

"What's that supposed to mean? That Amber got macho and bought herself a snowmobile?"

"No. Think about it."

Silence spun out for a few moments and then Sam said, "Wait a minute, Doogie doesn't actually believe that she . . ."

"Used it as an accelerant when she supposedly burned down Junior's trailer?" Suzanne said. "That's exactly what he thinks. Doogie, in his frenetic pursuit to solve two crimes, seems to have jumped to a rather erroneous conclusion."

"What if it's not erroneous?" Sam asked. "What if Amber really did it? What if she murdered Allan Sharp, too?"

"*Why* would she?" Suzanne said, sounding a little shrill.

"You told me that Allan Sharp harassed her."

"Yeah, but . . . do you think she'd go nuclear over something like that?"

"We may not know the full extent of what happened," Sam said. "Amber may have been extremely traumatized and forced to hold in much of her anger and emotions."

"You mean like PTSD?"

"Something like that, yes."

"And then she exploded? Like . . . bam?"

"Could happen," Sam said. "Stranger things have."

"I suppose," Suzanne said. "Still, murder combined with arson is a pretty quirky combo . . ." She was fumbling for words now. "I mean . . . I'm not sure what to think . . . what to do."

"I have a gnawing feeling—and I'm pretty sure it's not acid reflux—that you're going to ignore my warning and dig a whole lot deeper."

CHAPTER 14

THE Driesden and Draper Funeral Home wasn't exactly pleasing to the eye architecturally. In fact, with its turrets, finials, shabby gray paint, and blacked-out windows at the rear of the building (where they carried out the embalming), the building resembled the proverbial haunted house.

Even iced with snow, an appealing factor that made other homes and buildings appear soft and poufy, almost like gingerbread houses, the funeral home still appeared ominous. But that's where Suzanne, Toni, and Petra were at this exact moment. Fussing around in Slumber Room A— what George Draper was now calling the Somnus Suite— hurrying to set up their coffee, sandwiches, and pastries in anticipation of guests dropping by for the visitation.

Ah yes, the visitation. Allan Sharp, the deceased, was most definitely present and accounted for. In fact, he was lying in final repose on the opposite side of the room, spiffed up in a charcoal three-piece suit and stretched out

in a top-of-the-line walnut and brass executive-model casket. What George Draper called their Triton Model.

Toni pretended to ignore Sharp's body, but every once in
a while she dodged halfway across the room, put a hand
over one eye, and emitted a shrill little mouse squeak.

"Get back over here," Suzanne said. "Stop worrying
about Allan Sharp's dead body and help us get this food
set up."

Suzanne had spoken to Toni a little more harshly than
she'd intended, probably because she still felt jittery about
Amber being unceremoniously hauled away by Doogie.
She was also rattled by the fact that Doogie, and apparently
Petra, thought the girl was capable of murder.

"Sorry, Toni," she said as Toni wandered back over to
the refreshment table. "I didn't mean to bark at you."

"That's okay," Toni said. "I was kind of wigging out and
you helped bring me back to reality. Still, this place gives
me the creeps. All the dusty velvet draperies and swags of
black fabric. Then there's the flowers. I really do hate that
funky funeral smell."

"It's funny, isn't it," Petra said. "You pick flowers in your
garden and they smell so lovely and fragrant. Then you
bring a perfectly good bouquet into a funeral home and
suddenly they're tinged with that awful hint of decay."

"Now you're really creeping me out," Toni said.

"I think it's the chemical smell that pervades everything," Suzanne said. "It's not the flowers' fault."

In reply, Toni pinched her nose closed.

"So we've got the three different tea sandwiches,
brownie bites, bars, and coffee," Petra said. She was talking
to herself, reassuring herself, as she arranged cups, saucers, plates, and napkins just so on the hastily set-up folding
table.

Toni unpinched her nose. "Maybe we should have brought a couple bottles of cheap Chardonnay." She sounded vaguely hopeful. "Help take the edge off the evening."

"Shame on you," Petra said. "This is a visitation in a funeral home. Vigil lights will be lit. *Prayers* will be said. This isn't supposed to be happy hour at Bub's Bar."

"Hey, no harm done," Toni said. "It was only a suggestion."

UNLIKE today's Christmas Tea, the visitation *did* attract fewer people on account of the snow. Even after George Draper lit the candles, dimmed the lights, and put a soft funeral dirge on the sound system, Slumber Room A looked desultory. Like a party that wasn't going to happen.

Then Earl Sharp, Allan Sharp's brother who lived in the neighboring town of Jessup, arrived. Along with Don Shinder, the law partner.

Close on their heels came another half-dozen guests. And then Mayor Mobley strutted in, his face pink from the cold, the entire city council trailing behind him like a gaggle of baby ducks.

"Looks like we've got customers," Petra whispered.

"Finally," Suzanne said. She was beginning to feel sympathy for the dead-and-almost-forgotten Allan Sharp.

Mayor Mobley's bulk sidled up to the refreshment table almost immediately.

"What have we got here?" he asked, his beady eyes roving across the sandwiches and bars.

"Let me fix you a plate," Suzanne offered.

Mobley lifted a pudgy hand and waved her away. "That's okay, I can manage perfectly well on my own."

Right, Suzanne thought. Managing on his own meant

stacking eight brownie bites on top of six sandwiches—which Mobley was currently doing. He reminded her of customers at a Bloody Mary bar where you were only allowed one pass, so everyone used toothpicks to creatively cantilever shrimp, buffalo wings, pickles, cheese hunks, olives, jalapeños, bacon, and beef jerky sticks off the sides of their glasses.

Good thing the rest of the mourners weren't so greedy.

Teddy Hardwick showed up and took only a single sandwich with his cup of coffee.

"Are you sure you wouldn't like a bar, too?" Petra asked.

Hardwick shook his head. He looked dejected and deflated, as if he'd just taken a hard punch to the gut.

"I'm sorry about your play being cancelled," Suzanne said to him.

Hardwick's expression seemed to collapse even more. "This cancellation is a tremendous disappointment to everyone involved. Cast, crew, all of us. We've worked doggone hard to make this play happen, all for the town's enjoyment. And now . . . it's been taken away."

"Do you know who made the decision to call off the play?" Suzanne asked.

"Not exactly," Hardwick said.

"Maybe Mayor Mobley?"

"I don't know. But I'm going to make it my mission in life to find out."

That's funny, Suzanne thought. *I'm going to make it my mission in life to find out who killed Allan Sharp. And set Junior's trailer on fire.*

Hardwick reached out and touched Suzanne's sleeve. "Have you . . . do you know?" he stammered. "Has Sheriff Doogie shown up here yet?"

"Not yet," she said. "But I'm sure he will."

"I need to . . . talk to him. About something," Hardwick said. He took a sip of coffee and almost choked.

"Are you feeling okay?" Suzanne asked.

But Hardwick just shook his head again and wandered off, looking dazed and a little lost.

Suzanne watched Hardwick practically collapse on a folding chair, one of several black folding chairs that were arranged in a semicircle like a coven of scrawny crows.

"What's with him?" Toni asked. "He's taking the cancellation of the play awfully hard, isn't he?"

"Yes, he is," Suzanne said. She wondered if Hardwick really was horribly disappointed or if he was battling a guilty conscience. And what exactly did he want to talk to Doogie about?

Suzanne's thoughts were quickly cut off as Don Shinder came over to greet her.

"This is just wonderful what you did here," Shinder said. "The sandwiches and bars, the coffee, just wonderful. I know Allan would have so appreciated your efforts."

"We were happy to help out," Suzanne murmured.

"I was thinking that—" Shinder stopped suddenly. Reverend Ethan Jakes had just walked into the room. "Ah, I see our minister has arrived." Shinder seemed sadly pleased.

"I didn't realize that Allan Sharp was a member of the Journey's End Church," Suzanne said.

"He wasn't," Shinder said. "But Reverend Jakes contacted me when he heard about Allan's death . . . his murder. He offered his condolences and asked if he could help in any way."

"And now here he is," Suzanne said. *Interesting.*

"He's also going to conduct the graveside services tomorrow morning."

"There won't be a church service?" Petra asked. She sounded shocked—and a little disappointed.

"No, but I do hope you ladies will attend," Shinder said. "It would mean so much to Allan's brother."

"Of course we will," Petra said.

They all fell silent as Reverend Jakes took his place directly in front of the casket. He waited for the conversation to die down; then he held up a black prayer book. "If you could all come forward," he said with a brisk motion of his hands. "I'd like to lead everyone in a few prayers."

Toni glanced at Suzanne. "I don't think he means us heathens."

"Shh," Petra said.

Reverend Jakes was certainly no slouch in the prayer department. He whipped through the Lord's Prayer, veered into several Bible verses, and then positively galloped through the Valley of Death psalm. His voice was deep and resonant as he gazed out over the mourners with a slightly aloof look on his face.

"'Scuse me," said a gruff voice at Suzanne's elbow. She turned and there was Sheriff Doogie, reaching for one of the coconut-pecan bars.

"Here you are," she said, a note of disapproval evident in her voice.

"Happy to see me?" Doogie gave her a friendly nudge with his elbow.

"Not really," Suzanne said. "I was even less happy when you crashed my party this afternoon."

"Couldn't be helped. Jeez, I love these church basement funeral bars," Doogie said.

Suzanne frowned. "Why does everyone call them that?"

"Because that's where you always see them. In a church

basement following a funeral." Doogie finished his bar and reached for another one.

"Not so fast, Sheriff. I have a few questions for you."

"Yeah? Shoot." He chewed his second bar and chuckled. "That was a little law enforcement humor there in case you didn't notice."

"I want to know about the fingerprints you were so anxious about," Suzanne said. "Were Amber Payson's fingerprints on that can of gasoline your deputy found?"

Doogie shook his head. "No."

"No?"

"Whoever handled it must have been wearing gloves."

"You think?" Suzanne said. "Since it's, like, ten degrees below zero outside."

"You don't have to get all snarky about it," Doogie said. "I told you I wanted to talk to her, not arrest her."

"Do you have any evidence at all that Amber might have set Junior's trailer on fire?"

Doogie turned and stared at her with steely gray eyes. "Nope. But it was arson all right. Chief Finley found traces of an accelerant."

Suzanne noted that nugget of information and continued. "Do you have any evidence at all that Amber murdered Allan Sharp?"

"Only what I'd call circumstantial evidence. Amber worked for Sharp, he fired her, and there were bad feelings on both sides."

"Bad feelings," Suzanne said. "That's how you refer to sexual harassment? As bad feelings?"

"Before you get on your high horse and pack me off for a week of sensitivity training, Suzanne, please realize that this is one of those 'he said, she said' type of situations."

Suzanne wanted to bite back at him, but deep down she

knew Doogie was probably right. It was Amber's word against a dead guy's. And the dead guy wasn't talking anymore.

"Have you taken a careful look at anybody else?" Suzanne asked.

"Of course I have," Doogie said. "I'm investigating my butt off. Jeez, you sound just like Allan Sharp's brother. Take a look at this suspect, take a look at that suspect."

"So what about Mayor Mobley? And Teddy Hardwick? Are they viable suspects?"

"Whoa, whoa, whoa," Doogie said, holding up a hand. "What did I say about poking your schnoz into my business?"

"You can toss your warnings right out the attic window," Suzanne said. "Because I'm already involved. Have been ever since that ghost threatened to slice me open with his knife."

"Whose fault was that?" Doogie grabbed another brownie, tilted his head back, and tossed the whole thing into his mouth. "Yeah, you're involved, all right. But you shouldn't be," he mumbled as he walked away.

Suzanne was ready to explode with rage. Unfortunately, at that exact moment, a half-dozen people descended on their table for coffee and sandwiches. So she tamped down her anger, put on a faux-happy face, and got busy serving. Toni immediately pitched in to help, since Petra had wandered off to join some sort of prayer circle that Reverend Jakes was leading. As Suzanne poured coffee and plated food, she kept one eye on Jakes. Then Teddy Hardwick wandered back to the refreshment table.

"Petra told me that you've been looking into the murder," Hardwick said to Suzanne. "I think that's wonderful, since you already have a reputation for being a kind of citizen watchdog."

"I'm interested because I was peripherally involved," Suzanne said.

Hardwick's brows knit together. "I completely understand because I feel the exact same way," he said.

"I was wondering, did you actually *see* the murder take place?" Suzanne asked him. She was going to get to the bottom of this if it killed her. Even if her questions did come across as impertinent. "I mean, were you out in the audience watching the whole thing? If so, weren't you at all curious about what was happening up onstage? Because that whole dance of death episode surely wasn't in the script."

"Like everyone else, I thought it was a little weird at the time," Hardwick said. "But I was caught off guard and never thought to . . . what? Interfere? And even if I had stepped in, could I have confronted an armed killer?"

Like I tried to, Suzanne thought to herself.

"So you were right there in the audience," Suzanne said, her voice shaded with doubt.

Hardwick stared at her. "Yes, of course I was."

That wasn't what Dale Huffington had told her, but Dale could have been mistaken. Suzanne let it drop for the time being and said, "Did you ever find Sheriff Doogie and touch base with him? Earlier tonight, you said you needed to talk to him about . . . something."

"It'll have to wait." Hardwick sighed deeply. "I've got to take care of something else first."

"Problem?"

"Ah, there's an issue with my foundation. I'm expecting a contractor to drop by."

* * *

AN hour later, the visitation was all over except for the praying. Reverend Jakes was still mingling with a few of the mourners, holding hands and leading them in quiet prayer.

"That boy sure does love to pray, doesn't he?" Toni said.

"Must be some sort of land-speed record," Suzanne said. She didn't mean any disrespect; it just seemed a little over-the-top.

As they packed up leftover bars and sandwiches and dumped out the coffeepot, Petra wandered over to help. "Why don't you let me . . ." she said.

But Suzanne shooed her away. She and Toni could take care of it.

Finally, they carried everything out to Suzanne's car. Snow was still filtering down, coating trees, houses, and streets, turning everything into eerie white humps. Streetlamps were ringed with frosty haloes and cast a dim, almost grayish light on everything. It was difficult to tell where the sidewalk dropped down to meet the street.

Toni opened the rear door of Suzanne's Taurus and said, "I could try to wedge this stuff in your backseat, but I don't think it'll fit."

"That's because Junior's tools are still taking up space," Suzanne said. "Got any idea when he's going to come over and grab them?"

"Nope," Toni said. "Got any idea when his furry body is gonna stop stinking up my cramped one-bedroom apartment?"

"Point taken. I'll pop the trunk."

As they stashed everything in Suzanne's trunk, Reverend Jakes ghosted past them, head bent, lips moving, as he scuffed along through three inches of new-fallen snow.

"Excuse me," Suzanne called after him.

There was no answer.

"Could I have a word with you?"

Jakes kept on walking.

"Reverend Jakes?" Suzanne called again.

But Jakes never answered her, never turned back. He just climbed into his car and drove away.

CHAPTER 15

THURSDAY morning everyone in Kindred and the surrounding communities woke up to a winter wonderland. The heavens had dumped more snow overnight and snowplows were out in full force, struggling to keep the roads open.

Suzanne drove over to Toni's house and picked her up, then navigated a few more snow-clogged streets to get Petra. No sense everyone driving separately and risking getting stuck in a four-foot-high snowdrift or skidding into one of the enormous white piles of snow that the plows were depositing all over town.

"Kindred is starting to look like Santa's village," Petra said as they drove through town. Snowplows muscled snow around, piling it wherever there was space. Shop windows were frosted in white. Trees were iced in white. Bundled-up snow-shovel-wielding shopkeepers and residents were working valiantly to clear their sidewalks.

They drove another ten or twelve blocks through a residential section where sleds were parked in yards and a lone tricycle was iced in snow. They passed by a small office park and then headed out the lonely (but luckily plowed) road to Memorial Cemetery.

"It's fogging up in here," Toni said.

"That's because we're all breathing," Petra said from the backseat.

"I thought it was because we're all wearing eight layers of clothing and radiating enough body heat to melt the ice caps on Mars," Toni said. "And speaking of too much clothing, this getup makes me look like I've gained twenty pounds."

"I do it the old-fashioned way," Petra laughed. "By eating cookies. That way I don't need layers of nubby sweaters to make me look chunky."

Suzanne flipped the defrosters on high and the windows cleared just in time for her to see the black wrought-iron gates of the cemetery looming up before her. "So far, so good," she said as they glided into the cemetery on a narrow track that had been haphazardly plowed.

"Yeah, but are we gonna make it up and over the hills?" Toni asked. The cemetery occupied a hilly parcel of land, directly adjacent to a park reserve.

"Hope so," Suzanne said. She gunned the engine and fought hard to gain traction as she fishtailed up the narrow lane. Even so, she was climbing steadily with just a minor skid here and there.

"It's really a shame they're not holding this service in a proper church," Petra said.

"I like the idea of a graveside service," Toni said. "Easy in, easy out. Like pulling off the freeway for a Howard Johnson's. You know, real convenient."

"I've never heard convenience and graveside services mentioned in the same breath," Petra grumbled.

"There's a first for everything," Toni said. "In fact, I even heard about a funeral parlor in Florida that offers drive-through visitations. I dunno, maybe they bought an old Long John Silver's or something."

They churned past a stone statue of a kneeling angel with a damaged wing as wind whipped the snow across the windshield, creating a temporary whiteout.

"Guys," Suzanne said, "I'll just be happy if we don't get stuck." She turned on her wipers and was peering around, trying to figure out where exactly they were and where exactly they were supposed to go. She saw stands of bur oak and lots of tombstones, but where was the spot for the memorial service?

"There," Petra called out. "I see a row of parked cars up ahead."

"Thank goodness," Suzanne said.

Toni pressed her nose against a window. "And I see a tent off to our left. Well, I suppose it's more like a canopy flapping in the wind."

Suzanne pulled in behind three cars and an SUV and they all piled out. Luckily, someone had already established a beaten path through the snow so they didn't have to break trail like a bunch of sled dogs. Still, they skidded and slipped along in their winter boots until they reached the security of a large expanse of green plastic funeral grass. Folding chairs had been set up on that little oasis, so they each scrambled to grab one.

Then a dozen more people showed up, stomping snow from their boots as they stepped onto the green carpet. The funeral bier had been set up a few feet away. It was a low contraption, all polished wood and stainless steel, with hanging modesty panels of black velvet to conceal the actual grave. One thing was clearly missing, however.

"Where's the guest of honor?" Toni whispered.

Suzanne gave her a nudge. "Look over there."

They all turned to watch as a long black hearse slid to a stop in front of a grove of shaggy blue spruce trees. Behind it was another black funeral car. George Draper got out of the hearse as six men, all dressed in black, exited the other car. They all headed for the back of the hearse. Draper pulled open the rear door and a motorized tray carrying the casket of Allan Sharp slowly slid out. The six men lined up, three on either side, to grapple with the casket. They slid the casket out farther, bent low, and hoisted it onto their shoulders. They staggered under the unexpected weight as everyone watched with bated breath. Would they drop it? No. Good. Then the men proceeded to carry the casket to the graveside and rest it on top of the bier. Reverend Ethan Jakes followed closely behind the casket, wearing a long black robe over his winter coat.

Jakes again, Suzanne thought to herself. She glanced around and realized they were in the older section of the cemetery. It was a place of Civil War graves, marble obelisks, and a few mausoleums. She wondered if Allan Sharp had family buried around here. If he had a prepaid, reserved spot. She shuddered. It wasn't a pleasant thought.

Reverend Jakes stepped in front of the casket and lifted both hands in the air as if he were about to bestow a blessing. Which he kind of was.

"Friends," Jakes began, in what Suzanne thought was an overly dramatic oratorical voice, "we are gathered here to honor and say a final good-bye to our dear departed brother, Allan Sharp."

Down front, Earl Sharp, the deceased's brother, blew his nose and dabbed at his eyes with a white hanky.

Reverend Jakes went on to deliver a fairly standard homily concerning death and resurrection. Once again, Suzanne wondered why Jakes had stepped in to handle these services. After all, he'd had nothing but vitriol for Allan Sharp after Sharp had rebuffed him about holding a day of prayer. Was Jakes feeling a sudden abundance of forgiveness? Or could it be guilt? Had Jakes possibly had a hand in causing Sharp's death? The notion unsettled Suzanne because it would mean he was also the one who'd threatened her.

At this last thought, Suzanne glanced around quickly, looking for Sheriff Doogie. But Doogie's khaki bulk wasn't anywhere to be seen. Maybe this was a good sign. Maybe Doogie was busy doing something else, like interviewing a possible witness or following up on a new clue. On the other hand, maybe Doogie just didn't like funerals.

One thing Suzanne knew for sure. Today was Thrifty Thursday at the Cackleberry Club, which meant you could get a stack of six buttermilk pancakes for a dollar ninety-nine. Since Doogie responded positively to pancakes dripping with butter and maple syrup, he would undoubtedly drop by. She'd get a chance to grill him while he was eating and at his most vulnerable. But for now, Suzanne tried to refocus, to pull herself back to the moment. Reverend Jakes had just finished his prayer and was now gesturing for someone else to come up and address the small group of mourners.

Suzanne shifted on the cold, uncomfortable folding chair. The low temperature was getting to her—to all of them—so she hoped whoever delivered this eulogy would be quick about it.

Then Mayor Mobley lumbered to the front of the group and Suzanne inwardly groaned. Mobley was a blowhard, his speeches dragging on for what felt like hours at a time.

"I thought Mobley and Sharp hated each other," Toni whispered to her.

"Death makes strange bedfellows, doesn't it?" Suzanne whispered back. She spent the next ten minutes tuning out Mobley and shivering like crazy. True to form, Mobley droned on about how Allan Sharp had helped with his election campaigns, had been a pillar of the community, and, of late, had won a coveted seat on the Kindred City Council.

Since Mobley reigned as mayor, Suzanne wasn't sure how coveted that position really was, and she managed to drift off again, focusing instead on how awful the garish green funeral grass looked against the pristine white of the snow.

When Mobley finished, Don Shinder stood up to deliver a tearful eulogy for his old law partner. But he had to conclude his remarks three minutes in because he was so upset. Then Jakes led everyone in a final prayer and a shaky a cappella rendition of "Amazing Grace." With the song's final notes hanging on the wind, the service was blessedly concluded.

"Thank goodness, it's over," Petra whispered. "My buns were almost frozen to the seat of that chair."

More snow started drifting down as the mourners began to disperse. Suzanne gave Petra a hand as they shuffled back toward her car.

Toni, on the other hand, kept glancing back at the grave site. "After everybody leaves, are they going to bury him?" she asked. "Lower his casket into the ground?"

"I don't know what they do in winter," Suzanne said. She hunched her shoulders and pulled her scarf tighter around her neck. "The ground does seem awfully . . . frozen."

Back in her car, Suzanne cranked up the heater and

made a clumsy K-turn. Luck was with her and she managed not to get stuck in the snow. She headed back down the hill, skidding a bit, noting that the narrow road now felt more like a toboggan run.

"Before we hit the Cackleberry Club, can we stop at the Kindred Bakery?" Petra asked. "I have to pick up an order."

"What?" Toni said. "You're *buying* sticky buns now instead of making them from scratch?"

"Just picking up a couple dozen croissants," Petra said. "What with the visitation last night I didn't have time to mix the dough, roll it out, and then proof it."

"Not a problem," Suzanne said. She wasn't in a big hurry to get to work. She had lots to think about. Like the fact that two of her so-called suspects, namely, Mayor Mobley and Reverend Ethan Jakes, had featured prominently at the service. But neither Amber Payson nor Teddy Hardwick had been there. Did that mean something? Probably. She just didn't know what.

SUZANNE drove down Main Street and stopped directly in front of the Kindred Bakery. "You need any help?" she asked Petra. "You want us to come in with you?"

But Petra was already scrambling out of the backseat. "No, no," she said. "You two stay in the car and keep warm. I won't be but a second."

"You think this snow is ever going to stop?" Toni asked. "I saw this made-for-TV movie once—I think it was written by Stephen King—and there was this gigantic snowstorm that just wouldn't quit. Finally, all the buildings collapsed and everyone was buried."

"That's just lovely," Suzanne said.

Toni held her hands up to the heater. "Well, you know

what I mean." She wrinkled her nose, tried to clear some fog off the side window, and said, "Hey, look over there."

Suzanne turned to see Don Shinder getting out of his car across the street. His head was bowed and he looked exhausted. Two men came out of the building where his law office was located to greet him. They all started talking and nodding.

"Poor Don," Toni said. "Do you think he's interviewing for law partners already?"

Suzanne studied the two men who had greeted Shinder. They looked serious and were well dressed, in suits and topcoats, so they might very well be lawyers. They were also stomping their feet to ward off the cold and keep the circulation going. "Or maybe he's talking to a couple of headhunters," Suzanne said.

"For some reason that term makes me very queasy."

"Still . . . Shinder's business, his law firm, has to keep forging ahead. I'm sure he's got clients who are dependent on him for legal help, so chances are he's going to need someone to step in right away. A partner or a junior partner at the very least."

"Kind of like you have me," Toni said.

Suzanne smiled. "And I couldn't ask for a better partner."

CHAPTER 16

ONCE they were back at the Cackleberry Club, Suzanne, Toni, and Petra allowed themselves a scant twenty minutes of prep time before they officially opened for business. Petra had made an executive decision to combine breakfast and lunch today since attending the graveyard service had put them a good two hours behind. So a brunch menu.

"Give me the details," Suzanne said to Petra. She was dancing on the balls of her feet, ready to get cracking. Still trying to warm up, too.

"Chicken salad on croissants, mushroom and cheddar quiche, our dollar-ninety-nine pancake special, and salmon cakes with fried green tomatoes."

"Easy stuff," Toni said.

Petra smiled as she grabbed a bunch of celery and slapped it down on her cutting board. "If you think it's so easy, kiddo, why don't we trade places? I'll pour coffee and take orders while you man the kitchen and whip out all the food."

Toni lifted both hands in surrender and backed away. "Just kidding, just kidding."

"I know you were, sweetie," said Petra. "Say, would you mind doing me a big favor?"

"Name it," Toni said.

"Run into the Knitting Nest and grab me a fresh apron. This one's got a nasty splotch on it."

"Petra's as fastidious as a cat," Suzanne said.

"Nothing wrong with that." Petra smiled.

"I'll do it in a sec," Toni said, heading into the café. "I just want to get the coffee brewing first."

Suzanne sliced and buttered a dozen croissants, arranging them on plates with some strawberries for garnish. She glanced at her watch and said, "I'm going to hang our Open sign, okay?"

"Go for it," Petra said. "I won't be any readier ten minutes from now."

But as Suzanne walked into the café, a bloodcurdling scream suddenly rent the air. It rose, spiraled out of control, and then dissolved into a slow moan. And it came from . . .

The Knitting Nest!

"What the Sam Hill was that?" Petra rocketed through the swinging door, almost colliding with Suzanne.

"I don't know," Suzanne said. "But it came from . . ."

"Toni?" Petra said. "What did that poor girl . . . ?"

They rushed into the Knitting Nest to find Toni quaking like a leaf and doing a sort of jitterbug dance. She was pointing a finger at what appeared to be a ghost. And not just any ghost; it was the cowled ghost that had murdered Allan Sharp!

"It's the same ghost!" Toni cried. "Come back to haunt

me." She looked utterly frantic. "You both see it, too, don't you? It's not just a filament of my imagination?"

"Figment," Suzanne said.

"Whatever. It's for sure a real-life apparition," Toni said, backing away, shivering and shaking with fear. "We should, like . . ." She raised a clenched fist. "Kill it!"

"No, no," Petra interrupted. She was almost, but not quite, on the verge of laughter. "That's not a ghost, Toni; it's a ghost *costume*."

Toni whirled about to face her. "Whuh?"

"Remember the other day when Teddy Hardwick came in? He brought that costume along with him and asked me to make some changes," Petra said.

"You mean it's the same costume that Bill Probst had been wearing?" Suzanne asked.

"That's right," Petra said. "So I can guarantee it's perfectly harmless. And that it wasn't involved in the murder."

Toni's teeth were still chattering like castanets. "Holy baloney, is that really true?"

Petra nodded. "Didn't I just explain myself?"

"But I really thought it was a ghost! Or that Allan Sharp came back from the dead to haunt us."

"Oh, for cripes' sake, Toni," Petra said, getting a little stirred up now. "There's no such things as ghosts."

Toni pointed at the costume that Petra had hung on a quilting frame. "That haunt sure looks genuine to me."

"You're just freaked-out from the visitation last night and the funeral this morning," Petra said. She moved closer and touched a protective hand to the ghost costume. "I worked very hard on this."

"Teddy Hardwick asked you to change it?" Suzanne asked Petra. So that's why Hardwick had been meeting with her.

"In a few places, yes," Petra said. "He wanted a few modifications made. So this ghost would look significantly different from . . . um . . ."

"From the killer's ghost costume," Suzanne said. She immediately thought of Reverend Jakes buying all that cheesecloth. Now she definitely had to question him.

"I guess that's about right," Petra said.

Suzanne studied the spooky gray-green costume. "Well, even though the play's been cancelled, that costume does look convincing."

"It convinced me," Toni said.

CUSTOMERS showed up, coffee was poured, and brunches were cooked to order. As more customers arrived, so did the postman with the morning mail.

"Look at this," Toni said. In between customers, she'd been paging through the *Bugle*. Now she handed it to Suzanne. "You made the front page of the newspaper. Your name was prominently mentioned in Gene Gandle's article. You're semifamous."

"Semifamous how?" Suzanne asked, grabbing the newspaper and scanning the front page.

"The article says you were the first one to figure out that a fake ghost killed Allan Sharp. That you chased after the ghost and that it turned and threatened you with a knife."

"I wonder where Gene got his information."

Toni affected a look of complete innocence. "I have no idea."

"Toni!" Suzanne shrieked. "Did you spill the beans about this?"

Toni started to protest, then gave it up. "Me and like a dozen other people. If you recall, it was nutcakes that night.

Allan Sharp was oozing blood onstage, everybody was screaming their fool heads off, and you dashed after that killer ghost."

"Only it wasn't a ghost," Suzanne said. "And now the killer knows exactly who I am."

"He didn't before?" Toni asked.

"No! It's not like I introduced myself." Suzanne turned, poured herself a cup of coffee, and downed half of it quickly. She was hoping the caffeine would hit her fast so she could sort her thoughts out more clearly. "Now he knows my name. And can probably figure out where I live."

"Damn," Toni said. "That ain't good at all."

"No, it's not." Suzanne wasn't so worried about herself as she was for Sam. He was what you'd call . . . trusting. If somebody called the house and cried emergency, he'd dash out the door, no questions asked.

"There's also a sidebar article about Junior's trailer burning to the ground," Toni said.

"Am I mentioned in that one, too?"

"No, but I am."

"Aren't we the lucky ducks."

A half hour later, Sheriff Doogie walked in. He stood there stomping snow off his boots and surveying the crowd in the café as if he were hunting down Russian spies for the CIA. Then he walked over to the counter and hoisted himself onto his regular stool.

Suzanne poured Doogie a cup of coffee, set it in front of him, and said, "We missed your smiling face at Allan Sharp's graveside service this morning, Sheriff."

Doogie swept his hat off his head and set it on the stool next to him. "I'm not big on graves or services," he said. "In case you hadn't noticed." He shrugged out of his brown parka and tossed that on another stool.

"Even when the service is for a murder victim?"

"What's that supposed to mean?"

"There's zero hidden meaning in what I just said," Suzanne told him. "Sharp was murdered in cold blood; his killer is still on the loose. I'm thinking that maybe, just maybe, he might have turned up at the service this morning."

"Is that what you think happened?" Doogie asked.

"I don't know, isn't that what always happens in the movies? The killer comes back to gloat? But of course I don't know because I'm not privy to the really critical information."

Doogie took a sip of coffee and made a big production out of savoring it. Then he said, "You think you could help figure this out?"

"I'm probably smarter than your average deputy."

Doogie grinned. "Ya got me there, Suzanne. But can you shoot straight? Can you hit a moving target? Could you shoot an actual person?"

"I don't know, I've never tried."

Doogie cranked his head sideways and squinted at the chalkboard. "Buttermilk pancakes, huh? Sounds pretty good."

"I'll put your order in right away," Suzanne said.

"Wait one." Doogie held up a finger. "Can you have Petra add a rasher of bacon?"

"Sure. Regular or turkey bacon?"

Doogie scowled. "Turkey's for Thanksgiving. And that's already past."

"Whatever."

Suzanne put in Doogie's order, then busied herself

delivering a half-dozen entrees that had just come up. And even though they were offering an abbreviated menu, the Cackleberry Club was blessed with a full house today. Which meant that, halfway through lunch, Toni had to get out a mop and bucket and swipe up all the water that had puddled at the front door. The joys of a winter storm.

When Doogie was down to his last pancake, Suzanne circled back to talk to him.

"So who's at the top of your suspect list?" she asked.

Doogie stared at her.

"Let me guess. Amber Payson and Mayor Mobley are enjoying top honors?"

Doogie hunched his shoulders in a noncommittal shrug.

"What about Teddy Hardwick?" Suzanne asked. "You know, he was looking for you last night at the visitation. Did the two of you ever connect?"

"Nope." Doogie sopped up syrup with his last bite of pancake. "What'd he want?"

"I don't know. Maybe he wanted to confess."

"Very funny," Doogie said.

"Not really, since I already told you that Hardwick had been all lathered up about Allan Sharp. Because of the cracked foundation in his new town house."

"But Hardwick was busy directing the play the night of the murder."

"Sure he was, but he managed to mysteriously disappear at the moment the murder took place."

"And you think that makes Hardwick guilty?"

"I think that makes him a legitimate suspect," Suzanne said. She paused. "And another thing. Reverend Ethan Jakes bought umpteen yards of cheesecloth last week at that fabric store, Fabrique."

"What's cheesecloth?" Doogie asked. "You mean for wrapping up cheese?"

"It's a kind of fabric, what the ghost costume was made out of."

Doogie gave a slow reptilian blink. "You're kidding." He was suddenly digesting more than just his pancakes.

"No, I'm not."

"But he's a . . . an ordained minister," Doogie said.

"Who was severely rebuffed by Allan Sharp when he suggested the city council hold a day of prayer."

"And you think Jakes nursed a grudge over *that*?"

"Jakes is strange," Suzanne said. "He's got this gleam in his eye. Like he has some sort of messianic calling."

Doogie looked thoughtful. "You give me a lot to chew on, Suzanne." He stifled a burp.

"It is a lot. And I know most of my suspicions are based on what you always call circumstantial evidence," Suzanne said. "But you have to start somewhere, right?"

Doogie lifted a hand. "It's one of the ways you start building a case."

"Okay, then," Suzanne said. "Can I ask you about Allan Sharp?"

"What do you want to know?"

"Allan Sharp lived alone?"

"You know he did," Doogie said.

"Have you been able to account for his comings and goings on that particular day?"

"You mean the day he was murdered?"

"Yes," Suzanne said. "I'm wondering if Sharp got into an argument with someone. Did he happen to deliver some bad news? You know, the kind of thing that might push someone over the edge and make them angry enough to retaliate."

"Not that I've found so far," Doogie said.

"What about enemies?" Suzanne held up her hand and said, "I know Sharp was roundly disliked all over town, but I'm talking about real enemies. Serious enemies."

Doogie squinted at her. "Mayor Mobley?"

"Sharp and Mobley *did* have a serious falling-out. But investigating Mobley is tricky," Suzanne said. "He's got a coterie of spies and tattletales all over town."

"Tell me about it."

"What about Allan Sharp's brother? Were there any problems between them?"

"None that I've found so far. Earl's your basic mild-mannered accountant and it seems like they got along fairly well."

Suzanne thought for a minute. "Is there anything more on who might have set fire to Junior's trailer?"

"Nope."

Suzanne leaned on the counter. "Huh."

"Yeah," Doogie said. "It's a pickle, ain't it?"

CHAPTER 17

SUZANNE was brewing a pot of Earl Grey tea when Reverend Ethan Jakes walked in. He was wearing a faux-faded fleece hoodie that said Jesus Washed Away My Sins on the front, dark slacks, and pac boots. Jakes glanced toward the counter, let his eyes pass over her, then turned and sat down at the small table by the window.

Suzanne wondered if Jakes was avoiding her or if he might be a trifle shy. On the other hand, if he was avoiding her, he wouldn't have come in here in the first place. Okay, so this was her chance to talk to him and maybe even confront him about the cheesecloth he'd bought.

Suzanne grabbed her list of teas and headed for Jakes's table.

"Afternoon, Reverend," she said. "That was a very nice service you conducted this morning."

"Thank you."

"With the day being so cold, I have a feeling that a nice

hot cup of tea might warm you up." She set the tea menu down in front of him.

Jakes glanced at the tea menu, then looked at her. "I was thinking about a cup of coffee. But since you mentioned it, tea does sound interesting."

"What kind would you like?" Suzanne asked.

Jakes wrinkled his brow. "That's kind of a problem. The only tea I've ever tasted is Chinese restaurant tea. So I'm your basic tea neophyte."

"Tea's not so tricky," Suzanne said. "There's black tea, green tea, and white tea."

"That's it?"

"Well, they all have umpteen variations. Tell you what: I could brew a pot of Ceylon tea for you. It's light, bright, and refreshing. Kind of a starter tea. Or I could brew a flavored tea."

"What kinds of flavors are there?" Jakes asked.

"Pretty much anything you want. Spiced plum, rose hips and hibiscus, lemon verbena; I've even got a chocolate tea." Suzanne was aware that their conversation had suddenly turned friendly. Good. When she quizzed him later about the cheesecloth, she might get a straight answer.

"I think I'd like to try your spiced plum tea."

"Along with a cream scone?" Suzanne asked.

Jakes bobbed his head. "That might be nice."

Under Toni's watchful eye, Suzanne brewed a single pot of spiced plum tea, then plated a scone and added small dishes of Devonshire cream and strawberry jam.

"You're really buttering him up," Toni said under her breath.

"Trying to anyway."

When Suzanne carried the tea tray to Jakes's table, she

lingered. Instructing him in the art of cutting his scone crossways, adding the jam first, and then dabbing on the Devonshire cream.

"What happens if I do it the other way around?" Jakes asked.

"Tastes the same, just a little messier."

Jakes chuckled. He really was loosening up. Which meant it was time for Suzanne to pounce.

"I was in Fabrique the other day and one of the ladies who works there mentioned to me that you'd bought almost an entire roll of cheesecloth," Suzanne said.

Jakes stared at her, unblinking, like an old turtle.

"Which got my overactive mind to wondering," Suzanne continued. "What would a man of the cloth do with so much cheesecloth?"

"Is that supposed to be a joke?" Jakes asked. Now there was a touch of steel in his voice.

"No, it's a legitimate question."

"Then my overactive mind has to wonder why you'd bother asking."

Suzanne slid into the chair across from him. "I'm going to tell you why, Reverend Jakes. Because the ghost, the theater ghost that killed Allan Sharp, was wearing a costume made out of cheesecloth that had been dyed a dark gray-green color."

There. She'd laid it all out on the table like a spooky banquet from "The Fall of the House of Usher." The question now was . . . would he bite?

Jakes took a sip of tea and pursed his lips. Then he looked at her, expressionless. "And you think I concocted a phony costume so I could murder Allan Sharp?"

"I don't know. Did you?"

Jakes set his teacup into his saucer with a tiny clink. "No. I did not. In fact, I'm highly offended that you'd even ask."

"I'm not always subtle with my questions," Suzanne said. Did she believe Jakes? She wasn't sure.

"I see you're anxiously awaiting a complete explanation," Jakes said. "So even though it grates on me, I'm going to give it to you." He drew a deep breath and said, "Our youth group is planning to take a summer camping trip. I suggested we do a weekend prayer retreat instead, but the kids are insistent on camping. They've got camping in their heads and they won't let it go." He shrugged. "What can you do?"

"So you're going to use the cheesecloth to make . . ."

"Bug screens that will fit over the front of their tents."

"Bug screens. Okay. And the kids have already purchased these tents?" Suzanne asked. She knew she was giving him the third degree, really holding his feet to the fire, but she didn't much care.

"In a manner of speaking, they have. Kuyper's Hardware store gave us six nylon tents on credit. Now we have to raise the money to pay for them."

"How are you going to do that?"

Toni wandered over with a steaming pot of tea, ready to give Jakes a refill. She was also dying to know what they were talking about.

"For one thing," Jakes said, "we're hosting a cross-country ski event tomorrow evening at Jordan Park Reserve." He nodded at Suzanne and then at Toni. "You both should come."

"What is that exactly?" Toni asked.

"A cross-country ski loop. The kids have named it the Cocoa Loco Loppet," Jakes said.

"Oh sure," Toni said. "I've seen your posters all over town announcing it."

"The Cocoa Loco Loppet wasn't my idea; it's something I inherited," Jakes said. "Anyway, our youth group has marked out a four-mile trail with various stops along the way for skiers to warm up and enjoy hot cocoa and cider." He spread a gob of jam on his scone, then pointed the silver butter knife directly at Suzanne. "So now you know. And, in exchange for my honesty, I think you should both come out and support us."

"You mean actually go cross-country skiing?" Toni said. "With skis and poles and everything?"

Jakes offered them a thin smile. "With so much new snow, you might find it refreshing."

AFTER Reverend Jakes had left, Toni said, "So you believed his story? About the tents and cheesecloth and stuff?"

"If he was lying, it was a very well-crafted story," Suzanne said.

"But . . ."

"But I'm still suspicious. Yes."

"What are you two yakking about?" Petra asked. She'd emerged from the kitchen and was pulling on her winter coat. "It better not be about that stupid ghost costume again."

"When are you going to get that thing out of here?" Toni asked. "It gives me the creeps just knowing it's here." She pushed up the sleeve of her pink sweater. "I think I'm starting to break out in hives."

Petra sighed. "I'll probably take it with me now. I need the room for my quilting club ladies." She plopped a knitted cap on her head. "My friend Samantha is picking me up and I'll ask her to help schlep that costume over to the Oakhurst Theatre. Lord knows, it's doing no earthly good here."

"That's because ghosts aren't earthly creatures," Toni said.

"Will you put a cork in it?" Suzanne said to Toni. Then to Petra: "Would you like me to take care of that costume for you? I go right by the theater on my way home." She also figured delivering the costume would give her a dandy excuse to talk to Teddy Hardwick.

"Thank you," Petra said. "That would be a great relief."

Suzanne glanced at Toni. "You want to ride along?"

"No, thanks," Toni said. "If I need a ride, I can always call Junior. Besides, I've got a lot to do around here. Take out the trash, mop the floors, straighten out the books . . . you know, stuff."

"We've got an overhead light bulb that's burned out, too," Petra said.

"No problem, I'll add it to my to-do list," Toni said.

SUZANNE set the ghost on the seat next to her and drove over to the Oakhurst Theatre. A winter sunset painted the horizon with luscious pinks and oranges, dabbing in a swirl of blue here and there. Very calming, even with a ghost as a passenger.

When Suzanne arrived at the theater, she was lucky. One of the hardworking snowplow guys had cut a wide swath in front of the door so she was able to park directly in front.

Grabbing the filmy, slithery ghost, she ran through the cold and slipped inside the theater.

From the moment the heavy door thudded behind her,

Suzanne was aware that the place was dark, quiet, and almost deserted. Or was it? She walked through the lobby, where swags of dark green velvet curtains seemed to deaden her footfalls and suck any sound out of the air.

Then she pushed open another door and walked into the small theater.

The theater was hushed and dim, with only a few overhead lights glowing down near the stage.

"Hello?" Suzanne called out. "Is anyone here?"

She walked halfway down the center aisle, the rounded velvet seatbacks vaguely reminding her of rows of tombstones. The air felt thick and oppressive.

"Teddy? Mr. Hardwick?" The hair on the back of Suzanne's neck started to tickle. It *felt* like someone was here.

Then there was a rustling sound from backstage and a voice called out, "Hello?" Teddy Hardwick emerged onto the stage and gazed out into the darkened theater. He shaded his eyes from the overhead lights and said, "Who is it? Who's there, please?"

"It's me, Suzanne." She hurried down the aisle toward the stage.

"Goodness' sakes," Hardwick said. "What brings you out in this awful weather?"

Suzanne held up the ghost costume. "I brought your costume back." She walked around to the side of the stage, climbed the four steps, and handed it to Hardwick. "It's the one you asked Petra to work on."

"I'm afraid we won't be needing it now," Hardwick said, taking the costume from her. He sounded completely down and disheartened.

"I know. It's so unfair how things turned out," Suzanne said. "I know you put considerable effort into producing this play."

"Casting calls, assigning parts, costumes and sets, directing the play," Hardwick said. "I put my heart into it and look what happened. It got ripped out."

"Who . . . ?" Suzanne began.

Hardwick made a sharp grimace. "You can thank Sheriff Doogie for our last-minute cancellation. He persuaded the Logan County Arts Committee to call off the play. He said cancelling it was the safest thing to do in light of all the strange occurrences around here."

"I'm sorry about that," Suzanne said. *Am I really? No, maybe not.*

"This hasn't been a very good time for me," Hardwick said. "It feels like everything is collapsing at once."

"Your play . . . and I guess your home's foundation," Suzanne said. "Any news on that? Any resolution?"

Hardwick's laugh was a sharp bark. "Hah. Nothing."

Suzanne glanced around the darkened theater. For some reason she felt a tad uneasy being here alone with him. "But you're still here. You must be working on . . . something?"

"Just packing up costumes and storing some of the sets," Hardwick said. "Tightening up loose ends." He moved a step closer to her. "There's just so much work to be done."

Suzanne took a step backward. "I'm sure there is."

"And I take a certain degree of comfort in working in this theater," Hardwick said. He gazed out toward the empty rows of seats, then up into the rafters. "I feel at home here, as if I truly belong." He shrugged. "You never know, I may end up working here all night."

Really?

"The thing is, I'm always planning," Hardwick rushed to explain. "My mind is always whirling, constantly thinking ahead. People in Kindred are fearful right now because they believe a maniacal killer is on the loose."

"Uh-huh," Suzanne said. *Because there really is a maniacal killer on the loose.*

"But once this nasty business is finally resolved, I'm hoping we'll be able to get our theater program back on track. I'd really love to stage a light operetta this spring. I'm thinking Gilbert and Sullivan's *HMS Pinafore*."

"Do you think you can find enough people in town who can sing? And who have the courage to get up onstage and sing and dance in front of a packed house?"

"I don't know," Hardwick said. "But I'm certainly going to try."

BACK in her car, Suzanne decided to check on Amber Payson. She hadn't talked to the girl since Doogie had practically dragged her out of the Cackleberry Club yesterday afternoon, and she was wondering how Amber was feeling.

She drove down Mason Street and stopped in front of a brick duplex. It had a short set of steps that led to a porch with a white railing all around it. A snow shovel leaned up against the wall next to the door on the right. Which led to the half of the duplex where Amber lived.

But when Suzanne knocked on Amber's door, there was no answer even though she could see lights on inside.

She knocked again. "Amber? It's Suzanne. Are you in there?"

Two full minutes went by; then Amber opened the door about an inch. All Suzanne could see was a hank of auburn hair and a single eye peering out at her. An eye that was red and puffy. Amber had obviously been crying.

"May I come in?" Suzanne asked.

Amber sniffled. "Why?"

"I wanted to see how you were doing. I'm so sorry Sheriff Doogie came barging in like that at yesterday's tea."

"Are you really?" Amber asked.

"Yes, of course I am."

"You didn't tell him to accost me like that? You didn't tip him off that I'd be there?"

"No! Of course not."

Amber crooked the door open another two inches. "Because I heard that you two were pretty good friends."

"Well, sure, I'm friendly with the sheriff," Suzanne said. "He's basically a pretty decent guy. But I would never set you up like that. You have to believe me. I had no idea he was going to come charging in like that."

"Okay," Amber said. She started to close the door.

"Wait a minute. Please?"

"What?"

Suzanne was back to staring at a single eye again. "You seem terribly upset, Amber. May I come in? Can we talk this through? Maybe I can help."

"No. You've done enough." Amber not only slammed the door this time; there was the telltale sound of a dead bolt clicking into place.

"DOGGONE," Suzanne muttered as she drove back through downtown. She was upset with herself that she hadn't tried harder with Amber. But what could she have done? How could she have come across as more sympathetic and understanding? And why was Amber suddenly pulling an I-vant-to-be-alone act? It was positively baffling.

Suzanne turned down Main Street, passed a snowplow

with flashing amber lights, and cruised past Rudd's Drugstore, Root 66 Hair Salon, Beckman's Gift Shop, and Kuyper's Hardware.

Wait a minute!

Suzanne spun her head around, scouted traffic, and decided she was in the clear. She executed a quick U-turn and parked her car just a few doors down from Kuyper's Hardware.

When Suzanne entered the store, there was the familiar *ding-ding* over the front door, and, a few steps in, she found herself inhaling the mingled aromas of fresh sawdust and paint. Since it was so close to Christmas, there was a huge display of kids' toys near the front of the store. And then, in descending order, came housewares, paint and shelf paper, tools, spools of chain, and then ladders, shovels, and snowblowers.

Bert Kuyper was standing at the wooden counter, wrapping a package in brown paper. He wore a beige cotton painter's apron over his blue work shirt and jeans, and his eyes gleamed from behind rimless glasses. He looked like an old-timey shopkeeper, which he kind of was.

When Kuyper saw Suzanne, he smiled and said, "Howdy, neighbor. Are you perhaps in need of a snowblower? I've got a deal on Toros. No interest until spring, when you no longer need it."

"Already got a snowblower," Suzanne said.

Kuyper grabbed a metal snow shovel and held it up. "How about the low-tech model?"

"Got one of those, too."

"Then how can I help you?" Kuyper asked.

"I have a question about tents," Suzanne said.

"Pretty cold out for winter camping," Kuyper said.

"I'm more interested in the tents the youth group at the

Journey's End Church got from you. You really gave them the tents on credit?"

Kuyper nodded. "Kids gotta have something to look forward to, you know? Not just online games and stuff but the kind of real outdoor adventure that stirs the soul."

"I hear you," Suzanne said.

"And I figure the kids are good for it. They'll put on a bean feed or sell magazines to earn the money." Kuyper brightened. "They're even sponsoring a cross-country ski event tomorrow night." He pointed toward the front window. "Got one of their posters in the window."

"You're a kind and generous man," Suzanne said.

"I know what kind of heart you have, too, Suzanne," Kuyper said. "You'd do the same for those kids."

"Just out of curiosity, how much money does the youth group owe you?"

"You going to make a donation?"

"Maybe."

Kuyper closed one eye. "Let me see . . . for six tents and four hunting knives, that'd be around six hundred eighty dollars."

"Wait a minute," Suzanne said. "You said tents *and* hunting knives?"

"That's right."

There was a sudden whooshing sound in Suzanne's ears. Must be her heart beating a little faster. "What do the, um, knives look like?" she asked.

"Come on over here and I'll show you."

Kuyper led her to the back of the store, where Coleman stoves, heavy-duty work gloves, Realtree jackets, and hunting knives were on display.

"Right here." Kuyper picked up a knife and slowly slid

it out of its dark brown leather sheath. "This is the kind they wanted. The fixed-blade model by Buck Knives."

The stainless-steel knife with its clip-point blade gleamed wickedly under the lights, causing Suzanne to utter a surprised gasp. The knife looked terrifyingly similar to the one that had been leveled at her the other night.

"What is this kind of knife generally used for?" Suzanne managed to squeak out.

"It's all-purpose," Kuyper said. "For cutting ropes and cords, filleting fish, skinning hides."

Dear Lord, Suzanne thought. *It's maybe even perfect for committing murder.*

CHAPTER 18

IT was four-forty-five, almost full-on dark, when Suzanne drove back to the Cackleberry Club. She pulled into the back parking lot and knocked loudly on the kitchen door right before she let herself in. She didn't want to just burst in and scare the pants off Toni.

"What are you doing back here?" Toni asked when she came to the door. She pulled it open and Suzanne hurried inside, anxious to get out of the cold.

"I've been tramping through a spooky theater, talking to a distraught Amber Payson, and looking at the type of hunting knife that almost killed me," Suzanne told Toni.

"All that and you still have time for a madcap social life," Toni said. "Aren't you the busy little bee."

They made a pot of hot chocolate and sat down at the counter. Then Suzanne elaborated on delivering the costume to Hardwick, getting rebuffed at Amber's place, and then popping into Kuyper's Hardware.

When Suzanne was finished, Toni sucked a marshmallow into her mouth, swallowed hard, and said, "You *have* been busy."

"It's all pretty weird, huh?"

"Like you fell down the rabbit hole into another dimension," Toni said. "So let me get this straight. Teddy Hardwick is mooning around in a deserted theater like the Phantom of the Opera. Amber is feeling sorry for herself and crying her eyes out. And maybe, just maybe, Reverend Jakes borrowed one of those hunting knives so he could stab Allan Sharp."

"And then threaten me," Suzanne said. "Don't forget that part."

"And you're sure it was the same kind of knife?"

Suzanne lifted a shoulder. "Pretty sure. But all hunting knives look the same to me."

"If you want to shove all this information in Sheriff Doogie's face, you're going to have to pick your number one suspect. And your positive ID on the knife is going to have to be a whole lot better," Toni said.

"That is a problem because I'm *not* positive. Sure, Reverend Jakes is on my suspect list, but now I've got an even worse feeling about Teddy Hardwick." Suzanne shuddered. "Toni, if you could have seen him all alone in that dark theater. It was Halloween-style creepy."

"And now he's got the ghost costume," Toni said. She leaned back and stared at Suzanne. "So what do you want to do?"

"My head tells me we should make a left-hand turn and try to investigate Teddy Hardwick."

"How do you propose we do that?" Toni asked. "And, yes, I noticed you're using the 'we' word." When Suzanne didn't answer, Toni said, "Uh-oh. Are you thinking what I'm thinking?"

"I don't know," Suzanne said. "What are you thinking?"

"That you want to spy on him up close and personal?"

"Not at the theater; that's for sure. I don't want to go back there. But . . ."

"Oh jeez," Toni said, her eyes going wide. "You want to creepy-crawl Hardwick's house, don't you?"

"Don't you?"

"No!"

"Come on," Suzanne urged, "you're my partner in crime."

"'Crime' being the operative word. What if we get caught? There are laws on the books against breaking and entering."

"Why are you worried? You don't have a police record."

"And I don't intend to start now," Toni said. "Who needs a crazy Lindsay Lohan–type mug shot? That stuff is guaranteed to find its way onto the Internet and stay there forever. Nope, this chickie-poo ain't interested."

"But if I asked you real nice, then would you say yes?"

Toni sighed deeply. "Ah, I don't know. Well . . . maybe. I suppose if I imbibed a cocktail or two, that might take the edge off. A little liquor always helps me think straight."

AND that's how Suzanne and Toni found themselves at Schmitt's Bar. Sitting in a battered wooden booth, "Devil with a Blue Dress On" blaring over the speakers, the clink of beer mugs and pool balls ringing in their ears.

"Whatcha gonna order?" Toni asked. She had a draft beer sitting in front of her as she studied the one-page menu. Suzanne had a margarita.

"Burger basket," Suzanne said. "What else?" Freddy, the hippy-dippy bartender and owner of Schmitt's Bar, had a secret method for cooking burgers. He sizzled them on a grill that was black as the coals of hell. And once those burgers were done, all charred and plump and juicy, he slipped them inside a nice, smooshy bun and served them with Parmesan fries.

The waitress, a gum-chewing woman in a pink tank top and low-slung blue jeans, took their orders and brought them each a second drink.

"I'm sorry," Suzanne said, "but we didn't order these."

"It's happy hour," the waitress said, snapping her gum. "Double bubble. Two drinks for the price of one."

"Hot-cha," Toni said, lifting her glass. "That's the kind of math I can understand."

"Start Me Up" by the Rolling Stones suddenly spilled out over the speakers and Toni began wiggling, doing a gleeful little seat dance.

"Careful there, girlfriend," Suzanne said. "You could attract some undue attention."

"Au contraire," Toni said. "I'd consider it my due." She snapped her fingers in time to the music and squirmed around, looking at all the men who were lined up two-deep at the bar.

"If Sam saw me here, right now, I do believe he'd call off the wedding," Suzanne said.

"No way. That man worships the eggshells you walk on."

"You think I've been tiptoeing around? That I haven't exactly been candid with him?"

"Sure. But that's because you don't want to cause him any worry," Toni said.

"You have a wonderful way of rationalizing everything, don't you?"

"Hey, don't knock a good stiff rationalization," Toni said. "They've gotten me through lots of tight spots."

Their burgers arrived and they tore into them.

"Mmn, guh," Toni said, talking with her mouth full.

"Uh, guh," Suzanne agreed. She swallowed hard and said, "But how on earth can you polish off a double burger with cheese and onions? I mean, you're like a hundred and ten pounds soaking wet."

"It's my killer metabolism. I'm like a diesel-powered Ford F-150. I can burn fuel faster than I can shove it in."

"That's amazing."

"Just lucky, I guess. By the way, exactly what did you tell Sam about tonight?"

"That I was grabbing a bite with you," Suzanne said.

"In other words, you have Sam on a need-to-know basis. And tonight he doesn't need to know."

"Only if we discover something exceedingly strange," Suzanne said.

TWENTY minutes later, their burger baskets polished off, they were finishing up their drinks.

"You sure you want to do this?" Toni asked. "We could just sit here and order another drink. String out the evening and let your plan go a little hazy. Eventually we'd forget all about it."

"No, I really want to investigate," Suzanne said.

"What if Hardwick's at home?"

"Then we won't go near his house or even peek in a window. But he told me he planned to be working late at the theater."

"So what exactly would we be looking for?" Toni asked.

"I'm not sure."

"What!"

"Maybe we'll know it when we see it?" Suzanne offered.

"That doesn't exactly sound like a well-laid plan. More

like one of those let's-invadc-Russia-in-the-winter plans. Never works out."

"I hear you," Suzanne said.

"Do you know which town house belongs to Hardwick?"

"Yes, but only because I looked it up on the Internet," Suzanne said.

"The stalker's guidebook to the universe," Toni chuckled.

"If you're having second thoughts, I completely understand," Suzanne said.

"You think I'd let you sneak into Hardwick's place all by yourself? No way. What if something really horrible happened?" Toni leaned forward and lowered her voice. "Like what if he caught you and threw you into a victim pit in his basement."

"Toni!"

"Well, you're the one who thinks sweet little Teddy could have murdered Allan Sharp. So what's to stop him from doing the same thing to you?"

Suzanne took a final sip of her drink and let it slide down her throat. "You make a good point, Toni. A darned good point."

FIFTEEN minutes later, Suzanne and Toni were cruising past Hardwick's town house in Whitetail Woods. A light snow was coming down, creating a kind of shimmering haze. Streetlamps cast dim yellow circles in the snow.

"There it is," Suzanne said as she slowed her car. "Second unit from the end." A burp of adrenaline pushed through her veins, making her heart bump an extra beat.

Toni caught her excitement. "You scared?" she asked.

"More like anxious."

"Me, too." Toni reached into her pocket, pulled out a

stick of Juicy Fruit gum, and unwrapped it. "You want a stick?"

"No."

Toni crumpled the gum into her mouth. "Calms the nerves, kinda like chewing tobacco. Only there's no nasty spitting involved."

"The lights are off at Hardwick's place, so it doesn't look like anybody's home," Suzanne said.

"On the other hand, Hardwick could be sitting in the dark watching TV. Or nursing a stiff drink," Toni said. "Grumbling about his cancelled play."

"I'm thinking we should park around back so as not to attract any undue attention."

"Go for it," Toni said.

Suzanne continued down the block, turned right, then made another right into a well-plowed alley. Back here it was darker, with barely any lights to mark the detached garages. Suzanne eased her way into a single parking spot directly adjacent to Hardwick's garage. No lights were tripped by motion sensors, and Hardwick's place looked completely dark from back here, too.

"So now what?" Toni asked.

"I see a small deck and, I'm pretty sure, a set of sliding doors."

"You think that's a way to get in? That they might be unlocked?"

"I don't know. Let's go find out."

They climbed out of the car and stood in the dark for a few moments, looking down the row of town houses, gauging things from the back side. Each town house looked pretty much identical to the next, and all had blue plastic trash bins with the words Randy's Sanitation stenciled on them. A hint of burning wood hung in the air. Somebody had their fireplace going tonight.

Hardwick's sidewalk, leading from his garage to his back door, had that scraped-by-a-snowblower look. His deck did not. That didn't stop Suzanne and Toni. Slowly, carefully, they climbed the two steps onto his deck, floundered across it through a foot of snow, and pressed their noses against the sliding glass door.

"Not much to see," Toni said.

They were looking in at what appeared to be a small room with a beige sofa, matching beige chair, and two innocuous-looking lamps.

"I thought theater people were supposed to be flamboyant," Toni said.

"What did you expect?" Suzanne whispered. "Theater posters and playbills?"

"More like plush red furniture, gilded frames, and tons of tchotchkes."

"Sounds awful." Suzanne drew a deep breath and said, "I'm going to try this slider."

She tried it, really leaned into it, but the sliding door didn't budge.

"Rats," Suzanne said.

"Back door," Toni whispered.

They clumped back down the steps and tried the back door. Locked tight. Suzanne took out her cell phone and shone a pinpoint of light at the lock on the doorknob. It looked fairly uncomplicated and a little cheap.

"Just the doorknob lock, no dead bolt," Toni said.

"Guess not." Suzanne knew that if Allan Sharp had cut corners on the construction of the townhomes, he'd probably done so on the finishes as well. And this door lock looked prime for kicking in. Or picking. She hesitated for all of one second, then dug in her bag and pulled out a metal nail file.

"You think you can pick that lock?" Toni asked.

"I'm going to try."

"Wait a minute." Toni pounded on the back door. "Anybody home?" she yelled out. "Teddy, you crazy fool, are you in there?"

"Good thinking," Suzanne breathed. After all, Hardwick *could* be in there. And the last thing she wanted to do was stumble in and find him flaked out on his sofa watching old black-and-white movies. Or sharpening his knife.

Toni knocked again and then said, "He's not home. I knocked hard enough to wake the dead." She nodded at Suzanne. "Time's a tickin', so you better go for it."

Suzanne stuck the tip of her nail file into the lock. She moved it back and forth slowly, not feeling anything click, not really finding any wiggle room. After a few more jabs, she said, "I don't know if this is going to work. Maybe his lock is better quality than I thought."

"Wait a minute," Toni said. Now it was her turn to dig in her purse. "I got something that might . . . if I still have it." She unzipped a plastic cosmetic bag, poked through a jumble of lipsticks, tins of blusher, and eyebrow pencils, and said, "Okay. I do still have it."

"Have what?"

Toni held up a funny-looking key.

"What's that?" Suzanne asked.

"Something Junior gave me. It's a bump key."

"I thought bump keys were urban legends."

"Naw, lots of lowlifes have them."

"Like Junior?"

"Actually, Junior made this one. He just bought a basic

house key at the local hardware store. You know, one that fits a standard cylindrical lock. Then he filed off some of the teeth and deepened a few grooves."

Crazy, Suzanne thought. She couldn't believe it was that easy to make a key that would get you inside someone's house. Or was it? "Will the key work?" she asked.

"I don't know. Let's find out."

Toni pushed the bump key all the way into the lock, then pulled back slightly. From there she jiggled it, joggled it, and coaxed it back and forth.

"No dice, huh?"

"Ah, these things take a little time." After another two minutes of trial and error, Toni said, "I think . . ."

There was a loud *click* and the door to Teddy Hardwick's town house swung wide open.

Toni grinned. "Shazam."

CHAPTER 19

"You did it," Suzanne breathed. She stood there, stunned, gazing in at the darkened interior, knowing in her heart that they'd just broken all sorts of laws. What would Sheriff Doogie think? Better yet, what would Sam think? Of course, she could stop right now, with no harm done. They could walk away from this little caper while they still had the chance.

But Toni was the one who pressed to keep going.

"C'mon," Toni said. "We're in. We can't stop now."

Suzanne stepped across the threshold, her heart bumping inside her chest. Toni followed her in and closed the door behind them.

The place was dark and dreadfully overheated. Suzanne also had the strangest feeling, as if something bizarre had happened or was about to happen.

Determined to shrug that off, Suzanne glanced about the bland room and said, "I think this is supposed to be the family room."

"What do they call a family room if you don't have a family?" Toni asked.

"Back in the sixties and seventies I think they called them rec rooms."

"You mean like a car wreck?"

"'Rec' for 'recreation,'" Suzanne said.

"Ah."

Toni put a hand on Suzanne's shoulder and followed her into the kitchen. There were the usual red and green indicator lights—from the toaster, the microwave, the dishwasher—so that made it a little easier to see. The kitchen was small but well-appointed, with oak cabinets and marble counters. Hardwick was a tidy homeowner—a mortar and pestle, spice rack, bottle of olive oil, and silver bowl filled with apples were the only things on his counter.

"This kitchen isn't half bad," Toni said. "Lots of built-ins, plus all the appliances are stainless steel. How much does a place like this cost?"

"I think the units sell for around two hundred and fifty thousand dollars."

Toni gave a low whistle. "That's a lot of bucks for a town house. Especially since you still gotta pay a monthly association fee and you don't own any of the land around it."

"But that works for some people," Suzanne said as they stepped into the dining room. Only it wasn't being used as a dining room at all because there wasn't any table and chairs. Just a computer on a desk, a swivel office chair, and a card table set up next to it.

"Hardwick must use this as his office," Toni said. Then: "What does he need an office for? He directs plays, for gosh sakes. How complicated is that?"

"I think he has to write a lot of grant requests to the state arts board to get grant money and things. Remember he

honchoed that photo show at the county museum last
year?"

"Oh yeah," Toni said. "That was—"

Briiing!

The front doorbell sounded, loud and harsh.

"Get down!" came Suzanne's shocked whisper. "Hit the
deck!"

They both dropped to the floor and flattened themselves
against Hardwick's carpet. It was new and scratchy and
smelled of chemicals. Adhesive, probably.

"Who's at the door?" Toni whispered. "You think they've
got a key?"

"Don't know. Hope not."

"You gotta take a look!"

"Me?" Suzanne said. She hesitated for a few moments,
then pulled herself to her knees and gingerly crawled across
the dining room floor. From behind a panel of curtains, she
peeped out a window, only to see a woman in a pink coat
with a small white poodle in a matching coat.

"Woman with poodle," Suzanne whispered.

"What?" Toni started humping toward her like a human
inchworm.

"Never mind."

The doorbell rang again, the woman hopping from one
foot to the other, trying to keep warm. After about two
minutes, she turned and walked away. But not out to a
car—down the row to another town house.

"I think she's a neighbor," Suzanne said.

"You think the poodle lady saw us come in here?"

"I don't think so. She didn't act particularly worried."

"Girlfriend, then?" Toni asked.

"Who knows? Let's take a quick look-see and then

skedaddle out of here." Suzanne was beginning to realize this was a really bad idea.

"Yeah, this place is starting to give me the creeps," Toni said.

They tiptoed across the tiled floor of the entryway and into the living room. Suzanne turned on her flash again so they could see. This room was furnished with a little more pizzazz. A beige leather sofa, glass cocktail table, two large, colorful hassocks, and a piano in the corner.

"Not bad," Toni said. "Hardwick must do all right."

"I'm going to run upstairs real quick," Suzanne said. "You can wait here if you want."

"Okay."

Suzanne turned off her flash and started up the narrow stairway into the pitch-dark. She knew the two-story town house was fairly narrow, so a short stairway would inevitably lead to a small landing where you'd turn and take another few steps up to the second-floor loft.

Suzanne was two steps below the landing when a car bumped down the street. She turned, looked out the front windows, and hesitated. *Is Hardwick coming home?* The neighborhood was so quiet that she could even hear faint music coming from the car's radio. Then the car braked and swung around in a hasty U-turn. Beams of light splashed through the front windows and against the interior walls of Hardwick's town house. The rapid, bouncing light almost gave the impression of an old-time movie. Then the light from the headlights flickered against something pale and blue that floated just slightly above Suzanne's head.

What . . . ?

A sudden sick feeling seeped into every pore of Suzanne's body. And she instantly knew.

Suzanne reached out and gripped the banister to steady herself. Then she turned on her flash and shone it at the body that dangled just a few feet in front of her.

It was Hardwick all right, but it kind of wasn't him, either. His face had collapsed into a death mask, pale blue and shriveled from lack of oxygen. His eyes were bugged out, his tongue stuck straight out of his mouth, and a rope was twisted tightly around his neck.

Suzanne shone her wavering flash upward and saw that the rope was tied to the upstairs balcony railing. She shone her flash back down and saw that Hardwick's feet dangled just inches above the carpeting.

Suzanne's mouth was so dry, it took her a few moments before she could gather some spit. "Toni." Her cry was a hoarse croak as it came out of her constricted throat.

"What?" Toni called, her voice faint. She'd wandered back into the kitchen.

"Come here." Suzanne descended two steps. She'd had an instant, intense fear that Hardwick's cold, dead body might swing out and touch her. "Take a look at this."

When Toni was standing at the bottom of the stairs, Suzanne shone her light on Hardwick. It framed his puffy blue face perfectly.

"Jiminy jeez Christopher!" Toni gasped. She stared at Hardwick for a moment, then stepped back and dropped to her knees and made the sign of the cross. "What *happened* to him?"

"I don't know. He might have hanged himself," Suzanne said.

"He committed suicide?" Toni looked up, but this time she had her fingers covering her eyes.

"Or maybe . . ." Suzanne wasn't all that certain about cause of death.

"Maybe what?" Toni asked. She spread her fingers open and peeped out expectantly.

"Maybe someone helped him along?"

"You mean Hardwick was *murdered*? Oh shit. You think somebody came here and hanged him?"

Suzanne backed all the way down the stairs now. "I don't know," she said, her voice still tight and scratchy. "Only a coroner or an ME could determine the exact circumstances."

"You mean someone like Sam?"

"Oh jeez, Sam. He's gonna kill me when he finds out I was here. This time he's really gonna let me have it."

"Let's put that particular issue on the back burner. What are we gonna do *right now*?" Toni asked. "I mean this very minute."

"Much as I'd like to, we can't just boogie out the back door and pretend this didn't happen," Suzanne said. "That we didn't *see* this."

"Yeah." Toni reached up and pinched her nose closed. "The neighbors would figure it out sooner or later."

"We have to call Sheriff Doogie," Suzanne said with a heavy heart.

"Which means he'll alert every deputy and officer in the tri-county area. We'll be looking at a major bugout."

"And Doogie will most certainly call Sam."

"Okay," Toni said. "Then we better go in the kitchen, turn on some lights, and make that call."

They did. And it went horribly.

"*Dead*, you say?" Doogie shouted once Suzanne had him on the line and was able to cough out a halting explanation. "Hanged? Holy Hannah! Did you call an ambulance? Did you try and cut him down?"

"No, it's too late. Hardwick's definitely not breathing," Suzanne said. "I mean, his face is completely blue."

Doogie asked a few more rapid-fire questions and then said, "Do not touch the body or move an inch, Suzanne, until I get there. Do not allow anyone onto the premises until I get there. Do you understand?"

Suzanne moved the phone away from her ear because Doogie was screaming so loudly. "I understand."

"I can't tell you how important it is that you follow my instructions to the letter."

"I will," Suzanne said. She gazed at Toni. "We will."

She hung up her phone and said, "Doogie says we're not supposed to leave the premises."

"I could hear him shouting. People living ten miles away could probably hear him shouting. People in the next state . . ." Toni swallowed hard and said, "Are we in deep doo-doo?"

"I don't know. It's too early to tell."

"On the one hand, we're guilty of breaking and entering. On the other hand, we discovered a murder. If Hardwick's body had gone undetected until tomorrow, then his killer's trail would be ice-cold and that much more difficult to follow." Toni stopped abruptly, cupped a hand to her mouth, and whispered, "Wait a minute, you don't think the killer is still here, do you? I mean, he could be hiding in an upstairs closet or something."

"Don't even go there, Toni."

Toni sagged against the refrigerator. "You don't really think Hardwick killed himself, do you? I mean, suicide is a mortal sin."

"Even though I've had all of two minutes to process this whole thing, I *don't* think Hardwick killed himself. You saw him hanging there, Toni. Do you think he strung himself up there like a piece of meat on a factory farm?"

Toni shook her head. "I don't know. I just kind of *glanced* at him." She wrinkled her nose. "Still, when his play was cancelled, he took it awfully hard."

"Let me tell you something, Toni. Nobody, but nobody, takes cancelling an amateur play *that* hard."

SHERIFF Doogie was quick to agree with Suzanne when he showed up five minutes later wearing jeans, a rumpled sweatshirt, and a dark blue parka. He took one look at Hardwick's body, examined the noose and rope, and said, "Murder. Plain and simple."

"Not that simple," Deputy Driscoll said, studying Hardwick's still-suspended body. "It could have been self-inflicted."

"Trust me, it wasn't," Doogie said. Three more deputies had just arrived and were milling about in the tiled entry along with Suzanne and Toni.

"What do you want to do?" Driscoll asked.

"You and Robertson get the crime scene kit from the car," Doogie said. "We'll take photos, bag his head and hands, take fingerprints from whatever surfaces we can, as well as front and back doors." He glanced at his other deputies. "Deputy Reed, you go out and start knocking on doors. Talk to the neighbors, ask them if they've seen anybody around, any strange cars, in the neighborhood. Deputy Orson, you go set up a roadblock. I don't want anybody driving in here unless it's the meat wagon." He cocked a sharp eye at Suzanne and Toni. "You two ladies, I want you in the kitchen right now."

Suzanne and Toni marched into the kitchen, where Doogie turned and unleashed on them.

"What the hell were you *doing* here?" Doogie demanded. "I know Hardwick didn't invite you in because he was busy dangling from the business end of a rope."

"You're right," Suzanne said. "We weren't invited in."

"Was the door open or did you bust a window?" Doogie asked.

"Neither," Suzanne said.

Doogie put his hands on his ample hips. "Well?"

"Show him, Toni," Suzanne said.

"Do I have to?" Toni asked.

"Yes!" Doogie shouted. He frowned at Suzanne. "Show me what?"

Toni held up the bump key.

"What've you got there?" Doogie asked.

"Bump key," Toni said.

"Sweet holy croakers," Doogie said. "Are you freaking serious? Don't you know those things are illegal?"

Toni shook her head as Doogie deftly plucked the key from her hand.

"Where'd you get this?" Doogie asked.

Toni shrugged. "I don't remember."

"Why do I think that dimwit Junior might have a hand in this?" Doogie fumed. His mouth worked furiously for a few moments even though no words came out.

There was a loud clumping sound and then Deputy Robertson came into the kitchen. "We're processing the body," he said. "Anything else we should be looking at?"

"We're going to have to go through all these kitchen cupboards," Doogie said. "And look at all his computer stuff."

"Looking for a suicide note?" Robertson asked.

"I don't believe it was suicide," Doogie said. "Still, we gotta examine all the angles." When Robertson left, he spun around in the kitchen and then faced Suzanne and Toni again. "You realize what we've got here, don't you?"

Both Suzanne and Toni held their breath, not sure what Doogie was about to say.

"It's a double murder," Doogie said. "A double homicide."

"You think Allan Sharp's murder is connected to Hardwick's?" Suzanne asked.

Doogie touched a hand to his forehead, as though feigning deep thought. "Let me see now, Allan Sharp was murdered in a play that Teddy Hardwick was directing." He exhaled hard. "If that's not connected I'll eat my hat."

"You know," Suzanne said, "Hardwick wasn't supposed to be here."

"What are you talking about?" Doogie asked.

So Suzanne told him about dropping the ghost costume off at the theater and how Hardwick had told her he'd be working there late.

"Something caused him to come home, then," Doogie said. "Or someone. And then they snuck in here like a greased weasel and hung him."

"Hanged him," Suzanne said.

"Huh?" Doogie's brows beetled together.

"Never mind."

"Don't get technical," Doogie said. "Dead is dead."

They stood in the kitchen, pondering Doogie's words for a few moments. Suzanne glanced through the dining room and out a front window. Red and blue lights strobed and flickered off frosted car windshields and snow-covered trees. It looked as if Santa had arrived early—only with a police contingent.

"There could be a small upside to this," Toni said.

"What might that be?" Doogie laced his fingers together and cracked his knuckles.

"Hardwick was kind of a suspect, but now he's been eliminated."

"Yeah, permanently eliminated," Doogie said. He rolled his eyes toward the ceiling. "Heaven help me."

THERE was no celestial intercession, but Sam did arrive a few minutes later in full-on doctor-coroner mode.

"Now what have you gotten yourself into?" was Sam's first question to Suzanne. But before she could come up with a decent answer, he brushed past her to take a look at Hardwick.

"Sam doesn't look too upset," Toni observed.

"No, he's plenty upset," Suzanne said. "The vein in his temple was throbbing like crazy. He's already hit DEF-CON 2."

Doogie walked back into the kitchen. "I got more questions for you two."

"Sure," Suzanne said.

"Plus we're going to have to fingerprint you as a matter of elimination."

"Yuck," Toni said.

So Driscoll did his fingerprinting and Doogie asked a ton more questions. Suzanne and Toni answered as best they could, with Doogie sometimes asking the same question over and over, but coming at it from different angles.

"Okay, I'm satisfied," Doogie said finally.

"That we're not criminals?" Suzanne asked.

"Killers?" Toni asked.

"No, I'm satisfied knowing that you're both foolhardy, obtuse, and blockheaded."

"Flattery will get you everywhere," Toni said.

There was a knock on the back door and then Gene Gandle stuck his head in. "Sheriff? Can I come in and look around? Looks like we got ourselves another front-page news story."

"Did Orson let you through the barricade?" Doogie asked.

Gandle nodded. He was a pencil-necked string bean of a middle-aged man who was dressed in a brown JCPenney suit. He was normally in charge of ad sales for the *Bugle* and wrote the occasional high school sports report. But Gandle had always fancied himself a newspaperman in the fashion of Carl Bernstein, one of the *Washington Post* reporters who broke the story on Watergate.

"I'm gonna kill that dimwit Orson," Doogie said as he wandered off.

Gandle looked at Suzanne and Toni. "You saw Hardwick's body?"

"Yes," Suzanne said. "Though I sincerely wish I hadn't."

"He still hanging in there?" Gandle gazed in the direction of the living room.

"Hanging from the upstairs balcony. The loft," Toni said.

"You think he offed himself?" Gandle asked.

"Doubtful," Suzanne said. She could hear the officers moving about in the other room. Catching an occasional strobe of light and Sam's flat, almost clinical tone, she surmised that one officer was taking photos while Sam was dictating into an audio recorder.

"Did you see any sign of a struggle?" Gandle asked. He was starting to take notes.

"Like what?" Toni asked.

"Was he shot?" Gandle asked.

Suzanne and Toni exchanged glances. Then Suzanne said, "I don't think so."

"Somebody got the best of him," Gandle said. "Come on, what more can you tell me?"

"Not a thing," Suzanne said. "Doogie pretty much swore us to secrecy."

"But this is a major news story," Gandle said. "Haven't you ever heard of freedom of the press?"

"Not when Sheriff Doogie's in charge," Toni said.

FINALLY, it was all over. Hardwick had been bagged, tagged, cut down, and hauled away. Doogie had asked a myriad of questions. The deputies (well, most of them) had done their jobs fairly well.

Sam walked into the kitchen and found a half-asleep Suzanne propped up against a counter. Toni was poking around inside the refrigerator, wondering if she could help herself to an orange.

"Another dead body," Sam said to Suzanne. "You're not just the town jinx; you're the Bermuda Triangle of murder." He gave a faint but tired smile. "Suzanne, what am I going to do with you?"

Suzanne could think of any number of exciting, romantic diversions, but Sam looked like he was going to be a tough customer tonight. No sweet words would melt his heart. No triple chocolate brownie would put him in a soporific mood. "For now, could you just take me home?"

Sam put an arm around her. "I can do that."

THAT night, Suzanne lay in bed next to a lightly snoring Sam and did something she hadn't done in a long time. She counted her lucky stars. She thought about her friends, the Cackleberry Club, her first husband, Walter, and now Sam.

And she thanked the Lord for all he'd given her. All these gifts and then some. Her good health, her curiosity, her ability to mostly see the good in people, her profound sense of justice.

Suzanne knew she had no business pursuing either of these murder investigations. It would be foolhardy and dangerous. And yet, her behind-the-scenes snooping had added a certain frisson to her life.

She closed her eyes and smiled as she drifted off to sleep.

CHAPTER 20

WITH the murder of Teddy Hardwick literally hanging over her head, Suzanne still had to honor her commitment to WLGN radio this Friday morning. After all, she was scheduled as a guest on Paula Patterson's *Friends and Neighbors* show in order to promote the Cackleberry Club's toy drive.

Walking down the hallway of WLGN, headed for Paula's studio, Suzanne was immediately buttonholed by Norm Steed, the station's news manager, who was also known (behind his back, of course) as Stormin' Norman. Steed was stocky with a practically square head, walked with a rolling gait, and wore black-frame glasses that were as large as pie plates.

"Just the person I wanted to see," Steed wheezed out to her. "Tell me everything you know about Teddy Hardwick's murder last night." He took a gulp of air and said, "It *was* cold-blooded murder, am I right?"

Suzanne tried to severely downplay her role in last night's fiasco. "I really don't know much of anything, Norman."

"That's not gonna work for me," Steed said. "Because I have it on good authority that you were there. That you and Toni were the ones who found Hardwick's body."

"Um, does everybody know about that?"

Steed's head bobbled. "Oh yeah. Sure. It's the red-hot news of the day. In fact, we're leading all our broadcasts with Hardwick's murder. Our listeners want to know what's going on out there. They want to know if there's a serial killer prowling around Kindred and maybe over into Jessup. Everybody's terrified that they're the next victim," he said gleefully.

"That's just awful," Suzanne said.

"Of course it is," Steed said. "But it's kind of great, too. When it comes to ratings, I mean." His eyes grew beady behind his glasses. "And ratings translate into revenue."

Suzanne tried to get by him. "Excuse me. I don't want to be late for Paula's broadcast."

"For you, she'll wait," Steed said. "Just be sure to lay out all the juicy details, okay? Like what did Hardwick look like? How long had he been hanging there?"

Talking about Hardwick was the absolute last thing Suzanne wanted to do as she slipped into Studio B. Luckily, there were no questions from Wily VonBank, Paula's longtime sound engineer. Instead, Wily smiled and touched a finger to his lips as he led her from the control booth into a small studio. It was semidark, warm, and baffled with blips of foam rubber that reminded Suzanne of egg crates. Paula sat at a small console talking into her microphone. In honeyed tones she crooned about a sale on carpets at Cal's Carpet Barn in neighboring Jessup.

As Suzanne sat down on a high stool, Wily placed a pair of headphones on her head and positioned a microphone directly in front of her mouth. Then Suzanne waited, feeling a little jittery, a little nervous, that Paula might drill her about Teddy Hardwick.

But Paula didn't do that. In fact, talking to her was an absolute dream.

After giving Suzanne a warm introduction and chatting back and forth, Paula said, "Tell us about the toy drive that's going on at the Cackleberry Club right now."

"We're collecting toys for kids who might not otherwise get a gift for Christmas," Suzanne said. "And it doesn't even have to be an expensive toy, just something fun."

"If people are in a gift-buying mood, what's the age range they should consider?"

"We're collecting toys for kids five years old on up to age sixteen," Suzanne said. She leaned in closer to her microphone. "You know, people love to buy cuddly teddy bears that appeal to young kids. But older kids, teenagers, are often forgotten."

"And they're still kids, too," Paula said. "Even though they'd rather die than admit that."

"But everyone loves finding something under the tree on Christmas morning."

Paula asked a few more questions, then gave the dates of the toy drive and the address of the Cackleberry Club.

"You folks know where it is," Paula said. "All you have to do is follow the aroma of fresh-baked sticky rolls." She hit a button on her console and her show music—what radio folks called bumpers—came up. And Suzanne was done.

"Painless, yes?" Paula said.

"Thank you for not asking me about Teddy Hardwick," Suzanne said.

Paula waved a hand. "It wouldn't have been appropriate." Her eyes twinkled. "Still, you have to run the gauntlet outside."

"Norm Steed already accosted me."

"And he probably will again," Paula laughed.

But for some reason, Steed was nowhere in sight. So Suzanne was able to rush out of the station and, she hoped, be on her way. She was a little late, but not too late. If she hurried, she'd arrive with fifteen minutes to spare before the Cackleberry Club opened for business.

Just as she reached her car, another car, a silver SUV, pulled in beside her. It was Don Shinder, Allan Sharp's old partner.

Shinder climbed out of his car, saw Suzanne, and said, "I heard about Teddy Hardwick. It must have been awful for you." His voice was kind and he had a sympathetic look on his face.

Suzanne just nodded. "Norm Steed just tried to pry the details out of me."

"Awful," Shinder said. "You know, being a lawyer, I'm used to people displaying that kind of morbid curiosity. Accidents and homicides, people always want to pick at you for details. It's macabre." He shook his head as if to dispel that irritating thought. "What brings you out here, Suzanne? You have aspirations to be a DJ, too? As if you don't have enough keeping you busy?"

"I was just doing a promo piece with Paula for our toy drive."

"Today must be good-deed day," Shinder said. "I'm recording a public safety announcement for snowmobile safety."

Suzanne reached over and squeezed his arm. "Good for you."

DRIVING back through town, Suzanne wondered what Sheriff Doogie would be up to today. Would he re-interview anyone? Had he found fingerprints at Hardwick's house that didn't belong and therefore could be construed as suspicious? How was Doogie planning to catch Hardwick's killer? And was it really the same person who'd killed Allan Sharp?

Suzanne figured it pretty much had to be. Then she shifted focus and decided to review her suspect list. Now that Hardwick was out of the picture, that left Mayor Mobley, Ethan Jakes, and Amber Payson.

Could Amber be the wild card in all of this? The girl had encountered serious issues with Sharp; that was for sure. But what about Hardwick? Did Amber and Hardwick know each other? Had they been having a relationship? Was Amber even strong enough to muscle Hardwick into a situation where she could get a noose around his neck and hang him? And if so, why would she want to kill him? What would be her motive?

All the suspects felt like possibilities to Suzanne, yet none of them felt exactly right, either.

"HEY, Suzy-Q," Petra called out when Suzanne walked in. "How's our big radio star?"

"Tired of dodging questions about last night," Suzanne said.

Petra's face crumpled. "I'll bet you are. Toni told me all about it." She touched a hand to her heart. "What a shocker. To find Hardwick hanging there like a sack of potatoes."

"It was the worst."

"I didn't catch the whole broadcast, but I'm hoping Paula didn't ask questions about it, did she?" Petra asked.

"No, but that awful news director peppered me with questions and pretty much hung all over me."

"Stormin' Norman Steed."

"That's the guy."

"He's a horse's patootie."

Toni came blasting through the swinging doors into the kitchen. "Hey, I listened to part of your broadcast. I had the radio on while I set the tables and filled the sugar bowls."

"Did everything sound okay?" Suzanne asked.

Toni gave a thumbs-up. "You were great. I bet people will be bringing in toys like crazy."

"Good," Suzanne said. "Then the stress was worth it."

"Didn't you once tell us, 'There's no such thing as bad publicity'?" Petra asked.

"No," Suzanne said. "I think that was somebody . . . in publicity."

IT was Frittata Friday at the Cackleberry Club and Petra had dreamed up a doozy. Three farm-fresh eggs with mushrooms, spinach, bacon, and Monterey Jack cheese.

"Say," Toni said to Suzanne as they both flitted about the café, serving customers, pouring refills on coffee and tea, clearing away plates. "Can you believe how freaking busy we are? Our frittatas are selling like hotcakes. Even our hotcakes are selling like hotcakes."

"Good, it'll help fluff the bottom line," Suzanne said. She kept a watchful eye on their margin and was always mindful of the vast difference between making a living and making a profit.

"But all our customers are buzzing about the murder. The *second* murder."

"Do they know we were there?"

"Most of them don't," Toni said. "Not yet, anyway." She motioned for Suzanne to join her behind the counter, where they'd have a modicum of privacy. "How are you doing?" Toni asked. "With Sam, I mean. Was he furious at you for sneaking into Hardwick's house? Did he call off your engagement?"

"That's the weird thing. I thought he'd be stark-raving mad; instead he just asked me if I thought breaking and entering was the smartest way to spend my time."

"Ooh, that's even worse than Sam going all bonkers on you," Toni said. "Don't you see what he did? He took the cool, rational approach. When somebody does that with me, I come down with a terrible case of the guilts."

"Except I don't feel particularly guilty."

"That probably means you're part sociopath. That your brain doesn't feel bound by normal rules and conventions."

"Really, Toni? Really?"

Toni gave Suzanne an evil grin. "Girl, I'm just yanking your chain."

The front door creaked open, letting in a gust of wind along with Gene Gandle, the reporter. "Suzanne," he said, crooking a finger.

Suzanne went over to Gandle. "Can I get you a table, Gene? Are you here for breakfast?"

Gandle's dark eyes seemed to twirl with light. "I'm here for the big story," he said.

Suzanne shook her head. "Sorry. No."

"But it's all over the radio," Gandle protested. "If WLGN has the story, why can't I?"

"If they have the story, they didn't get it from me."

Gandle put a hand to the bow tie that poked out from his long gray winter coat. "The thing is, we're thinking of putting out a special edition. An extra. Like major newspapers do when there's a huge story like a war or an impeachment. I don't think Kindred's ever had two murders in one week before."

"If you want the dirt, you'll have to get it from Sheriff Doogie," Suzanne said.

"But he's already barred me from the Law Enforcement Center!"

"Sorry, buddy, then I can't help you."

"Not even if I give you top billing in the article?"

"Especially if you give me top billing."

THE rest of the morning was just as trying and frantically busy. Of course, the death of Teddy Hardwick was the numero uno topic of conversation in the café. A few customers eyed Suzanne and Toni, but most were too polite to ask questions outright. Instead, they speculated about Hardwick's death, buzzed about a possible connection to Allan Sharp's murder, and floated their own wild and wacky theories. Serial killers, terrorists, maybe angry survivalists who'd descended from the bluffs around Kindred.

By the time lunch rolled around, rumors were flying even harder and Suzanne was ready to walk out the door.

"Be cool," Toni said. "Most of these folks are just plain scared. Two strange deaths in this town—really two murders—has everybody on pins and needles."

"Including me," Petra called from the other side of the pass-through.

"I wish Doogie would drop by for lunch," Suzanne said. "I've got about a zillion questions I want to ask him."

"Oh, he'll stop by," Toni said. "Don't worry about that. The man has an appetite that won't quit. But I don't think he'll be in the proper frame of mind to answer any of your questions. He's gotta be feeling tremendous pressure."

"Lunch orders are up," Petra called out.

Suzanne grabbed an order of Scotch eggs and a frittata,

while Toni grabbed two burger plates and a bowl of soup. Once Suzanne had delivered her orders, she looked around the café and took stock of the situation. All her customers were munching away, conversing with one another, and looking relatively contented. So, blessed be, something was going right. Then she heard the door open. A latecomer. She turned, hoping it was Doogie, ready to pounce on him, only to find . . .

"Sam!" Suzanne cried. "What are you doing here?"

"Hoping to get some lunch." Sam clapped his leather mittens together, making a soft whumping sound. "Are you not happy to see me?"

"No, no, I'm bubbling over with delight," Suzanne assured him. "I just didn't expect to see you this soon." Sam had run out of the house extra early this morning, chewing a piece of whole wheat toast and looking a little frantic. Had he been frantic about her? Was he starting to worry that they were no longer compatible?

"I have something I want to run by you," Sam said. He shrugged out of his sheepskin jacket to reveal his blue scrubs.

Suzanne led him to a table and dropped into the chair across from him. "What?" Sam looked even more serious now. *Uh-oh, is he going to break it off with me? Was the episode last night the straw that broke the camel's back? Is there anything I can do or say that will win him back?*

"My weekend suddenly got complicated," Sam said. "I told Bob Larabee that I'd fill in for him at the ER this weekend. He wants to drive up to Lutsen in northern Minnesota and take his kids skiing."

The wire that had been tightening around Suzanne's heart suddenly relaxed. Sam wasn't breaking it off with her. And thank goodness for that. In fact, now she felt deliriously happy.

"So, you're telling me that you'll be working at the hospital all weekend?" Suzanne asked.

"Yes. Starting tonight, in fact. Is that going to be a problem for us? I mean, if I'm reading you right, you look kind of happy about it. I thought you'd be disappointed."

"No, no, don't mind my moods. Your ER gig is fine with me."

"I wanted to make sure you didn't have anything special planned."

"You mean social calendar–wise?"

"Or maybe a special dinner. Like prime rib or your ultra-fabulous chicken Kiev?"

"Why, Dr. Hazelet, was that a subtle hint-hint I just detected?"

"Aren't you the perceptive little minx."

"Don't care to eat that hospital cafeteria food?" Suzanne joked.

"Now that you mention it . . . no."

"Maybe I could swing by Saturday night and bring you some homemade chili?"

"Suzanne, I would love that."

"And then you'll be working Sunday, too?" she asked.

"Only till four."

"Then I could probably fix chicken Kiev for you Sunday night."

"You see," Sam said. "I knew there was a good reason I asked you to marry me."

THE afternoon flew by and still Sheriff Doogie hadn't come in. Customers came in for coffee and pie, tea and scones, many of them dropping off toy donations. Finally, at three o'clock, when Suzanne was starting to give up hope, Doogie came slip-sliding into the Cackleberry Club.

"Gettin' cold and icy out there," was his mumbled greeting.

"Watch the floor, watch the floor," Toni cried. "I just mopped."

"Jimminy Christmas," Doogie yelped. "A guy can't be expected to stomp *every* dang chunk of snow and ice off his boots."

Toni poked at his feet with her mop, then followed him halfway across the café, swiping up bits of slush. Doogie did a comic hurry-up shuffle, then sat down on his favorite stool at the counter.

"Sheriff," Suzanne said. She was standing behind the counter, facing him. "I thought you might be in for lunch today."

"Haven't had lunch. Been too busy."

"Working on Hardwick's murder? Because that's what it was, right? Murder?"

"I thought we established that last night. But before we get to talkin', I'd like to order something. If the kitchen's still open."

"It's open," Petra called through the pass-through. "What do you want?"

"What do you guys recommend?" Doogie asked.

"The frittatas are real good," Suzanne said.

"Then that's what I'll have. With genuine vegetables and none of that funky kale, okay? That stuff's only fit for rabbits."

"I heard that," Petra called out.

"I meant you to," Doogie said.

Once Doogie's lunch was up, Suzanne gave him ten minutes to eat, even though he only needed five since he inhaled food like an old-fashioned Hoover vacuum cleaner. So she was back in no time at all, tempting him with a piece of marble cake. And asking questions.

"So where are you on all of this?" Suzanne asked. She set the cake down and shoved a clean fork at him.

"Hard to tell; these two murders have more twists and turns than a cheap garden hose."

"But you think they're connected?"

"Have to be," Doogie said. "I mean, what are the odds they're not?"

"Do you think knowing they're connected narrows down your pool of suspects?"

Doogie took a bite of cake and bobbed his head. "Maybe. Somewhat."

"Are you still looking at Amber Payson?"

"I paid her a visit just this morning," he said as he chewed.

"And?"

"And she was unhappy . . . what else is new?"

"Do you think Amber was having an affair with Teddy Hardwick?" Suzanne asked.

"She says not."

"Do you believe her?"

"I thought I had Amber cold for Allan Sharp," Doogie said. "After their big office brouhaha. But for Teddy Hardwick . . . I'm not so sure."

"I saw Amber at the Hard Body Gym a couple months ago and she looked . . . how would you say it? She had a fairly slight build. Maybe a little too small for muscling around a guy like Hardwick. I don't think it's easy to hang someone, even if you're holding a gun to their head."

"Was Amber lifting weights when you saw her?" Doogie asked. "Pumping iron?"

"She was taking a yoga and meditation class."

Doogie ate another bite of cake. "Huh."

"Does Hardwick have relatives around here?" Suzanne asked.

"Nope. Just his parents, and they live in Minneapolis."

"Have you talked to them yet?"

"Oh yeah, it's part of the job," Doogie said. "The bad part."

"What's the good part?" Suzanne asked.

"Catching the asshole who murdered their son."

CHAPTER 21

SUZANNE was straightening up the Knitting Nest when Petra came in to join her. Petra pulled off her apron, kicked off her Crocs, and flopped down in one of their springy-sprongy wingback chairs. "Thank goodness for this place," she said, exhaling slowly. "It's my refuge in a world gone mad."

Suzanne smiled. Since the Knitting Nest was chockablock full of yarns and fabrics, it did offer a warm and cozy vibe. All that was missing was a fireplace.

"Did you see my new display of shawl pins and closures?" Petra asked.

"I was just drooling over them. Some of the pins look positively vintage," Suzanne said. Petra had also hung some more sweaters, shawls, afghans, and hats on the walls. Examples of what she'd knitted, with many of them for sale.

Suzanne picked up a pair of smooth wooden knitting

needles. "These feel so incredibly smooth. Almost like ivory."

"That's because they're handcrafted out of beechwood," Petra said.

"So what project did you dream up for your class next week?" Petra loved her knitting and quilting classes and was threatening to hold an appliqué class this spring.

Petra tossed a quilted tote bag to Suzanne. "That's the sample for next week's Bag Lady class," she said. "A lot of people want to learn how to quilt but don't think they have time to make a full-sized coverlet. So I start 'em out easy by sneaking in a smaller project."

"A tote bag," Suzanne said, holding it up and turning it so she could study both sides. "This is very cool. Stylish, too." The tote bag was completely quilted, using small squares of purple and red velvet. Some of the squares were solid colors; others were shot through with gold thread.

"If you're stitching by machine, you can practically make it in one night." Petra grabbed a skein of yarn and handed it to Suzanne. "Here, take a look at this."

Suzanne took the yarn and studied it. The fibers were a rich cocoa brown and very lustrous. "Beautiful. What is it?"

"You know Claire Nelson who lives over in Jessup?"

"Sure."

"She has a pair of Belgian Tervuren dogs."

"Are you telling me this was literally spun from their fur?" Suzanne asked.

Petra grinned. "Pretty cool, huh?"

"Absolutely." Suzanne handed the skein back to Petra and said, "Are you looking forward to your wine and cheese party tomorrow afternoon?"

Petra shrugged. "I guess so."

"If you don't feel up to honchoing it, I can take over. It's no problem." Suzanne and Toni had already agreed to help out. For Suzanne, a little extra work wasn't a problem.

"Ah, I just need a good night's rest. With my tough Nordic constitution I snap back pretty fast."

They heard the door open in the café and then a man's voice called out, "Anybody home?"

"Now what?" Petra asked. She seemed reluctant to hoist herself out of her chair.

Suzanne jumped up and peered out into the café. "It's Junior."

Petra flipped a hand up. "Meh."

Suzanne went out to greet Junior, wondering what was on his mind. Something to do with Toni?

"Howdy do," Junior said with a friendly wave. He was dressed in camo pants, a matching jacket, and a faded T-shirt that said Army.

"What's up, Junior? Preparing for an invasion?"

"You can't be too careful, Suzanne." Junior glanced around the café. "You know, this place is pretty well situated. It'd make a good FOB."

"What's that?"

"Forward operating base, like the military sets up. A kind of command post."

"And what war or disaster would you be anticipating?"

Junior ticked off his list. "Could be anything. North Korea, global pandemic, extraterrestrials, a zombie . . ."

Suzanne held up an index finger. "Don't." Suzanne didn't like zombies and couldn't understand TV's current preoccupation with them. The last thing she needed was Junior talking about a zombie outbreak.

Toni came out of the kitchen. "What are you doing here?" she asked Junior.

Junior dug into a limp khaki bag that was slung over his shoulder. "I brought some toys for your toy drive." He pulled out two small teddy bears and handed them to Suzanne.

"They're cute," Suzanne said. "Thank you." Now she felt bad for jumping down his throat. Well, a little bit bad.

"You *purchased* these bears?" Toni asked.

"Well, yeah," Junior hedged.

"Where?" Toni asked.

"At the dollar store," Junior said.

"You can't contribute to buying groceries, but you can go out and buy toys?" Toni asked.

"There's a difference. These toys are for *charity*," Junior said. "Besides, who needs groceries when you never cook? Your oven is jammed full of stuff like shoes and makeup, and you practically live on Diet Coke and microwave popcorn."

"That oven is *occupado* because I have a slight storage problem," Toni said. "Not the least of which is you taking up space—"

"Anyhoo," Junior said, clearly trying to change the subject. "On a cheerier note, I stopped by to see if you ladies would like to accompany me to happy hour tonight. Schmitt's Bar is having a two-for-one on Fearless Rednecks."

"That's an actual drink?" Suzanne asked.

"Bourbon mixed with some kind of neon red energy drink," Junior said. "Makes you buzzed out of your skull, but you never get sleepy."

"I'll pass," Suzanne said.

"Okay, then." Junior blew a kiss to Toni. "Later, babe. I gotta go see a man about a tank."

"Whaaaat?" Toni said.

"Guy over near Cornucopia. He's got a World War II vintage tank parked behind his barn. I thought maybe we could tinker with the motor and get it moving again."

"Good luck," Toni said. "Try not to invade any countries or blow anything up." After Junior had left, Toni turned to Suzanne and said, "You know what *we* should do tonight, don't you?"

"I haven't the foggiest idea, but I'm sure you're going to tell me."

"We should go to that cross-country ski thing. The Cocoa Loco Loppet that the youth group is sponsoring."

"Skiing? Really?"

"Sure. It'll help burn off all that nervous energy you've been building up."

"You're the one with all the nervous energy," Suzanne said. "Besides, I didn't think skiing was in your wheelhouse. You're more indoorsy than outdoorsy. I see you as a Netflix and Junior Mints kind of gal."

"I have been a trifle sedentary of late, I'll admit that," Toni said. "But since my hips seem to be expanding as fast as the national debt, I thought I'd try widening my horizons, too."

"With cross-country skiing."

"Hey, it's what I got."

"And skiing will get you out of the house tonight because Junior is driving you nuts," Suzanne said.

Toni dropped her head. "Junior *is* driving me to distraction. When I got home last night and told him about Teddy Hardwick, all he did was ask creepy questions. What color was his face? Did his skin look all pasty and dead? Honestly, Junior's macabre questions gave me nightmares."

"Now we get down to the real reason for your sudden interest in cross-country skiing," Suzanne said.

"Yeah, yeah, I know. But on the other hand, think how much fun we'll have. All the calories we'll burn."

"You make a good point," Suzanne said. "One of these days I have to start shopping for a wedding dress."

"I love that Sam is still going to marry you. Even after last night."

"I know," Suzanne said. "What a pest. I can't seem to shake him."

"So we'll do the ski loppet? Or did you have plans with your *amour du jour*?"

"Actually, Sam will be working in the hospital ER all weekend long."

"You see?" Toni said. "It's kismet. Or karma. Or maybe a kilogram." She shrugged. "Whatever, we should go."

"You talked me into it," Suzanne said. "Harangued me, actually."

With the floors mopped and the tables all set for tomorrow, Suzanne was ready to turn out the lights. Until a soft knock sounded on the front door.

Uh-oh.

She pushed back a ruffled café curtain and peered out the window. Two figures, women, were huddled on the front step of the Cackleberry Club.

Pulling open the door, Suzanne thought, *This can't be good.*

And it wasn't.

Missy Langston and Amber Payson stared in at her, both looking cold and jittery, snowflakes hanging off the tips of their eyelashes. Finally, Missy said, "Can we come in?"

"Yes, of course," Suzanne said. She opened the door wider and the two women trooped in. "I'm afraid I can't offer you any—"

"No problem," Missy said. "We really just need . . . um . . . to talk to you."

They settled at a nearby table and Suzanne said, "So what exactly . . . ?" They were all three of them fumbling for words.

Missy glanced at Amber, who said, "Actually, I came here to ask for help." She swallowed hard. "Again."

"I'm not sure . . ." Suzanne really didn't know what to say since Amber had thwarted her efforts several times already. But she decided to be open-minded and listen to the girl.

"Sheriff Doogie is on my case again," Amber said. "Big-time. Now he thinks I killed Teddy Hardwick."

"She wouldn't, she couldn't, do an awful thing like that," Missy sputtered.

Suzanne held up a hand. "I'm going to be absolutely blunt about this." She looked directly at Amber. "Where were you last night?"

"At home," Amber said. "Alone."

Suzanne knew that wasn't much of an alibi. In fact, it was a terrible alibi. "You didn't go out at all?"

"No, I didn't. Wait a minute . . ." Amber looked shocked, or at least pretended to look shocked. "Not you, too. Do *you* think I killed Teddy Hardwick?"

"It doesn't matter what I think," Suzanne said. "Sheriff Doogie is the one you have to convince."

"He's not buying any of her answers," Missy said.

"Why not?" Suzanne asked.

"Because he's a jerk," Missy said.

"You really think that's the reason?" Suzanne asked.

Amber hunched her shoulders forward in a defensive posture and said, "Maybe because I dated Teddy Hardwick at one time?"

Suzanne wanted to grit her teeth. So there *had* been a previous relationship with Hardwick. Could Doogie be onto something after all? Was Amber really the killer?

"I thought your old boyfriend was somebody named Curt," Suzanne said.

"That was *before*," Amber said.

"So you told Doogie a bold-faced lie," Suzanne said. "Why would you do that?"

Amber ducked her head. "Why do you think? Because I was afraid. The sheriff's a scary old guy."

"Tell me exactly when you dated Hardwick," Suzanne said.

"I don't know, maybe a year ago?" Amber said.

"For how long?"

"A few months."

"And you broke it off . . . why?" Suzanne asked.

"We just weren't interested in each other," Amber said.

"Their relationship ended not with a bang but a whimper," Missy explained. "They were okay together, but nothing really sparked big-time. So now you can understand why Amber needs your help."

"I wish Amber would have been more forthcoming about this earlier," Suzanne said. "To me and to Sheriff Doogie."

Melissa blew right past Suzanne's statement. "Yes . . . well, Sheriff Doogie has undoubtedly convinced himself that Amber and Hardwick had a horrendously bad, emotional breakup, when they didn't at all. And that she's been plotting to destroy him."

"If I had told Sheriff Doogie the truth, he'd for sure think that Teddy rejected me and that I *killed* him because of it," Amber said in a pleading tone. "I mean, do you see how bad this looks?"

Suzanne leaned back in her chair. "I know you ladies came here seeking help, but I just don't have the right answers." *In fact, I don't have any answers.*

Missy and Amber gazed at her, unhappiness written all over their faces.

"So now what?" Amber asked.

"I can give you some solid advice. Which is the same advice I've been giving you all along," Suzanne said.

"What's that?" Amber asked as Missy leaned forward anxiously.

"Get a lawyer."

Amber just dropped her head in her hands and groaned.

CHAPTER 22

TONI was completely befuddled. They'd arrived at the ski loppet, signed in, and rented their cross-country skis and ski poles. Now Toni was trying to figure out if there was a left ski and a right ski.

"I think it's like socks," Suzanne said. "They're interchangeable."

"You think so?"

"Just give it a shot," Suzanne said. She stepped into her skis, clicked the bindings closed, and grabbed her ski poles. "Along the way we can always make a few . . . adjustments."

They were both dressed like ski bunnies, Suzanne in a white nylon ski jacket with a furry collar and Toni in a shiny black ski jacket that had a trendy moto feel. Petra had given them each a knit cap with a pom-pom on top and a strap that went under the chin to keep them extra warm. And they were layered up in long underwear, slacks, and knitted socks (again thanks to Petra) that went up to their knees.

"This is kind of a big deal, isn't it?" Toni said.

Suzanne looked around. The young sponsors were there in full force, all of them dressed in fleece hoodies that said Journey's End Youth Group. A dozen light stanchions, borrowed from the City Works Department, had been set up in the starting area. A food truck sold coffee, donuts, and hot dogs, there was a ski rental area, and at least twenty skiers were milling about, all geared up and ready to head out onto the trail.

Suzanne also noticed that Reverend Ethan Jakes was there. Right now he was deep in conversation with Mayor Mobley. The mayor wasn't suited up for skiing but was bundled up in a dark green parka and an ugly plaid knit cap. As Mobley conversed with Jakes, he looked around, posturing importantly. Every once in a while, he glanced over in Suzanne's direction. Not making eye contact, but letting her know that he was there watching.

"You ready to go?" Toni asked Suzanne.

"As ready as I'll ever be," Suzanne said. She drew a deep breath of fresh cold air and tried to clear her head. She didn't want thoughts of Jakes or Mobley crashing in to distract her, ruining their moonlight ski trip.

Toni patted a fringed suede bag that hung down below her jacket. "You might have noticed, I brought along my trusty goatskin wine bag. Just in case."

"And I'm guessing it's filled to the brim?"

"With my favorite five-buck Chardonnay. And I got a bag of trail mix, too, in case we get hungry."

"You realize that trail mix *sounds* like a healthy food, but it's really just a sneaky way to eat M&M'S," Suzanne said.

"Well, yeah. I knew that."

They skied (badly) up to the starting gate, which was marked by two bamboo poles with blue flags fluttering on top.

"This is your group?" the starter asked them. "Just the two of you?"

"What you see is what you get," Toni said. She'd already taken a generous hit of wine.

"Okay," the starter said. "We've been starting a different group every five minutes so skiers don't get all bunched up on the trail. That means you guys can go in"—he checked his watch—"about two minutes."

"Great," Suzanne said. Now that she was out here, she was looking forward to skiing. Yes, it was dark and a little bit cold, but once she got moving she figured she'd warm up considerably. She'd read somewhere that cross-country skiing burned at least five hundred calories an hour.

"Just so you know," the starter said. "The trail is clearly marked and there are a couple of stops for hot cocoa and cider along the way. Plus, there's a nice warming house at the halfway point in case you need a break." He looked at his watch and lifted an arm. "You can start . . ." His arm came down. "Now."

Suzanne and Toni both shoved off, excitement coursing through them, happy to be on the trail.

"This is great," Toni cried as she whooshed along. She was skiing out ahead of Suzanne, staying carefully in the ski tracks the youth group had cut into the snow.

"Watch the trail," Suzanne cautioned. "We don't want to make any wrong turns."

"No problem," Toni called back to her. "It's really well marked and I've got eagle eyes."

"How are you doing otherwise?" As Suzanne watched,

Toni seemed to be flailing a bit. She'd glide a few feet, then wave her arms as she negotiated a kind of stutter step.

"I'm a little tangled up on the actual technique," Toni said. "Do I coordinate my right arm with my left leg or is it the other way around? And when I get so focused on kicking and poling, I forget to glide."

"You're doing just fine," Suzanne said as she watched her up ahead. "Your arms and legs should move in opposition. That's called the diagonal stride. Think of it as running on your skis and adding a little glide."

"I think I can do that. Yeah, I know I can."

They skied across an open space where long brown prairie grasses poked up through soft snow. Then they wove their way through a stand of blue-green pine trees that offered shelter from the wind and, finally, skis whispering in the snow, back out into open country again.

"It's really gorgeous when you get out in the open," Toni said.

"Look at the stars," Suzanne said.

Toni glided to a stop with Suzanne pulling up right behind her. "So many stars," Toni said as she tilted her head back. "That really intense portion . . . in the middle. Is that what they call the Milky Way?"

"It sure is. With so much ambient light from cities and highways, it's usually impossible to see. But in this crisp, clear sky the Milky Way really stands out."

"It makes you feel small, doesn't it? I mean, compared to the entire universe."

"It sure does," Suzanne said.

"This sky, with all the stars, reminds me of one of Petra's dark blue cashmere shawls, strewn through with silver thread."

"She'd love that description," Suzanne said, still admiring the night sky.

"I overheard some of what you were talking about with Missy and Amber," Toni said. "She could be the one, you know. The killer."

"Amber?"

"If she hated Allan Sharp enough and then had a really bad breakup with Hardwick. Both of those things could have put her over the top."

"You could be right," Suzanne said, though she hoped Toni wasn't.

"I've heard of women who murdered for a whole lot less," Toni said. She shoved off, digging hard with her ski poles. "Of course, most of the killers were *married* women who'd had it with the jerks they were married to."

They skied along the top of a ridge until the trail started to dip.

"Get ready to pick up some speed. There's a downslope right ahead of us," Toni said.

"Is it steep?"

"I'll let you know," Toni called back.

But the hill wasn't too steep. Not steep enough to cause any falls, and in no time the trail evened out again and they were swooshing through a stand of oak trees. Bur oaks, very gnarled and picturesque, with a few crumpled leaves doggedly hanging on.

Twenty minutes later, Toni was seriously pooped. Her stride shortened as she bent forward, trying even harder. Finally, she coasted to a stop and leaned on her ski poles, breathing heavily. "Getting tired," she wheezed. "I'm not used to this much exercise. The most I've been doing lately is a little cardio at the shopping mall over in Jessup. Running from Baker's Shoes to Fashion Bee."

"You know what?" Suzanne said. "We haven't yet seen one of those hot cocoa stops."

"Probably just up ahead," Toni said. She grabbed her wineskin, took a glug, and offered it to Suzanne, who shook her head no. Then Toni pushed off, skied about twenty feet, stopped, and veered off to the right. "It's this way."

Suzanne followed in Toni's tracks. They skied for another fifteen minutes and then Toni stopped again.

"What's wrong?" Suzanne asked.

"I'm all itchy," Toni said, wriggling her shoulders. "I wore that sweater Petra gave me and I think the yarn was spun from musk ox tails or something."

"Knowing Petra, it could be."

"Plus this trail is kicking my butt. And on top of that, I think I'm getting frostbite." Toni turned around. "Is my nose red? Do I have the deadly warning signs of frostbite?"

"If you had frostbite, your nose would be turning white. And then black."

"Eew." Toni touched her nose. "I guess I'm okay." She glanced around. "Don't you think it's kind of strange that we haven't run into any other ski groups?"

"They were starting groups every five minutes, so there should be one on our heels anytime now."

But there wasn't.

"I hope we didn't miss a turn or something," Toni said as she poked along.

"Toni! You were supposed to be watching for trail markers."

"I thought I was."

"When we made that last turn back there, was there a marker?"

"I'm not totally sure." Toni was beginning to sound panicked.

"Okay," Suzanne said. "Let's ski a little bit farther, and if we don't see a marker, we'll turn around, okay?"

"Sounds like a plan."

But two minutes later, Toni let out an exuberant whoop. "I see the warming house just up ahead!"

"Thank goodness."

"We can rest up and warm our tootsies," Toni said. "Maybe even get a ride back to the starting point."

But when they pulled closer to the small wooden structure, there weren't any lights and they didn't see any other skiers.

"That's strange," Toni said. She sidestepped up to the door and rattled it. The door slid open a few inches. "This has to be it." She knelt down, released her bindings, and stepped out of her skis. Suzanne did the same thing, thankful for the break.

But when Toni slid the door all the way open, she said, "It's awfully dark in here and not a bit warm. That's strange. Do you think the event is over? That everyone packed up and went home?" She threw her ski poles down. "Jeez, some luck we've had."

Suzanne poked her nose in. "This is strange." She looked around at the rustic wood floor, the unfinished walls, the lack of windows. "There's not even a heater in here. Just some crates and . . . oh no!"

"What?"

Suzanne gave a shiver. "You see those long boxes over in the corner?"

"Yeah?"

"I've got bad news for you. We definitely took a wrong turn and missed the trail."

"Doggone it," Toni said.

"And skied way too close to the cemetery."

"What!" Toni cried.

"This is the shed where they keep the dead bodies."

"What!" Toni screeched again.

"You know, where they store the coffins over winter because the ground's too frozen to bury them."

Toni raised her arms over her head and let loose a horrified scream. "Whaaaaa!"

Suzanne tried to keep her wits about her. "Come on, let's just get out of here."

But the words had barely popped out of her mouth when the outside door slammed shut on them!

"What the . . . ?" Suzanne said. *Did the wind do that?* She rushed to the door, tried to shove it open, and was met with firm resistance.

"Is it stuck?" Toni screamed. "Man, I gotta get out of here. You know how creeped out I get by dead bodies!"

"The door's not opening." Suzanne was leaning into it hard, trying to shove it open.

Toni, in a blind panic, began pounding on the door with her fists. "You're telling me we're locked in here? Who would do that?" She spun around in a tight ball of fury and gave the door a hard kick.

"I don't know," Suzanne said. This adventure had suddenly turned serious.

"Was somebody *following* us?" Toni screamed. "Is this their idea of a joke?"

Suzanne was about to reply and didn't. She thought about Sharp and Hardwick being murdered. All the strange things that had happened recently. Her mind didn't want to go there, but . . . could the killer have come after them because they'd been snooping around?

Toni remained in a state of complete hysteria. "We gotta get out of here or I'm gonna lose it completely. No, I *have* lost it. Suzanne . . ." She clutched at Suzanne's jacket. "What are we gonna do?"

"Cell phone," Suzanne said, fumbling in her jacket pocket. "We need to call for a rescue."

"Here, I got mine," Toni said. "But who are we gonna call?"

"Not Sam," Suzanne said. "He's busy at the ER. Besides, this could be strike three. This time he really might kill me."

"Junior. I'll call Junior," Toni babbled. She punched in Junior's number and, when he came on the line, screamed, "Junior, I need you!" She put her phone on speaker.

"I've waited a long time to hear those sweet words come out of your mouth," Junior cooed. He sounded like he was half in the bag.

"No, I mean it. We need you to come rescue us!" Toni cried.

"What's up sugarplum? Somethin' wrong?" Junior asked.

"Has he been drinking?" Suzanne asked. She leaned toward the phone. "Have you been drinking, Junior?"

"I'm sober as a judge." Junior burped. "Only had two beers. Well, heh heh, maybe two and a half."

Suzanne figured that amount was acceptable. Junior was still compos mentis.

Toni explained about the ski loppet and their accidently going off the trail and ending up in the cemetery shed. It took her a couple of tries to get Junior to fully comprehend their plight because he wasn't the brightest bulb in the box. But in the end, Junior finally got it and promised to come immediately.

"Please hurry!" Toni begged.

CHAPTER 23

JUNIOR was as good as his word. Fifteen minutes later they heard what sounded like a strangled tractor chugging its way toward them; then the noise petered out. A few moments later the door to the shed rattled and then slid open. Junior peered in.

"Looks like somebody threw the outside latch," Junior said. "Locked you girls in here."

"No kidding," Suzanne said. She was shaking with anger as well as from the cold, but hugely relieved that Junior had come to their rescue.

Toni ran full tilt toward Junior and flung herself into his arms. "Somebody *did* lock us in," she wailed.

Junior looked puzzled as his arms encircled Toni and he gently patted her back. "Jeez. You guys were in here all alone with the coffins and stuff? Kinda like *Tales from the Crypt*? That's way too creepy. I wonder who'd do a rotten thing like that."

"I don't know," Toni blubbered. "But I was scared, so scared!"

Suzanne, on the other hand, thought she might have an idea about who locked them in. Possibly someone who'd seen her and Toni ski off tonight—like Mayor Mobley or Ethan Jakes. Here was something she could take to Sheriff Doogie. Maybe help point him in the right direction.

"I'm so cold," Toni whimpered as they walked outside. She fumbled around, trying to pick up her skis, but was getting nowhere.

"Let me do that," Junior said. "You just crawl in my old Blue Beater and get nice and warm." He hastily gathered up both sets of skis and threw them into his backseat. "My amped-up heater's like a blast furnace in a Pittsburgh steel mill. I could smelt iron if I felt like it."

Suzanne started to climb into the backseat of Junior's car, then hesitated. "I can't sit next to these stinky tires," she said. Junior hadn't bothered to move them since the fire.

"Come sit in front," Junior said in an agreeable tone as he scrambled into the driver's seat. "Toni, scrunch over toward me and we'll all be nice and cozy."

"Don't count on getting too cozy," Toni said. She'd not only warmed up; she'd calmed down.

"Gimme a break, will you?" Junior said. "I crawled out of a nice warm Barcalounger to come rescue you guys."

He reached into his jacket pocket and pulled out a can of beer. But before he could pop the top, Toni grabbed it and tossed it into the backseat. "No brewski while you're driving," she said.

"Really?"

"Really."

"Spoilsport," Junior muttered. Then: "Suzanne, you want me to take you right on home?" He'd turned his heater on high, hitting them with a blast of hot air that carried the piquant aroma of engine sludge and motor oil.

"Just drop me at the park reserve so I can pick up my car and drop off our ski equipment," Suzanne said. She was anxious to see if Mobley and Jakes were still hanging around there.

"Works for me," Junior said.

"By the way," Suzanne said as Junior bumped through the snow and cut onto the cemetery road. "When are you gonna come fetch your tools from my car?"

Junior sniffled, then wiped his nose on his sleeve. "All in good time."

Toni let loose a little shiver. "I can't wait to get home and jump in the bathtub," she said. "Make the water so gosh-darn hot you could cook a lobster."

"Sounds like the Maine event," Junior snickered.

"But not for you," Toni said.

SUZANNE picked up her car, glancing around to see if Mayor Mobley or Reverend Jakes was still there. They weren't. In fact, the half-dozen people who were still there were busy packing up equipment and taking down banners.

Then, on a whim, Suzanne decided to head over to the hospital. She drove through town, circled back behind the hospital, and parked in one of the reserved ER slots. She jumped out, hit the button for the automatic door opener, and hurried inside.

"Is Dr. Sam Hazelet available?" Suzanne asked the woman at the desk.

The woman looked up. "Do you have an emergency?" she asked. The woman was young, maybe twenty-two, and wore pink scrubs. Probably one of the techs.

"Not at all. I'm Dr. Hazelet's fiancée. I thought I'd just pop in to see him, but I don't want to interrupt anything if he's busy with a patient."

"Oh, well then." The woman smiled. "Luckily nothing major is happening right now. In fact, I just saw Dr. Sam, like, one minute ago. Let me run and grab him."

"Thank you."

Suzanne waited all of thirty seconds before she heard two sets of footsteps coming down the hallway. Then she saw the tech, smiling, followed by Sam, looking slightly concerned.

"I didn't expect to see you here," Sam said. He put an arm around Suzanne's shoulders and led her over to a padded bench by the window. "Everything okay? How was the cross-country skiing? Do you feel better now? Did you blow out all the carbon?"

"Toni and I just experienced a weird . . . well, I guess you could call it a detour. We somehow took a wrong turn."

"You should have left a trail of bread crumbs behind you," Sam joked.

Suzanne had been about to tell Sam about the incident at the cemetery shack, but something stopped her. If she told Sam about being locked in, he'd be hugely upset. He might even put his foot down concerning her freelance snooping. Instead Suzanne said, "What time do you think you'll be coming home tonight?"

"Mmn, it'll probably be a little after midnight. Why, are you planning to wait up for me?"

"I might do that."

Sam leaned forward and kissed her forehead just as his pager beeped. "That would be great. I can't think of a better way to top off the evening."

When Suzanne walked in the back door to her home five

minutes later, Baxter and Scruff were sitting on the tile floor in the kitchen, waiting for her.

"What's up, guys?" Suzanne asked.

Looking like a pair of sphinxes, they gave her their best doggy stares.

"I know, I know, I've been gone most of the day. But I'll tell you what. Let me pull on a warm pair of boots and we'll take a nice walk, okay?"

"Walk" was the operative word. Baxter and Scruff trailed after Suzanne as she grabbed a warm pair of mittens, then pulled on her Ugg boots.

Finally, leashes were clipped, Scruff had on his red sweater, and they were all three on their way.

Baxter, an older dog, was a contented loper. Scruff, on the other hand, was a frenetic charger. Every two feet, Scruff darted off the sidewalk into someone's yard or onto the boulevard, jerking the leash in Suzanne's hand, practically pulling her after him. She'd tried very hard to teach Scruff the fine art of walking beside a human companion, but so far that skill set had eluded him. After all, there were squirrels to be investigated, scents of other dogs to be pondered.

After four blocks of being jerked around like a marionette, Suzanne finally unclipped the leash from Scruff's collar. They were directly across the street from Founder's Park and there were no cars on the street. So why not let him run?

This was the question Suzanne was pondering thirty minutes later when she still hadn't found Scruff. She'd whistled and called him, she'd discovered his erratic trail through the snow, but there was still no sign of her pup.

"Baxter," Suzanne pleaded. "Let out a bark or something, give me a hand, buddy. Let Scruff know that we're looking for him."

Baxter just stared at her with placid brown eyes. He knew it had been a major mistake to let Scruff run around on his own. Why hadn't she known that?

"Scruff! Scruff!" Suzanne called again. She'd caught a sliver of red up ahead. "I see you, you little monster. Get over here."

But when Suzanne and Baxter ran to where they thought Scruff had been, he was already gone.

"Doggone," Suzanne said. "Dog gone." Now she understood how the phrase had originated. It had first been screamed by some crazy dog owner who'd had the bad sense to let her pooch run free.

Suzanne darted into a grove of birch trees, calling Scruff's name. Just as she heard a slight flutter—was it Scruff?—she glanced up and saw a large owl take off from a branch above her head. The bird flapped as it flew skyward, silhouetted for a moment in the sky, looking powerful and magnificent, and then it was gone.

Suzanne knew that the Native Americans regarded the owl as a spirit animal, a messenger of change. And wondered if something was about to change in her life.

She pushed through the grove of trees out into a clearing and stood there, hoping for the best, thinking that if she stopped chasing Scruff, he might come to her.

And just when Suzanne was about to give up on Scruff—or possibly call out the National Guard—there he was, running toward her. Scruff's pink tongue hung out; his eyes were bright and shining. He looked as if he'd been having the time of his life.

CHAPTER 24

BACON popped and sizzled, oatmeal bubbled, and French toast turned golden brown on the griddle this Saturday morning at the Cackleberry Club.

Petra was in an upbeat mood as she shuttled between her cast-iron skillet and her industrial-strength oven, where she was checking the progress of her cheddar cheese popovers.

"So you two had a good time last night?" Petra asked. "On your cross-country ski trek?"

"Pretty good," Suzanne said.

"It was okay," Toni said.

They'd agreed not to tell Petra about veering off course and getting locked in the cemetery shack. It would scare her too much and they didn't want to upset her hours before her wine and cheese party at Hope Church.

"Skiing I can understand," Petra said as she opened the oven door and pulled out her popovers. "Now, snowshoeing, that strikes me as a weird form of locomotion."

"Lots of people around here do it," Toni said. "Hunters, especially."

"I guess snowshoes would make it easier to follow your trail back home," Petra said. "So you don't get lost in the woods."

Suzanne and Toni exchanged glances.

"What?" Petra asked. "What did I just miss?"

"Nothing," Toni said. She grabbed an apron and slipped through the door into the café.

"Is there something going on that I should know about?" Petra asked Suzanne.

"I think Toni's just upset that Junior's still bunking at her place."

"Ah, he's a bad roommate, all right. I'm sure four days is beginning to feel like four years. Junior has the innate ability to create a weird kind of time warp."

The menu Suzanne printed on the chalkboard was abbreviated today. French toast and bacon, oatmeal with apples and cinnamon, cheddar cheese popovers with chili, and California burgers with sweet potato chips.

Toni looked at the menu, then took a pencil from behind her ear and used it to scratch the top of her head. "What time are we closing today?"

"I'm guessing one, one-thirty," Suzanne said. "As soon as we can shoo everybody out and still be relatively cordial about it."

"Then we have to schlep everything over to Petra's church?"

"Just the cheese part. Bill Probst will be delivering French baguettes right from his bakery and Mark Pieri from Quicker Liquor is delivering all the cases of wine."

"What kind of wine?" Toni asked. She looked genuinely interested for the first time that morning.

Suzanne gave a casual shrug. "I don't know. Sacramental wine, I suppose."

Toni's mouth dropped open. "What!"

Suzanne pointed a finger at her. "Gotcha! I'm just kidding, Toni-O. I'm sure there'll be a lovely assortment of vino to choose from."

"I hope there's Chardonnay."

"And I hope the church gets a good turnout."

"Yeah, that too," Toni said. She walked to the front door and turned over the sign that said Open, and three minutes later they were busy seating customers and taking orders.

They did their brunch ballet for the next couple of hours, serving entrees, grabbing plates, spinning table to table with coffee- and teapots, dipping back to deliver the checks. By eleven o'clock there was a welcome lull. Which is when Kit Kazlik burst through the front door.

"Look who's here!" Toni screeched at the top of her lungs, causing Suzanne to turn in surprise and Petra to stick her head out the kitchen door to see what all the fuss was about.

Still pretty and blond, but six months pregnant now, Kit was starting to move a little slower as Toni swept her up in an excited but gentle hug.

Suzanne and Petra also welcomed her with warm hugs. Kit had occasionally filled in as a part-time waitress at the Cackleberry Club. Now, of course, she was biding her time until she became a full-time mom.

"You look so beautiful," Toni exclaimed. "Glowing."

"Healthy," Suzanne said.

"When are you due, honey?" Petra asked. They were all talking at once, the buzz of excitement about Kit's pregnancy absolutely contagious.

Kit patted her tummy. "Exactly three more months to

go." Then she dug in her shoulder bag and pulled out a pair of Raggedy Ann and Andy dolls. "Here, I even brought along toys to donate to your holiday toy drive."

"Thank you," Suzanne said.

"Blessings on your head," Petra said.

"I hope you did more than that," Toni said. "I hope you also brought along that guest list I asked for."

"That's right," Suzanne said. "Because we plan on throwing you the fanciest shmanciest baby shower this town has ever seen."

"Got my list right here," Kit said.

"How's Ricky?" Toni asked. Ricky was the dad-to-be.

"Still with the National Guard but coming home next month."

"Wonderful," Suzanne said.

"Come on in, sit down," Petra urged. "Can we get you a cup of tea? Raspberry and mint teas are supposed to be good for pregnant women. Or maybe something to eat?"

"I'm afraid I can't stay," Kit said as she handed her guest list to Toni. "But it's so wonderful to see you all."

"I'm thinking six weeks from today," Suzanne said. "For your baby shower. We'll send the invitations out right after Christmas."

"That sounds fabulous," Kit said. And then, as they all huddled around her again, Kit added, "You're all so kind. Thank you so much." Her eyes misted over as she looked directly at Suzanne. *Thank you, Suzanne,* she mouthed.

What seemed like eons ago, but had only been a year, Suzanne had convinced Kit to quit her job as an exotic dancer at Hoobly's Roadhouse. When Kit tearfully agreed, Suzanne had loaned Kit some money and given her a part-time job. And that one simple kindness had helped turn her life around.

Suzanne kissed Kit on the cheek. "You and your family deserve all the happiness in the world."

WHEN the little hand was on twelve and the big hand was on three, Sheriff Doogie came creeping through the front door like a cat tiptoeing after a mouse. Maybe he was trying to remain inconspicuous; maybe he was worried that Toni would accost him with her mop again.

Suzanne saw Doogie and wiped her hands on her apron in anticipation. Good. He'd shown up after all. Now she could share some critical information with him. Like how Amber had lied about dating Teddy Hardwick, and how she and Toni had been locked in the cemetery shack.

Doogie stopped short of the counter, cocked his head, and said, "What's shakin', Suzanne?"

"More than you can imagine."

Doogie sat down hard on his favorite stool and rested his elbows on the counter. "That right? Something I'm not privy to?" He glanced around quickly. "Maybe you should fill me in."

"Black coffee first," Suzanne said. She poured out a steaming mug and shoved it in front of him. "Because after I share a couple pieces of news with you, you'll need a hot cup of java to restart your heart."

"Then you'd better toss one of those donuts on a plate, too," Doogie said. When Suzanne reached for a glazed donut, Doogie said, "No, no, gimme the chocolate one with the pink and orange jimmies."

With Doogie slurping coffee and spilling jimmies down the front of his shirt, Suzanne leaned over the counter and spelled out everything that had happened in the last twenty hours. She enlightened Doogie on the fact that Amber

Payson had indeed admitted to dating Teddy Hardwick. Then she told him about getting locked in the cemetery shack the previous night.

Doogie's eyes grew bigger, his expression more disbelieving, as Suzanne delivered her stories. Then he stopped chewing his donut altogether, which was pretty amazing for Doogie since he was your basic down-to-the-last-crumb guy. When Suzanne finally finished, Doogie slammed a clenched fist down on the counter and said, "Doggone it, I knew that girl was lying. I could feel it in my bones."

Suzanne shrugged. "Who knew?"

"Nobody knew. But now, thanks to you, we all know. I tell you, Suzanne, the fact that Amber dated Hardwick changes the picture completely. Puts her right back at the top of my list."

"The one thing I can't get past is that Amber doesn't profile as a killer," Suzanne said.

"Profile? What do you know about profiling?" Doogie's face bloomed red all the way up to his receding gray hairline.

"I know some. And my contributions to your investigation haven't been completely inconsequential," Suzanne said.

"I'll give you that, Suzanne. You've been a big help in some ways. But in others . . . well, face it, Suzanne, last night you dropped your guard and let somebody lock you in a shack full of stiffs! And it could have been worse. The guy could have had a gun—and decided to use it! He could have been some crazy biathlon expert. You know, like they have in the Olympics? Skiing *and* shooting?" Doogie pulled out a white hanky and mopped perspiration from his brow. "What have I been warning you about all along, Suzanne? You gotta stay out of this investigation. Whoever killed Allan Sharp and Teddy Hardwick is a genuine monster. A stone-cold killer."

"Which brings up another question," Suzanne said.

Doogie peered at her with a certain amount of apprehension.

"Could Reverend Jakes be the killer?"

"I know you've had your suspicions about him all along, but I just don't see it," Doogie said. "Where's the evidence? Show me something concrete."

"I keep thinking that Jakes had something against Hardwick."

Doogie considered Suzanne's words. "You mean like some kind of grudge? I haven't seen anything that would indicate such hard feelings." Doogie took a quick sip of coffee. "But you say Jakes is a real Bible-thumper?"

"He's quite religious, yes."

"All I can think of is that Hardwick was a kind of artsy, free spirit," Doogie said.

"A libertine."

"And that somehow went against Reverend Jakes's strict sensibilities."

"Possibly," Suzanne said. It was as good an explanation as anything else.

Doogie shook his head. "I don't know. This whole thing is a horrible mess."

"If that's how you feel, maybe you should bring in reinforcements."

Doogie closed one eye. "What are you talking about?"

"You could ask Sheriff Burney from Deer County to lend a hand. Or at least a few of his deputies. Or even call in the state's Bureau of Criminal Apprehension." Suzanne leaned forward even more. "Please realize, you don't have to deal with these murders all by yourself."

Doogie lifted a shoulder. "I know that. But I am the duly elected sheriff. The two cases are under my jurisdiction. So . . . it's my duty."

"Well, you know you can count on me."

Doogie drew a deep breath and let it out slowly. "Suzanne . . . no."

At one o'clock, Suzanne and Toni began to discreetly clear away dishes and slip luncheon checks to their customers. By one-fifteen, most everyone had taken the hint and cleared out. Not only that; many of these same customers had generously half filled one of the toy bins with donations.

"Your stealth plan worked like a CIA operation," Toni said. She had a spray bottle and a rag and was busily cleaning tables. "I don't think our customers even realized they were being eased out."

"Gotta do it gently; that's the key," Suzanne said.

"Now that we finally have an empty parking lot, maybe our snowplow guy will come by and scrape it clean. Clear away some of those nasty ice ruts that have been building up. It's like a bobsled run in some places." Toni glanced out the window, curled a lip, and said, "Uh-oh."

"Why the sourpuss face?" Suzanne asked. Then her question was answered as Junior barged through the front door.

Junior looked left, then right, then whipped off his trapper hat complete with ear flaps. "Where is everybody?" he asked.

"Gone," Toni said. "Just like you're going to be."

"Junior," Suzanne said. "Thanks again for the rescue last night."

Junior waved a hand. "No problem. Anytime." Then he put a hand to his mouth and giggled noisily. His face pinched into a grin and he started doing a little tap dance on the run-down heels of his motorcycle boots.

"What's got you all revved up?" Suzanne asked.

"Ants in your pants?" Toni asked.

But Junior continued to dance and smirk, as if he had a great big secret to share.

Which he kind of did.

"Take a gander outside," Junior said.

Toni looked out the window, caught sight of something she hadn't seen before, and did a kind of double take. "What's *that*?" she asked.

"I've been busting my buttons to tell you guys. I just closed the deal this morning on a brand-new camper!" Junior said.

"Looks used to me," Toni said. "Beat-up, really. You paid good money for that piece of crap?"

"Traded for it," Junior said. "Even Steven."

Toni looked blank. "Traded with what, Junior? Your good looks and sparkling personality? You don't actually own anything of value."

"I hated to part with her, but I traded Old Yeller for the camper," Junior said.

"I thought that car didn't run very well," Toni said.

"Maybe the camper doesn't, either," Suzanne said.

"I'll be the first to admit the camper's got a few bugs," Junior said. "The tranny is a little squishy and the brakes are plumb shot. But I can fix it. I got the know-how; I've got the tools."

"Wrong," Suzanne said. "*I've* got the tools. The ones you stuck in the backseat of my car."

"And I thank you for hanging on to them because I'm gonna be needing them any day now," Junior said.

Suzanne looked out the window at Junior's new acquisition. It was a rounded little camper shell sitting atop a shabby truck. The camper part was painted a desultory aqua blue and white, the colors of an old swimming pool from the fifties. The entire rig listed badly to one side and reminded Suzanne of a small tugboat that was about to capsize.

Junior saw the look on Suzanne's face and said, "I have to outfit it with new tires, too. Increase the stability."

"Maybe you should work on your own stability first," Toni said.

"That camper looks awfully small," Suzanne said. "Can you even fit inside?"

"That's why I'm going to have to downsize," Junior said.

Toni snickered. "You own two pairs of saggy jeans, some ratty T-shirts, and a leather jacket. What else do you have to cram in there?"

"Got my golf equipment," Junior said.

"That set of used women's clubs you found at the dump?" Toni asked.

Junior wasn't put off in the least. "And I got my fishing tackle."

This time Toni really let loose a guffaw. "A Popeil Pocket Fisherman as seen on late-night TV and a stinky bait bucket hardly qualify as fishing gear."

"Gonna need that bait bucket for ice fishing," Junior said. "Got a big tournament coming up." Then he tucked his thumbs into his belt and grinned. "I'm happy to say, that camper's got all the comforts of home. A one-burner stove, a little icebox, and a table that folds down into a bed. You ever heard the term glamping?"

"You mean like glamour camping?" Suzanne asked.

Junior nodded toward his camper. "That's it right there. In a nutshell." He reached over, picked up Toni's spray bottle off the table and squirted the liquid into his mouth. "Breath spray?" he asked.

"Cleaning fluid," Toni said.

Junior coughed. "Does the trick, though."

SUZANNE was actually looking forward to the wine and cheese party this afternoon. Maybe it was the thought of getting away from the investigation for a few hours; maybe it was the camaraderie among the three of them as they diced and sliced cheese and arranged it on platters.

"This cheese smells funky," Toni said.

"Earthy," Petra said. "Because it's goat cheese. From Straw Ridge Farms, one of our local growers."

"What about this cheddar cheese?" Suzanne asked.

"That's from Annandale Farms," Petra said.

Suzanne nodded sagely. Even though the Cackleberry Club was predominantly a breakfast and lunch café, they prided themselves on sourcing products from local growers and producers. Apples came from local orchards, eggs from Calico Farm, poultry from local chicken farmers, bread from the Kindred Bakery. Even their jams, jellies, pickles, and preserves were made by hand by locals who prided themselves on their techniques and their recipes. They were a farm-to-fork restaurant, as Suzanne liked to say. A designation that gave them all pride.

"Do I stick colored toothpicks in all the diced cheese hunks?" Toni asked.

"Yup," Petra said.

"There sure are a lot of cheese hunks," Toni said.

"Good thing I bought a lot of toothpicks," Petra said. She glanced at Suzanne and said, "I overheard you talking to Doogie at lunchtime."

Suzanne flinched. "How much did you hear?"

"Oh, pretty much all of it," Petra said. "And what I couldn't hear I kind of surmised on my own." She paused. "I know the two of you got locked in that cemetery shed last night." She shook her head as if in disbelief. "And that Amber was dating Teddy Hardwick."

"So now you know it all," Suzanne said.

Petra held up a finger. "Give me a minute, I want to say a piece."

"Which is?" Suzanne asked.

"I'm upset, Suzanne, that after getting a stiff—no, let's call it a severe—warning from Doogie, you *still* want to investigate," Petra said.

"You don't think I should?" Suzanne asked.

"Duh," Toni said.

"I don't think your involvement is particularly prudent," Petra said. "And from everything I've heard, or overheard, you should probably steer clear of Mayor Mobley and that Amber person as well. At least until Doogie apprehends the killer. Or killers." She picked up a large knife and stabbed it into a wheel of Swiss cheese.

"And what if he doesn't?" Suzanne asked.

"He will," Petra said. "I have faith in our law enforcement officers."

"I'm glad somebody does," Toni mumbled.

Petra continued. "But until Doogie makes an arrest, I

think you should definitely take care. Don't go snooping down dark alleys or breaking into houses."

"Been there, done that," Toni said.

"It's not funny, Toni," Petra said as she sliced off two large wedges of cheese.

"Petra, I hear you and I will be careful," Suzanne said. "And the fact that you're so worried about me brings tears to my eyes. So I do promise to take extra care."

"I want to believe that," Petra said.

Suzanne smiled. "We could pinkie swear if that would make you feel any better."

"No," Petra said. "I guess I believe you. You're an honest, straightforward person, so . . . I trust you."

"Thank you, sweetie," Suzanne said.

"Oh, and I packed up some leftover chili for you to take to Sam," Petra said.

"Wonderful," Suzanne said.

"You know what we ought to do tonight?" Toni asked. "To stay out of trouble?"

"Whatever you're conjuring up, count me out," Petra said.

"What?" Suzanne asked. She didn't relish the idea of sitting at home while Sam worked in the ER for a second night. Maybe Toni had a sensible idea for once.

"We should take a nice leisurely drive over to Shooting Star Casino and have ourselves some fun," Toni said. "You can't get in trouble at a casino."

"Oh, yes, you can," Petra said. "Anytime you spin a wheel, pick up a deck of cards, or drop your hard-earned money into one of those infernal machines, it's right on the fine edge of sinning."

"You sound like Reverend Jakes from next door," Toni laughed.

"I know I do," Petra said. "Because he's a real hard-ass, too."

"Petra!" Suzanne said, looking stunned. "You *never* talk like that."

"That's because I've never met a reverend like Ethan Jakes before."

CHAPTER 25

EVEN though the wine and cheese party was held in the basement of Hope Church, the wine flowed freely and the cheese was a huge hit.

"Can you believe it?" Petra exclaimed. "People actually came. A whole lot of people!" She was standing behind a long line of tables laden with platters of cheese and colorful bottles of wine. She, Suzanne, Toni, and a dozen other volunteers all had tasks to do. Pour wine, put out clean glasses, slice more bread, put out another platter of sliced or diced cheese, answer questions, make nice with the guests.

"Probably one of the reasons you got such a big turn-out," Toni said, "is because the play got cancelled. People didn't have anything else to do."

"That's very hurtful, Toni," Petra said.

Toni looked startled. "I didn't mean it to be; I was just trying to be analytical. Practical. You know, I . . . Jeez, I guess it did sound kind of dumb."

"If that's an apology in the making, then I accept," Petra said. "Because I'm too jazzed about this turnout to hold anything against you for very long."

"Thank you," Toni said. She reached over and gave Petra's arm a friendly squeeze.

"Everything looks so pretty, too," Suzanne said.

The large room was strung with holiday décor, a small grouping of tables and chairs was arranged in one corner, à la French café, and a string quartet greeted guests at the door. Right now the strains of Schubert's "Die Rose" mingled with the clink of wineglasses.

"I love that we get to use real wineglasses," Toni said. "Instead of plastic Solo cups."

"Look at Reverend Strait over there," Suzanne said, pointing to a smiling silver-haired man in a conservative black suit. "He's ecstatic that your event is such a rousing success."

"This is a much better turnout than the chili supper we had last fall," Petra said.

"Well, yeah," Toni said. "Let's see now . . ." She held out cupped hands and moved them up and down as if she were weighing something. "Kidney beans versus a tasty Shiraz? Heck, ladies, it's hardly even a contest."

"I'm going to go over and talk to Reverend Strait," Petra said. "Congratulate him."

"I think Reverend Strait should be congratulating you," Suzanne said. "After all, this was your idea."

"With a little help from my friends," Petra added with a smile.

"Go talk to him," Toni urged. "We'll keep things hopping here."

Petra pulled off her apron. "If you don't mind . . ." And she was gone.

"Do you think we should open up these other bottles of wine?" Toni asked. She'd already grabbed a wine opener.

"I don't see why not," Suzanne said. "We've been pouring . . . what so far?"

"Rosé, Chardonnay, Shiraz, and merlot."

"And what else do we have?"

"There's a sparkling rosé, a Riesling, and a zinfandel. But the zin's from Australia, so I really don't know much about it," Toni said.

"Then let's open it up and find out," Suzanne said as she grabbed a wine opener.

"Works for me."

Suzanne and Toni popped corks, poured wine, and chatted with more guests.

"This is a real nice thing for Petra's church, huh?" Toni said when there was a break in the action.

"I'm betting they'll make this an annual event."

"They should. What'd they charge per head for this thing?"

"Ten dollars," Suzanne said. "So ten times all the people that are milling about here today."

"That's what? A hundred and twenty? A hundred and fifty people? And there's still more folks coming in," Toni said.

"Who doesn't enjoy a nice glass of wine?" Suzanne said.

"I could certainly do with a glass," a warm male voice said.

Suzanne looked up to find Don Shinder smiling at her.

"Hello," she said, greeting him. "Welcome. What can we start you off with?"

"Is that a sparkling rosé I see?" Shinder asked.

"From Schramsberg Vineyards in Napa. Want a taste?"

"I know a classic tasting means you should start with the white wines and work your way up to the reds," Shinder said. "But I like to bend the rules a little."

"These days, a lot of us are bending the rules when it comes to wine," Suzanne said. "I'm forever serving cabernet with roast chicken or pork."

"Good for you. It means you're fearless and have eclectic tastes."

Suzanne poured out a half glass of sparkling rosé and handed it to Shinder. "Here you go."

"Have you tasted this?" he asked her.

Suzanne shook her head. "I'm waiting on your recommendation."

Shinder took a sip.

"Well?"

"Delicious," he proclaimed. "It's got that mellow, fruity zip that I love in a good rosé. Now, what cheese do you recommend as an accompaniment?"

"I'd personally go with a semisoft cheese," Suzanne said. "A Gruyère or Havarti."

Shinder took a slice of Havarti, popped it in his mouth, and closed his eyes. "Sublime."

"And you should probably try the goat cheese, too."

"Don't tell me this is from Straw Ridge Farms."

"It is," Suzanne said. "They've been turning out some nice, rich, earthy goat cheeses in the last couple of years."

"Have you . . . ?" Shinder began. Then he stopped and shook his head. "No, this isn't the time or the place."

"For what?" Suzanne asked. She had a feeling about what he wanted to ask. "Go on."

"I was going to ask if you'd heard anything more about the investigation," he said. "Since you and Doogie are . . ." He made a whirling hand gesture. "Friends."

"Doogie warned me just this morning to stay out of the investigation," Suzanne said.

"Really? Because I thought you'd been somewhat help-ful to him."

"Mostly because I poked my nose in where it didn't be-long." Suzanne paused. "Wait a minute, you mean Doogie hasn't been keeping *you* in the loop? Especially concerning the death of Allan Sharp? He was your law partner, after all."

"I can't say Doogie's made any major revelations lately," Shinder said. Now he looked a little discouraged. "I was hoping there'd be some sort of closure on Allan's death. I know his parents are taking this awfully hard. His mother called me just this morning. Myself . . . I'm in the middle of trying to hire a junior attorney."

"We saw you outside your office, right after Allan's fu-neral. It looked like you had a couple of candidates."

"Yeah, well, I did. And I have to make a decision fairly soon. Problem is, my heart's just not in it."

"I can understand that. You know, it felt like Doogie was zeroing in for a while," Suzanne said. "And then Teddy Hardwick got killed and . . . well, that kind of threw Doogie off track. He started second-guessing himself. Was it one killer or two killers? What were their motives? Different? Same?" Suzanne shook her head. "It's very confusing."

"To say the least," Shinder said.

"Then when new evidence surfaced, Doogie seemed just plain angry. Though I think the anger was directed more at himself."

Shinder frowned. "New evidence. What do you mean?"

Suzanne lowered her voice. "It turns out Amber Payson *had* been dating Teddy Hardwick when she'd specifically told Doogie that they didn't know each other."

Shinder seemed stunned. "She lied about it?"

"Apparently so."

"But why? Hardwick was a single guy. He probably dated any number of women, don't you think?"

"Probably."

Shinder took another sip of wine. "Me, I still have a gut feeling about Mayor Mobley. He and Allan were so often at loggerheads. And Mobley's been involved in so many disgusting cover-ups . . ."

"Even his cover-ups have cover-ups," Suzanne finished.

"But the girl, Amber, I don't see it."

"I advised her to get an attorney," Suzanne said.

"Most definitely. But probably more as an offensive strategy than a defensive one." A bubble of people suddenly crowded up against the table, clamoring for glasses of rosé and cabernet. Shinder, still looking puzzled and a little bereft, stepped aside.

A few minutes later, Petra rejoined them. "Reverend Strait is over the moon about our success," she said. "Do you know they're still selling tickets at the door? People keep showing up."

"I hope we don't run out of wine," Toni said.

"Reverend Strait says he's got that covered," Petra said. "Mark at Quicker Liquor is on speed dial."

"I call that some forward thinking," Toni said.

One hour later and the cheese was dwindling and the empty wine bottles were starting to pile up.

"I'm gonna stick these dead soldiers in the empty cases," Toni said. "And move them out of the way."

"Thank you," Petra said. She glanced over at Suzanne. "Are we down to our last bits of cheese?"

"There's enough for about a dozen more mice; then we'll have to call it a day," Suzanne said.

"Wait," Petra said. "We've still got a bowl of cubed Monterey Jack."

"Then pour it onto the platter alongside the sliced Brie."

As Petra poured, a man's hand snuck in and grabbed a hunk of cheese.

Suzanne reached out as if to slap the man's hand in jest. Then she pulled back when she saw it was Reverend Jakes. He was wearing a camo-patterned nylon jacket and insulated pants. He looked like he'd been working outside. Chopping wood or something.

"Hello there," Suzanne said. "Come over to see how the other side lives?" She didn't mean her words to sound so snarky, but they'd come out that way. "I'm sorry, I didn't mean that the way it sounded. I didn't mean to be so weird and hypercritical."

"No problem," Jakes said. "And, yes, I'm in a very ecumenical mood today. Checking out another church's fundraiser, trying to keep an open mind." He glanced around. "This event seems to be very successful indeed."

Suzanne was kind of amazed that Jakes wasn't frowning today. He also wasn't spitting hellfire and brimstone or urging everyone to drop to their knees and pray for forgiveness. Maybe he'd tippled a glass of wine or two?

"How do you like our wine?" Suzanne asked, suddenly curious.

Jakes held up a hand. "Never touch it. Just not my style."

"But you're okay with turning water into wine, aren't you?" Suzanne asked.

"The Marriage at Cana. Oh yes. Absolutely. Can't fault the Good Book." Then Reverend Jakes's face took on a serious, almost somber, look. "How did you enjoy the cross-country ski event last night?"

"It was . . . very well thought out."

Jakes gave her a quizzical look. "I'm not sure how to interpret that."

"Aren't you?" Suzanne asked.

"Not really. I guess I'd better keep a careful eye on you."

"And I'm keeping an eye on you, Reverend Jakes." Suzanne leaned across the table at him. "If you had *anything* remotely to do with Allan Sharp's death, I'll make sure that Sheriff Doogie arrests you. Then, the next time we meet, you'll be wearing an orange jumpsuit compliments of Logan County Correctional Facility."

Jakes smiled at her. "That's an awfully big threat for such a small woman."

"Try me," Suzanne said. "Just try me."

"Ye gads, I'm glad that's over," Toni said as she and Suzanne walked to Suzanne's car. Suzanne was carrying an armload of empty platters. Toni had a half bottle of wine.

"You either have to glug down the rest of that wine or stick the bottle in the trunk," Suzanne said.

"Yeah, I know," Toni said. "I was just getting a jump start on the weekend. So I guess, um . . ." She looked uncertain, then said, "We'll stick it in the trunk."

"Good choice." Suzanne flipped open the trunk to reveal a jumble of tools. Junior's tools. There were even more tools in her backseat.

"I'll just set my wine next to Junior's punch pliers," Toni said.

"I'm impressed you even know what that is."

"Or maybe it's a riveter. I really don't know the difference."

"You feeling tired?"

"Naw, if anything, I'm kind of jazzed," Toni said. "Still thinking about hitting those slot machines over at Shooting Star Casino. Hint, hint."

"Gee, Toni, I don't know."

Suzanne's heart wasn't really into going to the casino, but she didn't exactly want to sit at home, either. She looked at her watch. It was five-thirty. She decided she'd drop off Sam's chili, go home and feed the dogs, and then slither into a pair of tight jeans and a ski sweater.

"Okay," Suzanne said to Toni. "I'm in."

AFTER stopping at the hospital, Suzanne took a detour. Tucked back behind the Cackleberry Club, on eighty acres of farmland, was a farm that she owned. It was currently leased to a farmer named Reed Ducovny and his wife, Martha. The Ducovnys grew corn and soybeans and watched over Suzanne's livestock, which consisted of a single horse named Mocha Gent and a mule named Grommet.

As Suzanne pulled into the farmyard, she noted that lights shone in the windows of the farmhouse, which was perched on a slight rise. Good. That meant Reed and his wife were home. With so many strange things going on around town, Suzanne wanted to be sure that Mocha and Grommet were safe.

And they were. She turned on the lights in the barn and walked past empty cow stanchions to the two large box stalls at the back. Both animals heard her coming and poked their heads over the gates of their stalls.

"How are you guys doing?" Suzanne asked. She walked over to Mocha first and scratched behind his ears. He pitched his ears forward and she ran her hand down the length of his muzzle and under his chin, enjoying the stubbly feeling. Then she leaned forward and exhaled a puff of air, the perfect way to tell a horse you were his best buddy.

Grommet was next. He was a big guy, almost seventeen hands high, with a shambling gait, which meant Suzanne rarely rode him. Yet, he was a rescue animal and the perfect stablemate for Mocha. So a good deal all around.

"Just the two of you now," Suzanne said. A month earlier, she had bought six horses that also needed rescuing. Now, thanks to help from Hoof-Beats Horse Rescue, they'd all been adopted into good homes. Or, rather, nice, cozy barns.

Suzanne reached into the oat bin, grabbed a scoop, and gave both Mocha and Grommet an extra helping. She watched them chow down for a few minutes, then turned and left, satisfied that they were happy and well cared for.

As she crunched across the snow to her car, she saw a shadowy figure standing on the side porch of the old house. Then a hearty voice called out, "That you, Suzanne?" It was Reed, wearing just a knit cap and denim overalls.

"It's me. Saying hi to the guys."

"Okay, then."

"Thanks for keeping a careful eye on everything," Suzanne said.

"No problem. Can't be too careful these days."

No, you can't.

Suzanne climbed back in her car. She decided that one of these days, when it quit snowing and the sun popped out, she would throw a saddle on Mocha's back and ride him up and down the long driveway. Work the kinks out. For both of them.

As she drove home, Suzanne thought about how simple life could be on a farm.

The farm was, of course, Suzanne's Plan B. If the world economy collapsed, if the country went back to a barter system, that was where she'd live. With her horses and a few chickens, pigs, and goats. Put in a vegetable garden, keep up the soybeans and corn. The place already had a well, so she'd be relatively self-sufficient.

All in all, it wouldn't be a bad state of affairs.

WHEN eight o'clock rolled around, Suzanne was as good as her word. She drove back over to Toni's apartment, honked the horn like a bad date, picked her up, and headed out County Road 65 to the casino.

Yes, she'd definitely succumbed to Toni's pleas to hang out at the casino tonight. But as a safeguard, Suzanne had brought along only thirty dollars. She'd play the slots and hope for the best, and if she couldn't ring a win out of the cherries and lemons, that would be it. She'd call it a night. At least she hoped that's how the evening would play out.

CHAPTER 26

TONI was jacked up like a hummingbird on speed. She talked a blue streak as Suzanne drove through the countryside, touching up her eye makeup in the small mirror on the visor, trying to glue on false eyelashes. When the eyelashes didn't pan out, she studied her hair, then pulled out a curling iron and plugged it into the cigarette lighter.

"I don't even know if that works," Suzanne said. She was amused and a little in awe at the full force of beauty artillery that Toni seemed to find necessary.

Toni touched a hand to her curling iron. "Yeah, it's heating up okay. Just because nobody smokes anymore doesn't mean the ciggy lighters don't work. They're still quite useful."

"I see that. Maybe we could even power up a set of hot rollers. Or a popcorn popper if we wanted a quick snack."

"The way I look at it, beauty isn't just an art; it's a science," Toni continued. "You need to do a lot of calculations

to figure out just the right shades of eye shadow and lipstick. Take what I'm wearing tonight, for instance."

"What are you wearing?" Suzanne asked. She'd done
her brows, brushed on some mascara, and added a smear of
pink lip balm. That was it.

"My eye shadow is called Blue Bayou. But if you've ever
studied prisms and color wheels and things, you know that
the color blue always has a touch of red in it. So what I did
was pair it with a lipstick called Red Hot Mama."

"What you did there"—Suzanne waved a hand around
her face—"looks good."

"Thanks. Because if I *don't* put on makeup, I come pre-
cariously close to looking like a bag lady."

"No."

"And I do wish I'd had time to hit a tanning salon for a
fake bake." Toni reached down, touched a finger to her curling iron, and said, "Ouch!"

"Hot?"

"Really hot." Toni started rolling and crimping her hair,
corkscrewing herself around in the front seat.

Szzzt! There was a loud sizzling sound, followed by a
puff of smoke.

"What was that?" Suzanne asked, clearly alarmed.

"Curling iron just grazed my Dynel clip-on curls," Toni
said. "I better be careful; I don't want my hairpiece melted
into a blob."

"We can't have that happening."

Toni finished her hair, then pressed both feet against the
dashboard and said, "What I'm thinking is, we can't go into
the casino all willy-nilly."

"We can't?"

"No. We need to have a plan, a gambling strategy."

"I was just going to play a few slot machines," Suzanne said.

"No, no, no, we gotta ease into the night with some blackjack. I'm feeling super lucky."

"I'm not sure I'd be good at blackjack; I'm not familiar with the rules."

"Blackjack is just twenty-one," Toni said. "Come on, I know you've seen blackjack tournaments on TV where a bunch of dissipated C-list actors sit around a table, smoking cigars and trying to outbluff each other."

"Okay, yeah. I guess I have seen that," Suzanne said. *For about two seconds. Then I turned it off.*

"What you wanna do is draw to twenty-one. But if you go over . . . kaboom. You go bust and the house wins."

"The house?"

"Suzanne, you're acting like you've never been in a casino before. Like you just woke up in a parallel universe."

"You know what?" Suzanne said. "I'll just wing it as we go along."

TEN minutes later found them walking through Shooting Star Casino, where lights blinked, buzzers buzzed, music blared, and everyone seemed to have lost their minds. Toni, in her tight jeans and gold lamé jacket, was pretending to be Sharon Stone in the movie *Casino* as they bopped over to a nearby blackjack table.

"Here, sit here," Toni said. "This table is a cheapie, only two dollars a hand."

They sat down in front of a somber-looking man in a white shirt and black string tie who looked more like a truck driver than a blackjack dealer.

"This is gonna be great," Toni said as they bought some chips. She winked at the dealer and popped the top two buttons open on her blouse. "We're gonna do great, I can feel it in my bones."

But Toni's bones were a little creaky tonight. And the hands were dealt so fast that, five minutes later, they were both down twenty dollars.

"How did that happen?" Toni asked as they walked down a row of slot machines. She seemed dazed and confused. "That guy was dealing cards so fast, the whole thing seemed like a blur. My brain can't work that fast."

"We need to slow down and take it easy before we both go broke," Suzanne said.

But Toni was starting to bounce back from her loss. "How about we try our luck at the wheel of fortune?" She pointed toward a large vertical standing wheel. "If we hit the right number, we could win that cute little Mercedes-Benz sports car that's parked next to it!"

Suzanne looked at the thin skim of dust that was on the car's hood and figured the cute little sports car had managed to outlast a lot of optimistic gamblers. But Toni was not to be deterred. She put down a dollar. And when that didn't pan out, she slapped down five dollars.

"Ooh," Toni said when the wheel stopped on the number ten. "I was so close."

"Maybe we should call it a night."

"I thought we'd get something to eat at the buffet. It's supposed to be cheap and pretty good."

So they went through the buffet line, loaded up their plates with ribs, chicken, and hunks of corn bread, and sat down at a table.

"Having fun?" Toni asked as she nibbled a wing doused in hot sauce.

"It's okay," Suzanne said. She was feeling bored but didn't want to completely rain on Toni's parade.

"I think we just need to readjust our attitude. I read in a gambling book once that you have to lose money before you can win some."

"We've got that covered," Suzanne said.

"So it would behoove us to try, try, try again."

So they did. After they finished dinner, they wandered into the middle of the casino, where a few exotic games were being played.

"Wait a minute, what's that?" Toni asked. She was gazing at an octagonal-shaped table with two neon red Chinese dragons hanging over it.

"*Pai gow,*" Suzanne said, reading the sign beneath the dragons.

"Sounds exotic."

"Sounds dangerous. Like you could lose a lot of money and not realize it because it's all done in a foreign language."

"Still, I gotta give it a shot," Toni said.

"How's your Mandarin?"

"Not so hot. Then again, neither is my English."

"Then why don't we just watch for a while? Try to get the hang of the game," Suzanne said.

But the longer they watched, the more complicated the game looked.

"Are you getting this?" Toni asked.

Suzanne shook her head. "Not even a little bit."

"I think it's like poker, only the dealer shakes the dice to see who gets their cards first."

"And each player is arranging their cards into two separate hands. I wonder if—" Suzanne stopped abruptly. She'd just seen a familiar face ghosting through the crowd.

"What?" Toni said. "What were you going to ask?"

Suzanne shook her head. "Nothing. No, I . . . I think I just saw Mayor Mobley go by."

"Where?" Toni turned around and searched the crowd.

"I don't know. He's gone now."

"Mobley's a gambler? Maybe this is where all the city's money is being squandered."

"I wouldn't put it past him," Suzanne said. Seeing Mayor Mobley had given her a funny feeling in the pit of her stomach. Something was blipping out a slow warning to her. Had Mobley followed them here? Or was it simply a coincidence? Was he just chilling out like everyone else?

"And every player takes a turn at being the banker." Toni's focus was back on the *pai gow* game, still trying to decipher its workings.

Suzanne grabbed Toni by the arm and pulled her away from the table. "Come on, let's go home."

"I guess," Toni said. They walked down a row of dollar slot machines that made enticing *plinkety-plink* sounds and headed for the exit, when Toni stopped dead.

"Now what's wrong?" Suzanne asked.

"I clean forgot."

"What did you forget?"

"I'm pretty sure I clipped a two-dollar gaming coupon out of the *Logan County Shopper*." Toni dug in her shoulder bag, pulled out a crumpled piece of paper, and studied it. "Yup. It says here this coupon is good for one free roll of nickels."

"What are you talking about?"

Toni fluttered the coupon in Suzanne's face. "If I redeem this coupon, we get to play the nickel slots using house money." She was jazzed up again.

"Seriously?" Suzanne had pretty much had it with the

casino. The cacophony of ringing bells and clattering coins, plus the evening's entertainment of a rockabilly band, were giving her the makings of a nasty headache.

"I'll split the nickels with you," Toni offered.

"No, that's okay." The way Toni played, popping in five nickels at once, Suzanne figured they'd be out of the casino in no time flat. "Where do you have to get your nickels?"

"Cash office."

They walked past the Lucky Deuce Cocktail Lounge and down a short hallway to where the cash office was located across from an exit door. There were two tellers plus an armed guard sitting behind bars and bulletproof glass. It looked like serious security, and Suzanne figured they might even keep a couple of trained Rottweilers back there, too, for good measure.

"Okay," Suzanne said. "You go ahead and get those nickels." There were five people in line ahead of Toni.

"You won't regret this," Toni said.

But five minutes later they kind of did.

"This is taking forever," Suzanne said.

"People cashing out their winnings," Toni said.

"I think you have to fill out some kind of tax form if you win above a certain amount."

"See?" Toni said. "That alone gives me hope. That there are actual big-time winners here."

But as they waited in line, they were suddenly aware of some kind of disturbance going on outside. Angry shouting. Loud protests. Punches being thrown?

"Do you hear that?" Toni asked. "That rock 'em, sock 'em sound?"

Suzanne nodded. "Sounds like there's a fight going on."

"Out in the parking lot?" Toni darted out of line, pushed open one of the exit doors, and stuck her head out. "Holy macarons!" she yelped. "Some poor guy is getting the stuffing beat out of him!"

Suzanne ran over to see for herself. And, sure enough, there were two guys in ski masks whaling on a guy wearing a burnt orange parka. They were punching, kicking, and swearing at the poor guy, who was sprawled facedown on the ground, struggling to protect his head.

"We have to call security," Suzanne cried. She spun around, with Toni on her heels, and ran back to the cash office. She cut to the front of the line and pounded on the window, rattling the glass. "Help, please. Two guys in your parking lot are beating somebody up!"

The guard immediately jumped up and held a radio to his mouth. Suzanne couldn't hear what he was saying but could see through the glass that he was calling for help. For reinforcements.

One minute later, four more security guards arrived. And in a flying wedge of black uniforms, they pushed their way through the exit doors. Only to find . . .

Nothing.

Stunned, Suzanne elbowed her way to the front of the pack. "Well, they *were* here."

"We saw them," Toni said. "Two guys beating the crap out of a third guy. Really tuning up on him."

"It's all over now," the guard from the cash office said. "They probably jumped in their cars and are long gone."

One of the other security guards shrugged. "Guess they must have resolved their differences."

"It seemed a lot more serious than just a disagreement," Suzanne said. "The guy in the orange jacket was really getting pounded." She'd seen fists flying, heard the sickening thud of flesh against flesh. Now she gazed out into the parking lot and saw only cars lit by the orange glow of sodium-vapor lights. A gentle snow had started to drift down. She lifted her arms in a gesture of futility and said, "Does this happen often? Fights in the parking lot, I mean?"

Another security guard with dark curly hair and a brush mustache shook his head and said, "Ma'am, you have no idea."

By the time Suzanne and Toni were back on the road, the snow was coming down with a lot more intensity.

"I think it's a good thing we left when we did. Some of the snow is starting to compact on the road and make it slippery," Suzanne said.

"Lots of twists and turns on this old road, too," Toni said. "Maybe I should have borrowed Junior's Blue Beater. It's got studded tires."

"Aren't those illegal?"

"Yeah, I guess. But he's really big into ice racing. A lot of dudes get together every Sunday over at Fish Lake. It's really fun to watch."

"I'll bet."

They continued along as County Road 65 ran through some of the prettiest country in Logan County. There were forests that swept all the way up to high ridgelines, ravines where creeks whooshed down through rocky gateways. And it was deserted out here, too, in this rough-and-tumble territory. It wasn't the kind of prime farmland that was found farther west of Kindred.

They spun through an S-curve and went down a steep hill. Towering fir trees rose on both sides, making the road close in more than ever. Suddenly, Suzanne's headlights picked up two bright eyes peering up at them from a ditch.

"You see that?" Toni cried out in surprise. "What was that critter?"

"Probably a fox," Suzanne said. "Or maybe a raccoon, though they're mostly hunkered down by now."

"Not many houses out this way," Toni said. She sounded anxious.

"Not too many." Suzanne had kept her eyes front and center on the road as she drove; now she glanced in her rearview mirror.

"Nothing much moving out here," Toni said.

"Except that guy coming up behind us. He's gaining on us like crazy. Must be doing seventy miles an hour."

"Maybe let him pass you."

"I've got no problem with that," Suzanne said. She eased off the gas and moved toward the right shoulder.

But the car didn't pass her. Instead it roared right up behind her, its bright lights shining through the rear window. The driver seemed content to stick hard on their tail.

"This sucks," Suzanne said. "I just wish he'd go around me."

Toni turned around to look. "Jeez, why does he have to have his brights on?"

"Because he's rude."

But that wasn't the half of it. Five seconds later the car nipped right up onto their rear bumper and gave them a nudge.

"Did that crazy driver just do what I think he did?" Toni asked.

"Bumped me. Must be desperate to pass."

Suzanne slowed down, but then the car behind her slowed down, too.

"Okay then, I'll speed up." She was starting to get

steamed. She didn't relish playing a game of chicken out here in the wilds.

"Holy crap," Toni said, glancing over her shoulder. "Now *he's* speeding up."

"I can't seem to lose this bum."

"Well, be careful," Toni said.

"Believe me, I'm trying to be careful."

"Probably a disgruntled gambler," Toni said. "Lost his entire paycheck at the craps tables."

"A familiar refrain."

Suzanne slowed again on a downgrade that had a tricky curve halfway through it. Which was the exact moment the car banged into them a second time.

"Get your cell phone out," Suzanne said. "Call the highway patrol."

Toni grabbed her phone, but before she could make her call, the rogue car smashed hard against their rear bumper. The jolt shook them both and caused the phone to fly out of Toni's hand.

"Hang on!" Suzanne cried. They'd hit an icy patch and she was fighting desperately to maintain control. She felt her car swerve left and steered into her skid. Then the car smashed against a low metal barrier and swerved right.

And that's when it all went to hell.

Suzanne fought to straighten her car, but it was simply not to be. A split second later, she felt her car's back end let loose completely and they spun crazily to one side. Then her front end dropped onto the frozen berm and clipped a ridge of hard snow. As if time had slowed to a crawl, the car began to tilt, and then it began a slow-motion, stomach-sickening roll. Suzanne felt her seat belt get uncomfortably tight as they rolled down the hillside and into a ditch far below. One second she was gazing through the windshield;

then she was upside down; then she was glimpsing a galaxy of stars through her moonroof. Another flash of white snow, and then stars again.

Dear Lord, Suzanne thought as her arms flailed helplessly and a cardboard box from the rear seat smacked her in the back of the head. *We're rolling all the way down the embankment!*

CHAPTER 27

DARKNESS, intense cold, and a jumble of limbs. That was Suzanne's first impression when she realized they'd finally come to an abrupt, heart-thumping stop. She blinked, drew a sharp breath, and fought to orient herself. She felt muddleheaded and woozy, and she was pretty sure that her car had landed upside down in the ditch. As more comprehension slowly dawned, she saw a huge gash in her windshield, all pointy and jagged like sharks' teeth. Snow and cold air were rushing in.

"Toni?" Suzanne cried in a weak voice. She looked around but didn't see her friend. Had Toni been thrown clear? "Honey, where are you? Are you hurt?"

There was no answer.

"Toni?" Suzanne released the seat belt, which was painfully cutting into her chest and shoulder. She dropped with a thud and called out again in what she hoped was a stronger voice. Her airbag hadn't gone off and she wondered why. Had it malfunctioned? Had the snow cushioned their descent that much? Maybe.

"I'm here," came a plaintive mewl.

"Toni." Suzanne glanced around and finally located Toni. She scrabbled farther back in the car, where Toni was bent over and huddled. Her airbag had gone off and her seat belt seemed to have released on its own. "Are you hurt?"

"I don't know," Toni managed to choke out. "My right arm is crumpled up and feels real funny."

"Can you move it?"

"No way, it hurts just to breathe."

"You stay here. I'm going to crawl out and get some help."

"Don't leave me alone, Suzanne. Please. I'm scared."

"I'll only be gone a couple of minutes," Suzanne said. "I promise. I need to . . . I need to . . . um. *What do I need to do? Because my head is still spinning. Oh yeah, I gotta find a cell phone and call for help.*

Suzanne crawled toward the windshield, hands searching frantically for her purse, wondering if she could kick her way out of the car. Or could she lever open one of the car doors?

That's when she heard the sound of boots crunching on snow.

"Somebody's coming," Suzanne said. A flicker of hope kindled inside her chest. *A rescue?*

"Who is it?" Toni asked.

"It must be the guy who hit us. I think he's coming to help."

"Jerk," Toni said.

A pair of legs stuck into dark green pac boots came into view and stopped just short of the shattered windshield.

"Hello?" Suzanne said. *Who is this?*

"Help us," Toni called out weakly. "Get us out of here."

The boots shifted. Whoever it was, it looked as if he was about to crouch down and try to pull them to safety.

"Are you injured?" a man's voice yelled out.

Suzanne was about to answer when she was struck with a wave of terror. She recognized that voice. Her mind reeled with fear and she shrank back into the dark recess of the car. Oh man, did she ever know that voice. It belonged to Reverend Ethan Jakes!

Dear Lord. Is he the one who rammed us from behind and forced us off the road?

"Get away from us," Suzanne screamed. Jakes was kneeling down now and Suzanne could see his face as he peered in. He looked worried as he reached a hand in through the broken glass and tried to grab her.

"No," Jakes said. "I didn't hit you . . . I was just driving by and saw your car go plunging off the road. I got the plate number of the car that . . ."

"I don't believe you!" Suzanne cried.

Suddenly, there was another scuffle of boots. As if a second person had just arrived at the crash scene. Suzanne heard Jakes say, "What are you . . . ?" And then there was a soft, muffled sound, like something heavy striking human flesh.

Right before Suzanne's startled eyes, Reverend Jakes's eyes rolled back in his head and he let out a loud groan. Then he toppled to the ground a few feet from her shattered windshield.

Stunned, Suzanne peered through the darkness at Reverend Jakes. Blood trickled down the side of his face and his eyes were scrunched closed now. The lights had definitely gone out. Someone had clobbered him on the head with something heavy. A tire iron maybe?

"But who?" Suzanne managed to stammer out loud. Who else was out there? A savior . . . or something else?

Snow scuffed as a man walked closer to the car and then knelt down next to the fallen Jakes. Seconds later, Don Shinder's face peered in at her.

"I didn't count on him coming along," Shinder said in an almost matter-of-fact tone of voice. "I thought I'd be killing two birds with one stone, not three." He sighed deeply. "Oh well."

Even in the dark Suzanne could see that Shinder was holding a tire iron. He was the one who'd clobbered Jakes on the head.

"Come on out of there," Shinder said. He clanged the tire iron noisily against the front bumper of her car and then poked it through the broken windshield, trying to prod her. "Let's get this over with."

Suzanne pulled farther back into the wreck, trying to tug Toni along.

"No," Toni moaned. "Hurts too much."

"Hang on, Toni." Suzanne grabbed Toni under her arms and inched her back into the scatter of junk—mostly Junior's tools—that had been dislodged during the crash.

"Hurts," Toni muttered again.

Seconds later, a flashlight beam probed the darkness.

"I know you're in there," Shinder said.

"Get away from us!" Suzanne shouted. In the reflected light from the flashlight, Suzanne could see that Shinder had two black eyes and a puffed lip. Was he the one she'd seen being beaten up outside the casino? Yes, it had to have been him. She recognized the burnt orange parka!

"I'm just here to help," Shinder said. "To bat cleanup."

"Get away from us," Suzanne cried again.

"Or what?" Shinder asked. "You'll crawl out and throw

a snowball at me? In case you haven't noticed, you don't exactly have a lot of negotiating power. You're basically rats in a trap."

"And you're a killer," Suzanne flung at him, reacting with both fear and rage. "*You're* the monster! Just wait until Sheriff Doogie gets his hands on you!"

"It's never going to happen, little lady. This time I hold all the cards."

"It was you back at the casino, wasn't it?" Suzanne said. "Getting the crap beat out of you."

"And it's all your fault!" Shinder bellowed, his voice rising in a horrifying shriek. "If you'd left well enough alone, I could have collected the business insurance on Allan and been just fine. Could have paid off my gambling debts and had plenty left over. But you . . . you had to poke your nose in my business every step of the way."

Suzanne digested his words and thought: *Oh shit! I'm right. Shinder really is the killer! He stabbed his own partner and then . . . he killed Teddy Hardwick?*

Now what?

Keep him talking?

I can try. I have to try.

"I can understand stabbing Allan Sharp to collect the insurance," Suzanne said, trying to keep her voice from quavering. "But why kill Hardwick?"

"To throw everyone off track," Shinder said. "Don't you see? Don't you get it? Amber Payson was about to go down for all of this."

Without warning, Shinder smashed his tire iron against the windshield. More glass cracked and popped as he moved the tire iron around, probing, dislodging hunks of glass, trying to create a larger hole. A hole that would be big enough for him to fit through. So he could crawl in and kill them!

"You're insane," Suzanne flung at him.

For some reason, her remark made Shinder chuckle softly. "I'm actually very clever and cunning," he said as he pulled the tire iron back and thumped it against his leather mitten. "Because I found out that people will do anything you want when you point a gun at them. Even slip their head through a noose."

"You won't get away with this."

"Of course I will. In about ten seconds I'm going to split your heads open like those poor dead squirrels you see lying on the highway. That's right, after I give you both a good hard knock, it'll look exactly like you lost control of your car, flipped into the ditch, and crushed your skulls in the ensuing wreck."

Suzanne tried to scrabble backward some more. She knew she had to do something. But what?

"Toni," she whispered. "Do you have your cell phone?"

"I . . . I think so," Toni said. "It should be here somewhere, only my arm hurts too much to try and find it."

"Let me . . ." Suzanne shifted her weight, trying to feel around.

Shinder, meanwhile, was getting even more ugly and restless. He started swearing and stomping around, poking at them. He was struggling to get enough leverage so he could take a swing.

What can we do? Suzanne wondered as Shinder dropped to his knees, huffing and puffing, sticking his face and now an arm through the broken windshield. He swung his heavy tire iron closer and closer to them. It was only a matter of time before he'd connect and bash their heads in.

Suzanne continued to search around inside her wrecked car, looking for something, anything, she could use to defend against him. Her fingers touched Toni's curling iron, but it had cooled off, so no good.

Shinder was crouched down on his hands and knees now. Gingerly, he thrust his head through the hole in the windshield and gazed at her. Then his shoulders slid in.

"Come out, come out, wherever you are," Shinder said in a taunting singsong voice.

Suzanne spun around to face him. If she gave Shinder a good swift kick in the head, maybe she could disarm him and hold him off. But for how long?

As Suzanne drew up both knees and positioned herself, ready to give him a hard, determined kick, she flung both arms out to stabilize herself. And at that exact moment, her fingers touched something . . . vaguely familiar.

"This is it," Shinder snarled. "End of story." He wasn't fooling around anymore. His mouth was pulled into a vicious snarl and his eyes shone with pure hatred.

As he stabbed violently at Suzanne with the tire iron, Suzanne wrapped her fingers around Junior's nail gun. With a hope and a prayer, she whipped the metal contraption in front of her, took careful aim, and pulled the trigger.

CHAPTER 28

TRAVELING at a velocity of ninety miles an hour, the three-inch steel nail hit Shinder's left shoulder like a turbo-charged hornet.

"Owww!" Shinder's bloodcurdling scream warbled pitifully in the still night air, and the impact of the nail sent him careening backward. Driven back outside the car, he landed hard, sprawling on his butt in the snow.

"Got him," Suzanne whispered. She felt no triumph, only relief.

But her relief was short-lived.

Like the wounded space creature from *Alien*, Shinder managed to pull himself up, spitting and swearing, saliva frothing and dripping from his mouth. Eyes crazed, a high-pitched bleat twisting out of his gaping mouth, he fumbled up his tire iron, staggered toward them, and came at Suzanne with another drunken jab.

And that's when she aimed for his right shoulder.

As she pulled the trigger a second time, the nail gun stuttered in Suzanne's hand and made a dull *ptuh-ptuh* sound.

That shot did the trick. Shinder let out a high-pitched keening sound as he dropped the tire iron and was driven to the ground. Even better, he stayed on the ground this time, writhing helplessly in the snow. His arms flopped out wide as if he were about to be crucified; then they flailed up and down as if he were trying to beat out a snow angel. Shinder spat out a string of curses, interrupted by pathetic little bleats. His manner of expressing pain.

Suzanne felt not a whit of sympathy for Shinder. Mostly because she didn't have time for sympathy. She scrunched forward, kicked a bigger hole in the windshield, then scuttled back to get Toni.

"I don't know if I can move," Toni moaned.

"Yes, you can," Suzanne urged. "You have to."

"Can you help me?"

"Of course. Just give it your best and try to crawl a little bit. I'll help you along."

Suzanne crawled out of the car, then turned around and grabbed Toni under her arms. Thirty seconds later they were both standing outside, looking down at Don Shinder, who was moaning pitifully.

"He tried to kill us," Toni growled. She was still cradling her arm but looked like she wanted to kick Shinder in the head. "He set Junior's trailer on fire as a smoke screen. Literally a smoke screen."

"Don't think about Shinder right now; just try to stay positive. Know that we're safe and out of danger." Suzanne pulled the crinkle scarf from around her neck and laced it around Toni's neck and left shoulder. Tried to fashion a sling that would take the pressure off her injured arm.

Toni stood there, head down, and let Suzanne work on her. Then she blinked a couple of times, as if she was just waking up, and gazed over at Reverend Jakes. "Who's that?" she asked.

"Reverend Jakes," Suzanne said. "He apparently saw the accident and came to try and rescue us. But Shinder smacked him on the head with a tire iron."

"Oh no. Is he dead?"

"I don't think so. Just knocked out cold."

"Well . . . can you do something?" Toni collapsed into a sitting position in the snow.

Suzanne went over to Reverend Jakes, knelt down, and touched the pulse point at the base of his throat. It felt fairly strong. And his breathing seemed quite regular and steady.

"I think he's going to be okay. He just needs a little time to wake up," Suzanne said.

Just as she spoke, Jakes slowly opened his eyes and stared up at Suzanne.

"Where am I?" he asked.

"You're in a ditch, lying next to my car. You tried to help me, but Don Shinder whacked you over the head."

Jakes blinked a couple of times, then lifted a hand and felt around on the top of his head. When he found the sore spot he winced. "Ouch. Hurts."

"I'm sure it does. You got hit pretty hard."

"Yeah, I kind of remember now."

"Now, just stay down, I'm going to try and find a cell phone. Call for some help."

"Use mine," Jakes said. He shifted slightly. "Jacket pocket."

Suzanne dipped a hand into Jakes's jacket pocket and pulled out his cell phone. "Thank God," she breathed.

"You better believe he's watching over us," Jakes said.

Still keeping an eye on Don Shinder, Suzanne called dispatch at the Law Enforcement Center and asked to be patched through to Sheriff Doogie.

"Help!" Suzanne yelled when Doogie finally came on the line. "We've been in a car crash!"

"What? Who?" Doogie asked. He was momentarily stunned.

"Me and Toni. And Reverend Jakes is hurt bad, too."

"You're all hurt? Where?"

"Toni's arm and I think—"

"No, I mean *where* where. Where are you? Where did you crash?"

"Oh, Don Shinder ran us off the road as we were driving back from the casino. On County Road 65, just past the old Miller place where the road dips way down. The thing is, our car rolled into a steep ditch and then . . . well, there was a shooting."

"What'd you say?" Doogie screeched. "A shooting? Somebody got *shot*? Who got shot? Was it Shinder?"

"Just get out here, okay? Fast as you can. And send an ambulance."

Suzanne punched off. Better to let Doogie come and see for himself.

She checked on Toni and Reverend Jakes again, and then dialed Sam's number. While she waited for him to answer, she jumped up and down, trying to warm up. Thank goodness Sam had his cell phone on him and picked up immediately.

"Suzanne?"

"Sam!" Suzanne almost cried when she heard his voice.

Sam was instantly on alert. "Sweetheart, what's wrong?"

Where to start? "Everything," Suzanne said in a quavering voice. "First we were in a car accident and then Reverend

Jakes got hurt, and then Don Shinder tried to kill us. And I think Toni's arm might be broken." Suzanne let loose a loud sob and said, "You're at the hospital? Still working in the ER?"

"No. You're not going to believe this, but I'm sitting in the front seat of the ambulance that's screaming its way toward you!" Sam cried.

"But . . . why? How?" Suzanne asked. She was stunned that Sam was on his way to their crash site.

"It was so quiet at the hospital that when Doogie called for an ambulance, I decided to jump in and ride along. See what I could do to help. Good thing, too. I had no idea that *you* were the one who was injured!"

"It's mostly Toni and Reverend Jakes," Suzanne said. "But please come quick, Sam. Please hurry."

"Dick Sparrow is driving this rig, pushing it up to sixty miles an hour on slippery roads. We're coming as fast as we can."

Tears ran down Suzanne's cheeks as she crossed her legs and sat down in the snow. "Can I just stay on the line for a little bit longer?" she asked. "Until you get here?"

"Of course. I'm right here for you." Then Sam switched from concerned boyfriend to ER doctor. "But tell me what's going on. You sound clearheaded and conscious, but is your respiration okay?"

"I think so." Suzanne hiccuped loudly.

"What about Toni?"

"She's not doing so well," Suzanne said. "She's rocking back and forth and cradling her arm."

"My arm's broken," Toni moaned.

"She thinks her arm is broken," Suzanne said. "I think it is, too."

"Try to keep Toni as warm as possible," Sam said. "You

said Reverend Jakes is injured as well? If you can scrounge any coats or blankets, wrap them tightly around both of them. And make sure they stay awake. Try to keep them talking."

"Reverend Jakes was driving by and tried to help us, but Don Shinder hit him on the head and knocked him out."

"Concussion," Sam said. "Again, be sure to keep Reverend Jakes as warm as possible, but don't move him. We don't want to trigger any sort of brain issues until I get a chance to check him out."

"And I . . . and I . . ." Suzanne had tried to remain relatively calm up until this point, but now the tears really started to come.

"Hang in there, sweetheart," Sam said. "Stay strong."

"No, I have to tell you what happened."

"You just did."

"There's more. I . . . I shot someone." Suzanne sniffled hard. "Well, not just someone, it was Don Shinder. But only because he tried to bash us with a tire iron."

"Dear Lord." Sam's voice grew hushed, as if he couldn't quite believe what he was hearing. "You literally shot him?"

"Shinder was coming after us. He was, like, ten seconds away from bludgeoning us to death . . . killing us."

"Suzanne, I . . ." Sam's voice caught in his throat. He didn't know what to say.

"Okay," Suzanne said at hearing the shock and disbelief in his voice. "I better hang up now and check on Toni and Reverend Jakes."

Suzanne sat in the stillness of the dark night, listening to the sigh of the wind through the trees. Sam had sounded utterly gobsmacked by her words. Had her confession about shooting Don Shinder upset him? She hoped not. But deep in her heart, she feared that it had.

CHAPTER 29

"ARE they coming?" Reverend Jakes called out to Suzanne. "The sheriff? An ambulance?"

"On their way," Suzanne said.

Jakes groaned and struggled to sit up.

"You're not supposed to do that," Suzanne said. "I talked to Sam and he's worried that you might have sustained a concussion."

"Got my bell rung good; that's for sure," Jakes said.

"You're not in danger of blacking out, are you?" Suzanne asked. She worried because he did sound awfully wonky.

"No, I'm a little shaky, but . . ." Jakes slowly got his legs under himself and tried to stand up. He didn't make it on the first try. "Whoa," he said as he collapsed back down in the snow.

Suzanne was instantly at his side. "Are you sure you're feeling well enough to stand up?"

"I'll be all right, just got the stuffin' knocked out of me." Jakes fought to stand again and this time made it to his feet. "But your friend over there . . ." Jakes nodded at Toni, who was sitting on the ground, rocking back and forth. "She's in a bad way."

Toni heard him and lifted her head. "I think I broke my arm," she said.

Jakes unzipped his parka and took it off.

"Don't do that," Suzanne said. "You're supposed to stay warm."

"Your friend needs it more than I do," Jakes said. He draped his parka around Toni's shoulders.

"Thank you," Toni said as she snuggled into it.

"Now we have to get out of here," Jakes said.

"Shouldn't we stay put?" Suzanne asked.

"If we can climb back up to the road, we can put Toni in my car and get her warmed up," Jakes said. "Us, too." He leaned down and wrapped his arms around Toni. "Does this hurt?"

"Not too bad," she said.

Jakes scooped her up easily and balanced her in his arms. "How about now, Toni?"

She leaned against his chest gratefully. "I'm okay."

"Just hang in there." Jakes adjusted Toni against the right side of his chest then extended his left hand to Suzanne. "Come on, Suzanne, let's climb this hill together."

And they did. With Reverend Jakes carrying Toni and leading the way, they climbed steadily up the steep incline they'd just rolled down. And every time Suzanne's foot slipped, Jakes was there to pull her back up.

"I'm sorry," Suzanne said when they were halfway up the embankment.

Jakes looked back at her. "For what?"

"For thinking you might have been involved in the murders. For being so harsh with you. You must think I'm a terrible person."

"I think nothing of the sort," Jakes said. He gripped Suzanne's hand tighter and pulled her up another few inches. "In fact, all things considered, I think you're amazingly brave. If I were ever in trouble, I'd want you by my side."

Ten minutes later, they were in Reverend Jakes's car, with the heater running full blast.

"This is a lot better," Toni said. Jakes had laid her out in the backseat with his parka still covering her. She'd stopped shivering and had actually smiled once.

SHERIFF Doogie arrived first. He skidded to a stop and jumped out of his cruiser, a blanket in one hand, his pistol in the other.

Suzanne climbed out of Jakes's car to meet him.

"Dear Lord, Suzanne," Doogie cried when he saw her rushing toward him. "Are you injured?"

"No, but Don Shinder is lying at the bottom of this ravine."

"Because you shot him?" Doogie didn't look happy.

"He confessed to killing Allan Sharp and Teddy Hardwick; then he tried to bludgeon us with a tire iron."

Doogie looked stunned. "Suzanne! For real?"

"Yes, for real. And Reverend Jakes was driving along when he saw our car plunge into the ditch. When he tried to help us, Shinder smacked him over the head."

"Hold everything. You have to start from the beginning," Doogie said. He holstered his gun and handed her the blanket. "I want you to explain everything that happened . . . and try to do it in a logical sequence."

"I will," Suzanne promised. "As soon as the ambulance . . ." She tilted her head to one side. A faint, shrill sound carried toward them on the wind. "Wait, I think I hear the siren now."

THE ambulance slewed to a stop a minute later. Dick Sparrow, the paramedic, jumped out and raced over to Reverend Jakes's car. Sam jumped out and ran toward Suzanne.

"Are you okay?" Sam asked Suzanne. He basically ignored Doogie.

Suzanne laid her head against Sam's chest and let him put his arms around her for all of two seconds. Then she pulled back and said, "I'm fine. But you need to take care of Toni. And check on Reverend Jakes."

"Are you . . . ?" Sam began.

But Suzanne waved him off. "I'm fine. Go."

Dick Sparrow and Sam got Toni into the ambulance, where Sparrow put an inflatable splint on Toni's arm. Sam ran through a quick concussion protocol with Reverend Jakes, then said, "I think you're okay, but I'd feel better if you rode back in the ambulance with us. Maybe spent the night in the hospital."

"I don't think—" Jakes began.

"That wasn't a suggestion," Sam said. "It's doctor's orders."

So Jakes climbed into the ambulance, leaving Sam with Suzanne and Doogie.

"What about Don Shinder?" Doogie asked.

"What about him?" Sam asked.

Doogie paused as another siren *whoop-whoop*ed from down the road. There was the screech of tires on pavement and a second cruiser slid to a stop. "Driscoll," Doogie said. He turned his attention to Sam. "Shinder is lying at the bottom of the ditch with a bullet in his head." Doogie looked both furious and scared. "Your fiancée here shot him to death."

"I believe she shot him in self-defense," Sam declared.

"Shinder's not dead," Suzanne said.

Doogie rocked back on his heels, his eyes practically popping out of his head. "He's not?"

"I only shot him with a nail gun," Suzanne said.

"What!" Doogie put both hands up to the sides of his head, as if his brains were about to blow out his ears.

"I shot Shinder twice, once in each shoulder," Suzanne said. "Because I had to somehow stop him. I mean, he hit Reverend Jakes over the head and then came after me and Toni." She choked back a sob. "He was going to kill us."

"So he's not dead?" Sam asked.

"We don't need an undertaker?" Doogie said.

"No, of course not. Shinder was crying and cussing a blue streak when we left him a few minutes ago. I don't think he's frozen to death quite yet," Suzanne said.

"With those nails, it sounds like he's going to have some rotator cuff issues," Sam said.

Suzanne shrugged. "Tough luck."

Doogie gestured to Deputy Driscoll. "Driscoll, grab a backboard from the ambulance and we'll go down and get him." Doogie paused and gazed at Suzanne again. "Nail gun?"

"You know, like roofers use to nail down shingles," Suzanne said. She put her hands together and pantomimed a shooting. "It was Junior's nail gun, from when he stuck all his tools from the explosion into the backseat of my car."

Doogie shook his head again, muttering to himself, as he and Driscoll walked over to the edge of the road and started down the snowy embankment.

A faint smile flickered on Sam's face. "So it wasn't a real gun?" Sam puffed out his cheeks and released a glut of air. "Here I had this terrible mental picture of you holding a Ruger or a Sig Sauer. Your lip curling as you blew away a puff of smoke."

Suzanne snuggled up against Sam, feeling his warmth and the fuzz of his chin stubble rubbing companionably against her forehead. "I don't think I'm really a gun person," she said.

"Good," Sam said. "Let's keep it that way." Then: "So it was Don Shinder all along. Not Mobley or Jakes or that girl Amber."

"You know what? Shinder actually *admitted* to killing Allan Sharp and Teddy Hardwick," Suzanne said. "He was gloating about it, right before he tried to kill me and Toni."

"Awful," Sam said.

"It really is." Suzanne tilted her head back and gave Sam a shy smile. "But the whole miserable thing is over, thank goodness. And I'm sorry to have caused you so much worry and pain. I just hope you're not terribly upset with me . . ." Her words practically caught in the back of her throat. "And that you still want to marry me."

Sam gazed down at her. "Suzanne, you scare me more than anyone I've ever known."

"But . . . ?"

Sam hugged her tighter. "But I still want to spend every terrifying moment with you."

Suzanne smiled as Sam smooshed her in his arms. For now, the world felt right. Perfectly, perfectly right.

Recipes from the Cackleberry Club

Jalapeño Grilled Chicken Sandwiches

¼ cup jalapeño jelly
¼ cup apple cider vinegar
½ tsp. salt
½ tsp. Tabasco sauce
4 boneless chicken breasts
4 hamburger buns
Lettuce and tomato for garnish

Over medium heat, melt jelly in pan, then stir in apple cider vinegar, salt, and Tabasco. Grill or fry chicken breasts, about 5 minutes per side. As you are doing this, baste generously with jelly and vinegar mixture. When chicken is cooked, serve on buns with lettuce and tomato garnish. Yields 4 servings.

Suzanne's Crabby Crab Cakes

1 lb. crabmeat
2 eggs
3 tbsp. mayonnaise
3 tbsp. mustard
4 slices bread, cubed
1 tbsp. Worcestershire sauce
1 tsp. baking powder
Butter or oil for frying

Gently mix all ingredients together and then form into 4 crab cakes. Fry in butter or oil until golden brown, about 5 minutes per side. Serve as an appetizer or with a side dish for a main meal. Yields 4 servings.

Slow-Cooker Sweet-and-Sour Pork

3 tbsp. soy sauce
¼ cup apple cider vinegar
2 tbsp. cornstarch
¼ cup brown sugar
2 lb. cubed pork
1 onion, diced
3 cloves garlic, minced
¼ cup apple juice
1 (½" square) cube ginger, grated
1 green pepper, cored and sliced
1 (20 oz.) can pineapple chunks, drained

Combine soy sauce, apple cider vinegar, cornstarch, and brown sugar in slow cooker. Add cubed pork and stir. Add onion, garlic, apple juice, and grated ginger. Cook on low for 8 hours. Add green pepper and pineapple and cook for an additional 10 minutes. Serve over rice. Yields 4 servings.

Peach Cobbler Pancake Topper

4 cups sliced fresh or canned peaches
1 cup sugar
1 tsp. vanilla
1 lemon, zested and juiced
1 tbsp. cinnamon
2 tsp. cornstarch

Place all ingredients in a medium saucepan and bring to a boil. Reduce heat and let simmer for 20 minutes. While sauce is in the last stages of cooking, start making approximately 16 of your favorite pancakes—either from scratch or from a mix.

Remove sauce from burner and let stand for 5 minutes to thicken. Place 4 pancakes on each of 4 plates. Top with peach cobbler sauce. Yields 4 servings.

Church Basement Funeral Bars

⅓ cup melted butter
1½ cups crushed graham crackers
1 cup coconut flakes

1 cup dates, chopped
1 cup candied cherries, chopped
1 cup candied pineapple, chopped
1 cup pecans
1 can sweetened condensed milk

Preheat oven to 325 degrees. In a bowl, combine melted butter with graham cracker crumbs. Pat crumb mixture into a 9" x 13" pan. Then press each ingredient, in a single layer, on top of the crumbs, starting with the coconut flakes, then adding the dates, cherries, pineapple, and pecans. Cover the entire dessert with the sweetened condensed milk. Bake for 20 minutes. Yields 15 to 18 bars.

Winter Salad

1 large head red leaf lettuce, chopped or torn into bite-sized
*   pieces*
2 tbsp. balsamic vinegar
1 tsp. Dijon mustard
½ tsp. sea salt
½ cup olive oil
1 large apple, chopped
½ cup walnuts
½ cup dried cranberries
½ cup feta or goat cheese, crumbled

Place the lettuce in a serving bowl. Put balsamic vinegar, mustard, and sea salt in a blender and blend on low for 10 seconds to combine. With the motor running on low, slowly pour in olive oil until the dressing is well combined. Pour the dressing over the greens and toss well. Add apple, walnuts, cranberries, and cheese. Toss again and divide among 4 salad plates. Yields 4 servings. (Note: For an entree serving, top the salad with a grilled chicken breast.)

Elvis French Toast

2 ripe bananas, mashed
2 cups peanut butter
4 tbsp. honey
½ tsp. nutmeg
8 slices bread
2 eggs
½ cup half-and-half
⅓ cup butter
Syrup
Powdered sugar

Mix together bananas, peanut butter, honey, and nutmeg. Spread mixture on 4 slices of bread, then top with the other 4 slices to create 4 sandwiches. Slice each sandwich into 4 triangles. Mix together eggs and half-and-half. Place butter in skillet and heat. Dip each triangle into egg mixture and cook in skillet, turning when one side is golden brown (about 1 minute per side). Place 4 triangles on each of 4 plates. Serve with syrup and a sprinkle of powdered sugar. Yields 4 servings.

Breakfast Burritos

1 (16 oz.) can any kind baked beans or refried beans
6 eggs

Salt and pepper to taste
2 tbsp. butter
6 strips bacon, cooked and crumbled
⅓ cup chopped green onions
6 (7" to 8") flour tortillas, warmed
½ cup shredded cheddar cheese
Salsa
Sour cream (optional)

Heat beans thoroughly in a small saucepan and keep warm on stove. In a medium bowl, beat eggs along with salt and pepper. Melt butter in a 10" nonstick skillet over medium heat. Add egg mixture and sprinkle in crumbled bacon and chopped onion. Cook, stirring occasionally, until the eggs are softly cooked. Divide the egg mixture into 6 parts and spoon one part into each warm tortilla. Top egg mixture with equal amounts of beans. Now top with equal amounts of cheese. Fold in the ends and roll up the burritos. Serve with salsa and sour cream, if desired. Yields 6 servings.

Chocolate Chip Scones

2 cups flour
4 tbsp. sugar
¼ tsp. salt
2 tsp. baking powder
½ cup butter
½ cup milk or half-and-half
1 large egg
1 tsp. vanilla extract
1 cup semisweet chocolate chips

Preheat oven to 350 degrees. Grease baking sheet. In large bowl, combine flour, sugar, salt, and baking powder. Cut in butter until mixture is coarse and crumbly. In small bowl, combine milk (or half-and-half), egg, and vanilla. Add milk mixture to flour mixture, then add chocolate chips. Mix with fork until mixture pulls together and forms a soft dough. Place dough on floured surface and knead gently 5 or 6 times. With lightly floured rolling pin, roll dough into a 7" circle. Cut into 6 or 8 wedges and place on greased baking sheet. Bake for 18 to 20 minutes, until golden brown. Serve warm. Yields 6 to 8 scones. (Note: Dough can also be baked in a scone pan.)

Pumpkin Breakfast Casserole

10 slices white bread, cubed
1 (15 oz.) can pumpkin puree
6 eggs, beaten
1 cup milk
1 (5 oz.) can evaporated milk
⅔ cup sugar
1 tsp. cinnamon
½ tsp. nutmeg
1 tsp. vanilla extract
⅛ tsp. salt

Lightly grease a 9" x 13" baking dish, then place bread cubes in the dish. In a large bowl, mix together pumpkin puree, beaten eggs, milk, evaporated milk, sugar, cinnamon, nutmeg, vanilla, and salt. Pour the pumpkin mixture over the bread cubes. Cover with plastic wrap and refrigerate overnight.

The next morning, preheat oven to 350 degrees. Uncover casserole and bake for 45 minutes, until mixture is set and toothpick inserted into center comes out clean. Yields 6 servings.

Sheriff Doogie's Three Little Pigs Breakfast Hoagie

Hoagie roll, sliced open and buttered
3 sausages, cooked
Hash browns, cooked
Fried egg

Stuff hoagie roll with sausages, then hash browns, then a fried egg. Enjoy!
Yields 1 giant sandwich.

Keep reading for an excerpt from
Laura Childs's next Tea Shop Mystery . . .

Broken Bone China

Available from Berkley Prime Crime!

RED and yellow flames belched from propane burners, inflating the hot-air balloons to heroic proportions and propelling them skyward. Hovering above the grassy flats of Charleston's Hampton Park, they bumped along on gentle currents, looking like a supersized drift of colorful soap bubbles.

"This is amazing," Theodosia cried out to Drayton as the wind blew her auburn hair into long streamers. "Almost as good as sailing." Her blue eyes sparkled with merriment, and a smile lit up her face as she reveled in her first-ever balloon ride.

With her fine complexion, natural endowment of hair, and pleasing features, Theodosia Browning was the apotheosis of what Lord Byron might have described as an English beauty in one of his novels. She was, however, modest to a fault and would have blushed at the very thought.

"Is this not the coolest thing you've ever done?" Theodosia asked as blips of exhilaration filled her heart.

"No, it's terrifying," Drayton Conneley responded. He'd wedged himself into the corner of their wicker basket, teeth gritted, knuckles white, as he hung on for dear life. "When you talked me into assisting with an afternoon tea for the Top Flight Balloon Club, I had no idea you'd twist my arm and make me go for an actual ride."

"It's good to live a little dangerously," Theodosia said. As the proprietor of the Indigo Tea Shop on Church Street, she was often tapped to host weekend tea parties. This one in Hampton Park, smack-dab in the middle of Charleston, South Carolina, was no different. Except that after pouring tea and serving her trademark cream scones and crab salad tea sandwiches, Theodosia had been offered a hot-air balloon ride. Gratis. And, really, who in their right mind would turn down a wild adventure like that! Certainly not Theodosia. To an outside eye, she might appear tea-shop-demure, but she possessed the bold soul of an adrenaline junkie.

"I believe the weather's beginning to shift," Drayton said. "Perhaps we should cut our ride short?" The sky, which had been pigeon-egg blue just an hour ago, now had a few gray clouds scudding across it.

"Wind's kicking up, too," said Rafe Meyer, their FAA certified pilot. He opened the blast valve one more time, shooting a fiery tongue high into the balloon's interior. "This will keep us at altitude along with the other balloons. But we should probably think about landing in another five minutes or so. Weather conditions do look like they might be deteriorating."

"Thank goodness for that," Drayton said under his breath. As Theodosia's resident tea sommelier and self-appointed arbiter of taste, he was definitely not a devotee of adventure sports. Sixty-something, genteel, with a serious addiction to tweed jackets and bow ties, Drayton's idea of high adventure was sitting in a wingback chair in front of his fireplace, sipping a glass of ruby port, and reading a Joseph Conrad novel.

"Take a look at that patchwork balloon over there. You see how it's descending ever so gently?" Theodosia said. "You don't have a thing to worry about. When we hit the ground you won't even feel a bump."

Drayton squinted over the side of their gondola. "What on earth is that whirligig thing?"

Theodosia was still reveling in her bird's-eye view and the hypnotic whoosh from the propane burner, so she wasn't exactly giving Drayton her full attention. "What? What are you talking about?" she finally asked.

"I'm puzzled about the small, silver object that appears to be flying in our direction."

Theodosia could barely pry her eyes away from the delicious banquet of scenery and greenery, history and antiquity, that was spilled out below her. Crooked, narrow streets. Elegant *grande dame* homes lining the Battery. The azure sweep of Charleston Harbor. The dozens of church steeples that poked skyward.

But as Theodosia turned, she too caught a flash of something bright and shiny buzzing its way toward them. Her first impression was that it looked like some kind of mechanized seagull. Only, instead of dipping and diving and surfing the wind, it was zooming right at them.

"I think it's a drone. Someone must have put up a drone," Theodosia said. She watched with growing curiosity as it circled toward them, coming closer and closer. The drone swooped upwards, then dipped down, doing a fancy series of aerial maneuvers. Finally, the drone zoomed in and hovered alongside their basket for a long moment. Curiously, the drone appeared to be making up its mind about something. Then it peeled away.

"What's it doing? Some kind of TV news thing?" Drayton asked. "You know, 'Film at eleven'?"

"I don't think it's a commercial drone. Probably someone who's filming the balloons for fun." Theodosia's attention had shifted to the weather as she scanned the sky to the east, in the direction of the Atlantic Ocean. More clouds had rolled in, turning the horizon into a dim blot.

"Such a strange buzzing thing," Drayton said. He gripped the side of the wicker basket even tighter. "Like some kind of giant, nasty hornet. Just having it circle around like that makes me nervous."

"There's really nothing to worry . . ." Theodosia began. Then her words ended abruptly as the little drone lifted straight up like a miniature helicopter or Harrier jet. Up, up, up it rose until it was flying level with the red and white balloon that hovered just ahead of them but at a slightly higher altitude.

"Isn't the drone edging precipitously close to that balloon?" Drayton asked as he continued to gaze upward.

"Yes, I think it is." Theodosia tapped their pilot on the shoulder, and when he turned, she pointed wordlessly at the drone that now hovered some forty feet above them.

The pilot glanced up and frowned, his expression telling her all she needed to know. "That shouldn't be there," he said.

"It's strange. Almost as if the drone is checking out each of the balloons," Drayton said. "Peeking in the baskets to see who the passengers are."

"Because it has a camera," Theodosia said. She glanced down toward terra firma, wondering who in the crowd below might be manipulating the drone—and why were they doing so? For fun or a joke or some kind of promotional film? But their balloon was too high to make out anything meaningful.

"I think the object is flying away," Drayton said. "Good riddance."

But the drone didn't fly away.

Instead, it circled back around, hovered for a few moments, revved its engine to an almost supersonic speed, and flew directly into the red and white balloon.

RIP. ZSSST. WHOMP!

A burst of brilliant light, bright as an atomic bomb, lit the sky.

Theodosia threw up an arm to shield her eyes, then watched in horror as the balloon was ripped wide open, top to bottom, like gutting a fish.

Flames shot everywhere and the hapless passengers screamed as the gigantic balloon exploded in a hellish conflagration. It sizzled and popped and wobbled for a few moments then began to collapse inward like a flaming deflated ball.

"Dear Lord, it's the Hindenburg all over again," Drayton said in a hoarse whisper.

Against the darkening sky, the burning balloon and dangling basket looked like some sort of Hollywood special effect. Then, almost in slow motion, the entire rig tumbled from the sky like a faulty rocket dropping out of orbit.

Screams rent the air—from the dying passengers as well as observers on the ground.

Hearts in their throats, eyes unable to resist this gruesome sight, Theodosia and Drayton watched the sickening spectacle unfold.

"What a catastrophe!" Drayton cried. "Can anyone survive this?"

Theodosia whispered a quick prayer. She didn't think so.

The burning balloon roared and rumbled as it continued its downward plunge, unleashing a blizzard of blistered nylon, hot metal, and exploding propane. Ash and sparks fluttered everywhere; the sound was like a blast furnace. Then, in a final ghastly incendiary burst, the balloon and its seared basket smashed down on top of Theodosia's tea table. Tongues of flame spewed out as bone china teacups were crushed, and a pink and green teapot exploded like a bomb.

And lives were surely lost.

Watch for the next Cackleberry Club Mystery

Battered Eggs

Between a truck heist, missing person, and gruesome killing, Suzanne hopes the "something borrowed, something blue" for her wedding doesn't turn out to be bloody blue murder.

And be sure to catch the new New Orleans Scrapbooking Mystery, also from Laura Childs and Berkley Prime Crime

Mumbo Gumbo Murder

During a French Quarter parade of spooky giant puppets, an antiques dealer is murdered and his dog left homeless. As Carmela and Ava work furiously to catch this violent killer, a new "paint and sip" shop and the mysterious Vampire Guild get in the way!

Find out more about the author and
her mysteries at laurachilds.com or
become a Facebook friend at
facebook.com/laurachildsauthor.

Writing as Laura Childs, this author has brought you the *New York Times* bestselling Tea Shop, Scrapbooking, and Cackleberry Club mysteries. Now, writing under her own name, Gerry Schmitt, she has created an entirely new series of sharp-edged thrillers.

Shadow Girl

an Afton Tangler Thriller
by Gerry Schmitt

In *Shadow Girl*, the second book in this series, a medical helicopter is blasted out of the sky, dashing the transplant hopes of a dying tycoon. It seems nothing can stop vicious crime boss Mom Chao Cherry from recovering her stolen narcotics—including more killing—unless Afton Tangler gets there first.

Gerry has ratcheted up the suspense and set the stakes even higher for Afton Tangler, single mom and liaison officer with the Minneapolis Police Department. Page-turning action, believable characters, and a ripped-from-the-headlines story.

Available in paperback from Berkley!

NEW YORK TIMES BESTSELLING AUTHOR

LAURA CHILDS

"Murder suits [Laura Childs] to a tea."

—*St. Paul (MN) Pioneer Press*

For a complete list of titles,
please visit prh.com/laurachilds